Praise for *Every*

"*Every Crooked Pot* is a beautifully nuanced tale about an
nary family and an even more extraordinary young woman. Not since Myla Goldberg's *Bee Season* has a first novel so deftly captured the complexities, joys, and frustrations of daughters and their families. It's hard to believe this is a debut—Rosen's voice is already as good as it gets. Keep an eye out for this rising star."

—Sara Gruen, *New York Times* bestselling author of *Water for Elephants*

"*Every Crooked Pot* is a funny, heartfelt, and beautifully perceptive novel. In her insightful character study, Renée Rosen takes the reader deep inside the heart and mind of a delightfully real protagonist. In her spirited portrayal of an ordinary—yet improbable—American family, Rosen illuminates great unspoken truths about young women, about daughters, and about all families."

—Adrienne Miller, author of *The Coast of Akron*

"It's so tempting to compare Renée Rosen's debut to similar auspicious literary starts—Anna Quindlen's *Object Lessons* comes to mind—but that would be doing the book a disservice, since *Every Crooked Pot* stands in a class by itself. Populated with vivid characters, at the center of which is resilient heroine Nina Goldman, this bittersweet novel will lift hearts while at the same time making readers wonder: Where has Renée Rosen been hiding all these years?"

—Lauren Baratz-Logsted, author of *Angel's Choice*

"Told with wit, wisdom, and characters so realistically drawn that they breathe, this poignant story of angst and redemption will touch the heart of anyone who ever longed to be 'normal' enough to be loved."

—Sandra Kring, author of *The Book of Bright Ideas*

"*Every Crooked Pot* is a work of courage, with a dose of sassy audacity thrown in for good measure. With humiliation, sorrow, tears, humor, and candor, this is a novel so full of heart and emotion, it's impossible to detach yourself from it. Renée Rosen is a rare find in today's jungle of women's fiction!"

—Carrie Kabak, author of *Cover the Butter*

"Realistic, sharp, and funny, Renée Rosen perfectly captures what it's like to be stuck on the outside longing to get in. A beautiful, poignant, and impressive debut—I didn't want it to end."

—Alyson Nöel, author of *Laguna Cove*

every crooked pot

every crooked pot

renée rosen

st. martin's griffin
new york

This is a work of fiction. All of the characters, organizations, and events portrayed in this novel are either products of the author's imagination or are used fictitiously.

www.stmartins.com

Library of Congress Cataloging-in-Publication Data

Rosen, Renée.
Every crooked pot / Renée Rosen. — 1st ed.
p. cm.
ISBN-13: 978-0-312-36543-1
ISBN-10: 0-312-36543-8
1. Ohio—Fiction. 2. Domestic fiction. I. Title.

PS3618.083156E94 2007
813'.6—dc22

2007010457

First Edition: July 2007

10 9 8 7 6 5 4 3 2 1

For my family,

especially my father, R. W. Rosen,

whose memory will live on forever

in the hearts and minds

of those who loved him so

acknowledgments

This book has been a long time in the making and many people have helped me in numerous ways, and to the following I will be forever grateful: my dear family, Deborah Rosen (Pyack), Pam Jaffe, Jerry Rosen, Andrea Rosen, Andy Jaffe, Joey Perilman, and Devon Rosen—my never-ending source of love and laughter.

My heartfelt thanks to my friends, old and new, who have been along for the ride, especially Karen Abbott, Nancy Abbott, Tasha Alexander, Amy Anderson, Anita Brick, Irma Bueno, Jessa Crispin, Susan Day, Mary Delany, Ken Hale, Gina Knapik, Fred Lochbihler, Linda Myers, Abigail Pickus, Dennis Rosenthal, Snake, Kathryn Stern, Marc Tolliver, Susie Weiner, and Joelle Ziemian. And to my true-blues: Jill Bernstein, Lisa B. Fine, Lisa Kotin, Beth Trebelhorn, and Paula Weiss—what would I do without you all?

To everyone at Backspace—finding all of you was a turning point for me. My thanks for their medical expertise go to Dr. Susan Taub of the Taub Eye Center and Dr. Amy Paller of Northwestern

University. Also, my appreciation for the teachings of Nichiren Daishonin, which helped shape this book. Thanks also to Celeste Trevino, who always knows best. And my appreciation as well goes to everyone at Rosen & Brichta.

And to my agent extraordinaire, Whitney Lee, who never gave up on me—there are not enough ways to say thank you for your encouragement and all your efforts on my behalf. And to my remarkable editor, Gina Scarpa, whose vision and guidance allowed me to see the real story I was trying to tell. From the very start, you championed this book with great care and wisdom, and I am so fortunate to have you in my corner. Without you, this would have been a much different book.

My special thanks go to Michael C. for planting the seed. And lastly, my debt of gratitude to three people who held me together and kept me going: Karen Call, who read this book in all its many shapes and sizes; Mindy Mailman (Bullwinkle), for keeping me laughing and for giving me a great title; and Joe Esselin, who has been there with me through every word and every line—I could have never done this without you.

every crooked pot

the saltwater remedies

The day we got pulled over for speeding, I was sitting in the backseat of the family station wagon—Lissy to my left, Mitch to my right, my Keds straddling the hump. My mother was riding shotgun with my father. It was mid-December of 1968 and I was seven years old. We were on our way to Florida for a business trip my father had disguised as our winter vacation. My father wanted out of the carpet business and thought this was his chance for a steady gig, playing clarinet at his friend's nightclub in Miami. It was a long drive down from Akron, and my father was set on making it to Savannah by the end of the day. That's why we got pulled over somewhere in southern Ohio, clocked at eighty-seven on the radar.

Even before the highway patrolman reached the car, my father was out of the driver's seat, walking toward the cop. "Officer," my father said, hands slightly raised, like the cop had him at gunpoint, "thank God you stopped us! I know I was speeding, but you've got to help me—I've got a very sick child in the car!"

Lissy, Mitch, and I looked at one another, confused, wondering who was sick. Then my mother reached back and gave my knee a squeeze, smiling at me with one brow raised.

I twisted around in my seat to get a better angle on the action. And while the flashing light on top of the patrol car went round and round, I tried timing my eye blinks just right, so that each time I opened my eyes, all I would see was red.

My father and the policeman were talking, but you couldn't hear the cop, just my father. "Officer," he said, "with all due respect, in the time it would take me to explain this to you, it could be too late."

The policeman came closer to the car.

"Listen," my father pressed on, walking alongside the cop, "it's very technical. If you really want to know, the orbital mass in her eye has ruptured." Followed by: "The retinal vascularization is swelling up and her festorial glands are coagulating!" My father was on a roll. There was no stopping him.

The cop muttered something into his ticket pad, his tongue working the inside of his cheek, rolling around like he had a jawbreaker in there. My father hadn't shaved that morning or slicked back his hair with Brylcreem. He looked a mess with his hair jetting out in all directions.

"All you have to do is look at her! Look at her eye! My God, the poor thing's hemorrhaging like crazy!"

I wasn't hemorrhaging. I always looked that way. It was my birthmark. The doctors said it was a hemangioma, but everyone else called it my port wine stain or my strawberry mark. To me it looked more like I'd been punched in the eye. The lid was always puffy and there was a big lump growing out of my eyebrow. The white of my eye was always filled with blood and the outside was all red and purple. The doctors told my parents it was because I had too many blood vessels in my eye.

"Officer," my father continued, "I've got a doctor standing

by. He's waiting for us at a hospital in Cincinnati—and if I don't get her there soon, she's gonna lose her sight in that eye!"

Lose my sight? I didn't even need glasses.

The officer tugged on his cap and leaned over to look at me. I made sure the cop got a good shot of my eye, and I knew better than to smile. My father was counting on me. I had a job to do. So I made my bottom lip curl under and scrunched my shoulders up close to my ears. My whole face went all sad, like a clown's. Normally, my eye never hurt, but right then it felt like it did. Given another minute, I could have cried.

The officer looked at my mother, offering her a half-nod, like the crossing guard at school giving you the go-ahead. He turned back to my father and the two men exchanged a few words, then shook hands.

My father got back in the station wagon, leaned his head back, closed his eyes, and started to laugh so hard that his shoulders were shaking. Then the cop pulled out ahead of us in his squad car and switched on his red sirens full blast.

"Hang on, gang! Here we go!" My father revved the engine and off we went, following close behind the police car. My father pointed toward the flashing light on the cop car and howled, "Here comes the Goldman express!" He pumped the accelerator as we whipped past another mile marker.

Instead of a speeding ticket, the officer gave us a police escort to the hospital. We ducked inside the sliding glass doors of the emergency room and waited until the cop drove off. Then my father herded us back to the car and hit the gas. Even with the detour, we made it to the Ohio-Kentucky border in record time.

Outside of Lexington, we'd started playing that license plate game where you try to get all the states. Mitch and I shouted out every plate we saw, even those states we'd already nailed. We could tell we were getting on Lissy's nerves, so we kept doing it just to make her cover her ears and lean as far away from us as she could. She was three years older than Mitch, six years older than me. She was a teenager now, which meant she was done playing with us.

For a long stretch, ours was the only car on the road. No license plates to be found. We were bored, with nothing to look at other than faded barns, weather-split with Mail Pouch slogans blanched out on the sides. Mitch kept kicking the back of my mother's seat, asking how much longer.

"Not too much," she said, keeping her eyes on the road, like she was the one driving.

My father was slouched in his seat, his shoulder pressed to the window, one wrist draped over the steering wheel, fingers free for snapping. "Do You Know the Way to San Jose?" was coming over the radio, accompanied by the squeaks from the Styrofoam cooler, which was sandwiched in between the suitcases. My father was singing along with all his heart, going, "I've got lots of friends in San Jose/Wo oh oh oh . . ."

When we got to the Holiday Inn that night, my father was in the adjoining room. He was lying on the bed with his right foot dangling off the edge, smoking his pipe as he read the Savannah phone book. That was what he did in every hotel room on every road trip we ever took: He read the Yellow Pages. He said you never knew what you might find.

Mitch and I were in the other room, fighting over my Etch-a-Sketch. He was holding it high above my head, making me jump for it.

"Give it back!" I said, slapping at his arms.

"Uh-uh-uh! Somebody's gonna get hurt." My mother stood watching us from the doorway of our connecting rooms. She was cleaning out the cooler, the lid tucked under her arm as she threw out half-eaten sandwiches and a bag of crumpled chips.

I kept slapping Mitch on the arm until he got mad, dropped the Etch-a-Sketch, and shoved me onto the bed. He leaped on top of me, sat on my stomach, pinning my arms back with his shins while his fingers played typewriter on my chest, hunting and pecking. "ChChChChChChCh—CHING!" He hit my cheek like it was the carriage return.

I wiggled out from under him, got back up, and charged toward him. He grabbed both my arms and turned my hands on me. "Why do you keep hitting yourself, Nina?" he said, whacking me in the head with my own fists. "Why do you keep hitting yourself? Huh? Huh!"

My mother came to my rescue. "Will the two of you just settle down and get ready for bed. We have another full day tomorrow."

"Tell what's-her-name to get out of the bathroom," Mitch said, now bouncing his Super Ball off the headboard.

"Mitchell, will you please— Lissy?" My mother rapped at the bathroom door with the Styrofoam lid. "C'mon now—you're holding everybody up."

Two seconds later, Lissy opened the door and stepped out. Her long blond hair was rolled in emptied-out cans of Tab, held in place by a strip of hair clips that looked like a band of bullets. She wanted to know why she had to share a bed with me.

"Nina snores."

"I do not snore!"

"Melissa," my mother said, "if you can sleep with all that hardware on your head, then you can sleep through a little snoring."

"But I don't snore!"

My mother bopped me on the head with the lid of the cooler. It made a hollow thump. She bopped Mitch too, then Lissy. It made us laugh.

My father was still in the other room, reading the phone book.

The next morning, we hit the trail at 6:30 A.M., and after stopping at a music store my father had discovered in the Yellow Pages, we arrived in Miami Beach. We passed a hotel marquee advertising Neil Diamond for Christmas Day and another one, next door, pushing lobster tails and Elvis Presley for New Year's Eve.

Mitch was clowning around, asking, "Hey Dad, where's the sign with your name?"

My father didn't answer and Mitch didn't ask again. It was the height of the season, and in bumper-to-bumper traffic on Collins Avenue, my father was no longer slouched in the driver's seat, no longer finding his way to San Jose. The back of his collar was damp with sweat by the time we pulled up to the Newport Hotel.

Inside, the lobby was loud and crowded. An oversized Christmas tree slowly rotated in the center while a dozen or more artists sat at easels, cartooning the tourists. A trio of musicians in matching vests, playing mandolin, trumpet, and conga drums, performed for people as they passed by.

"What do you think, gang?" my father said, tapping his foot to the music. "Is this not a hopping place, huh? Huh?" He was pleased with himself for having selected the Newport. "Not too shabby, huh, gang?" My father was stomping his foot now, clapping, gesturing to the conga player, who smiled back, nodding.

I stared at my father's loafers and started stomping my foot, wishing I could keep the beat the way he did. He looked at me and grabbed my hand, twirling me around like a Hanukkah dreidel.

After he'd spun me around a few more times, my mother told Lissy to go get Mitch, who had wandered over to the fountain. He was leaning along the marble ledge, his feet off the ground, his shirt all wet in front as he ran his fingers through the water, trying to scoop out the coins from the bottom.

I turned away and noticed a couple stepping off an elevator. He was tall and slim, with sideburns to his jaw. She had long frosted hair, kept her sunglasses propped up on her head, and wore a silver bracelet high up on her arm, way past her elbow. You didn't see women like her back in Akron. She reminded me of the fashion models in Lissy's magazines. She glided when she walked, and I was sure she always had handsome men following her around everywhere.

When I grew up, I wanted to be like her.

"Didn't I tell you? Didn't I say this was a great place?" my father said when it was just us five up in our rooms. The Newport Hotel was way better than the Holiday Inn, with blue-and-gold-striped bedspreads that matched the drapes and chairs. There was a big marble bathroom, with a tray on the counter that was filled with little bars of soap and miniature bottles of shampoo.

My father went to the window and pulled open the drapes. "Is that not gorgeous? Come here, kids . . ."

We all crowded around him, me slipping in place beneath his arm, a snag on his nylon shirt rising and falling against my cheek as he breathed. When he was happy like this, I just couldn't get close enough.

"Look out there," he said, tapping his middle finger to the glass. "You could take a picture—like a postcard. You kids have any idea how much extra it costs just to be on this side? Just to have this view of the ocean?"

❋

That night we kids sat three in a row on the side of the bed, voting for which color shirt my father should wear with which color suit. My father was color-blind, so I grew up watching him walk around the house half-dressed, going, "Does this go with these? Does that go with this?"

Back home, my mother had systemized his sock drawer: Black socks were tied, browns were rolled, and navies were folded. Shirts were hung from light to dark, with brown collars facing right, blues going left. Everything needed a specific order; otherwise, my father got into trouble.

Once he found a men's clothing outlet in the Peoria Yellow Pages and bought three pairs of chartreuse slacks. My father said they stood out on the rack. "Sharpest goddamn pants in the place!" No one could talk him out of them, not even the salesman.

My father couldn't see colors and couldn't dress himself, but he could sell carpet. He was a salesman all right, and he'd have customers buying wall-to-wall shag in a shade they never thought they'd own. My father was a frustrated musician, who hated what he did for a living, even though it was the thing he did best.

"Okay, gang, which one?" He draped four ties over his arm for us to choose from.

The neon sign outside Flipper's had a lit martini glass with an olive blinking on and off. Flip, the owner, was an old navy buddy of my father's. They'd been stationed together in Pensacola, and after leaving the service, my father went north and married my mother, while Flip went south and opened his nightclub.

My father stood under the awning, looking back at the parking lot. "Didn't I tell you, Sandra? Huh? Huh! Valet parking and everything!"

We didn't valet our car that night. Instead, we parked in the lot across the street. My mother made us all hold hands as we crossed the interstate. I don't think my father liked the idea of pulling up to Flipper's in his station wagon with QBC—Quality Brand Carpets—running across the sides and back, not when all the other cars were Cadillacs and Lincolns. We had a Cadillac back home—brand-new. That was the car my mother drove. We would have driven her car down to Florida, but my father didn't want to put that much mileage on it. But I knew that if we had brought that car down, my father would have valeted it, in a second.

My mother took a final drag off her cigarette before crushing it beneath the toe of her pump, giving a twist to make sure it was out.

"You kids have any idea who's played here? All the big names—big, big stars." My father said this without naming a single one. Then he wiggled the knot of his tie and took his clarinet case from Mitch. He took one last look at the parking lot and shook his head. "Valet parking and everything. Flip's done all right for himself . . ."

Flip was a large sunbaked man who had a gold medallion hanging from his neck. He greeted my father at the entrance with a big bear hug. Then he stood back and rapped his knuckles on my father's clarinet case. "Artie, I see you're still carrying that licorice stick around."

"Yeah, well . . . you know, haven't played much lately . . ."

My father had been rehearsing every day for the past three weeks. My mother had accompanied him on the piano, taking time out between numbers, darting into the kitchen to check on dinner.

"You know," my father said with a shrug, "I figured for old times' sake, I'd bring it along—give the kids a treat."

Flip laughed as he reached an arm around my mother, pulling her to his side, saying she was just as beautiful as ever. And she was, even though she looked older than my father. It was the hair that did it. My mother had been gray for as long as I could remember, but her face was young. She had high cheekbones, a perfect nose, and blue-gray eyes that everyone said were her best feature.

Lissy looked just like my mother and Mitch took more after my father. He had the same dark eyes, long face, and squared-off chin. People said I was a combination of the two, but I thought they were saying that just to be nice.

Flip led us down a flight of stairs and past the bar to a table close to the stage. "You're in for a real treat, Artie," he said as he pulled out a chair for my mother.

"Yeah? If these guys are half as good as we used to be, then you've got yourself a winner here." My father gave Flip a little jab in the side as he sat down.

All through the first set, my father danced in his chair and Lissy kept inching away from our table as far as she could get, until a cocktail waitress told her she was blocking the aisle. As she scooted in just a bit, my mother reached over and squeezed her hand. "Everybody's watching the show, Lissy. Nobody's paying any attention to him."

When the band took a break, Flip came over to our table and said, gesturing toward the empty stage with his thumb, "Aren't these guys outasight, man? Didn't I tell ya, Goldman?" He made a clucking sound. "Outasight!"

Flip pulled over a chair, turned it around, and straddled it, resting his chin on the back. While he and my father were talking old times, my mother reapplied her lipstick. Mitch had challenged me to a stare-down and Lissy kept elbowing me, trying to make me blink.

During the last set of the evening, Flip cut in on the piano player and called my father to the stage. They started off with "What a Wonderful Life," and after Flip soloed, it was my father's turn. Eyes shut, knees slightly bent, head bobbing left, then right, giving it his all, one note after the next.

I glanced over at my mother. She was smiling, her left hand on the tabletop, beating time to the music. Then people started to applaud, and for the first time since my father had gone onstage, I settled back in my chair, smiling big and proud. Even Lissy pulled in closer to our table, wanting to belong to him again.

My father and Flip played three more numbers. And my father looked like he belonged on that stage. He dazzled up there, joking with the audience between songs, making them laugh and clap even louder. He really did have what it took to be a star. Pizzazz, that's what my father had. And he knew he had it. He didn't even have to work at it. It was just there.

My father and Flip ended their set with the two of them standing before the microphone with their arms over each other's shoulders, singing "Fly Me to the Moon."

❋

The next morning, my father didn't say a word about Flipper's. After breakfast he went down on the beach with Lissy and Mitch, while I sat at the foot of my mother's chaise lounge, lobbying to go in the ocean without my goggles. The goggles, custom-made to protect my bad eye from the chlorine and salt water, had been accidentally left back home by my mother.

"But I'll be careful," I said, picking at the daisy appliqués on my mother's beach bag.

"Honey, I told you, if you want, you can go in the pool—in the shallow end—just as long as you don't get your face wet."

I knew from her tone that this was as far as I'd get. So I went over and sat at the edge of the pool, the bottom of my suit catching on the cement each time I moved. As I swirled my feet in the water, I looked out at the ocean, sulking.

Half an hour later, when my father came up from the beach, he crouched down beside me, told me it wasn't any fun down there anyway, and handed me a shell, all pink inside, like the roof of someone's mouth. My father kissed the top of my head, then went back over by my mother and spilled onto the chair next to hers. The bottoms of his feet were dusted with sand and a piece of seaweed was strung around his second toe. A long, dark lock of hair dangled down past his eyes, all the way to his cheek.

I got up and took the chaise on the other side of my mother. My father was already deep in conversation with the two men to his right—one wearing black socks with sandals, the other wearing a hat with fishing lures stuck all over it and a smear of white sunblock across his nose. They were discussing how the S&P was at an all-time high, and my father had launched into a speech, telling these strangers that they should invest in gold. A fresh audience. My father couldn't help himself.

The woman with the frosted hair, the one I'd seen in the lobby the day before, was tanning herself in the next row over. She wore a thin gold ankle bracelet and lay there, still, like she was sleeping. I closed my eyes, too, listening to the sound of bare feet slapping the wet cement and breathing in the smell of chlorine and coconut oil.

I was almost asleep when my mother leaned over and dabbed lotion onto my arm. "Honey," she said, rubbing it in, "you getting hungry, sweetie?"

We'd just eaten a big breakfast; she knew I wouldn't be hungry yet. I could tell she felt guilty about leaving my goggles behind. I knew I had her then. She was weakening and I wouldn't have to say another word. I just looked at the ocean and sighed. My mother turned toward the water, shading her eyes from the sun in a lazy salute. We could see Lissy from where we were. She was checking her tan marks, peeling down the shoulder strap of her bikini like the skin of a banana. My mother ran her hand along her throat and looked back at me.

"If I let you go down there, young lady," she said, "you have to be careful. You have to stay with Lissy and Mitch. And I want you to promise"—I heard her calling after me—"you won't go CRAZY! NINA, I MEAN IT!"

The three of us stayed in the ocean the rest of the day. Even Lissy played with us, jumping the waves. After each surge there was a moment's calm as that wave rolled past us and broke along the shoreline and another came roaring our way. Each wave brought a new kind of excitement. At just the right moment, we'd hurl ourselves into them headfirst, tumbling about, getting tangled in seaweed and losing our footing in a wash of foam, frothy as a bubble bath.

* * *

When we went back to our hotel room, the red message light was flashing: Flip had called. My father phoned back right away. "Yeah, Flip, Art Goldman, just returning your call . . ." He tugged on the drawstring of his swimming trunks, going, "Uh-huh, yeah . . ." Then finally: "Heh-heh—we didn't sound too shabby now, did we . . . Oh, it's an impressive setup you've got there . . . Uh-huh, yeah . . . Yeah . . ." He let go of the drawstring then, sat on the edge of the bed, and reached for his pipe in the ashtray. "You know me, Flip, I'm always up for a little business proposition . . ."

After he hung up, my father waved his fists in the air, going, "Yes, yes!" carrying on like he had the day he ran alongside of Mitch's Schwinn, letting go just in time to watch his boy pedal off, zigzagging his way down Burlington Road.

"Sandra!" he shouted. "This is it! THIS IS IT!"

"Yes, dear, I know," she said, smiling, patting his cheek.

He kissed her on the mouth, and not a second later, his eyes clouded over. "Oh me!" he said, patting his chest, half laughing, half crying.

My father cried a lot. Happy or sad, it didn't matter. He'd start up over anything, saying, "Oh me, here I go again with my waterworks."

"Didn't I tell ya, Sandra—stick with me? Huh? Huh!" He blew his nose in the handkerchief my mother had handed him. "C'mon, gang!" He dabbed his eyes. "Everybody get showered, get dressed!" He reached for his clarinet case and said, "Your Big-Joe-Daddy-O's taking everybody out for lobster dinners. How about that? Huh? Eh! Fresh Florida lobsters! We've got some celebrating to do!"

While I was in the shower, I heard my father playing his clarinet. I sang into my bar of soap, dance-stepping among the bubbles sudsing up the tiled floor: "Fly me to the moon/And let me play among the stars . . ."

We were getting dressed for dinner when my mother first noticed the change in my eye. "How does it feel, snookums?" she asked.

"Normal." I shrugged. It felt normal.

"Well, you know, it really does look good. And considering you were in the ocean all day—without your goggles . . . Can you see the difference?" She turned my head toward the mirror in the bathroom. It looked the same to me, maybe a little less red, or maybe it just looked that way because the rest of my face was so sunburned.

"I'm telling you, Artie," my mother said after she'd shuffled me over to my father in the other room, "it doesn't seem as red to me. Does it to you?"

"Let's have a look . . ." My father sat on the edge of the bed in his boxer shorts, inspecting my eye, spreading the lids apart with his thumb and forefinger to get a better look. "Well, well, well . . . Not bad," my father said, "not bad a'tall . . . Certainly doesn't look any worse. Who knows, maybe the ocean's good for it . . ."

"The corner isn't as red, is it, Artie?"

"All that salt water . . . Who knows . . ."

"And without her goggles . . ."

"Like Epsom salts or something . . ."

Their voices came rushing toward me. They were talking so fast, I couldn't catch it all. But the part I held on to was my father saying "The ocean's good for it." *The ocean's good for it!* That was all I needed to get me believing salt water had the power to cure me.

The next morning, I got up early, pulled on my one-piece, and stood swinging my beach bag back and forth, telling Lissy she looked fine. She had already changed her bikini twice and I was losing precious saltwater time.

I wasn't allowed near the ocean by myself. My mother said I had to have either Mitch or Lissy with me, and I wanted to get as much time in the water as I could. So after lunch, when Lissy decided to lie out by the pool, I egged Mitch on, challenging him to race me to the beach. Hours later, when he wanted to go inside for the day, I tried getting him to stay, telling him he could dunk me as much as he wanted and that I wouldn't tell on him or anything. I even promised him all the cherries from my Shirley Temples for the rest of the trip. I did what I had to do so I could stay in the ocean, concentrating on the salt water healing me, washing over my eye, washing away my birthmark.

☼

It was our second-to-last day in Florida and my mother had called us in early from the ocean because my father didn't want to be late. He was meeting with Flip and he wanted all of us to go with him. My father had a thing about going places by himself. At least one of us had to accompany him to the barbershop, to the delicatessen to get smoked fish and bagels, to the music store, the driving range, and even to the bank. And the thing was, once he got to wherever he was going, he'd almost always find some stranger to talk to. But even if he ignored you the whole time, you'd still be all excited to go with him the next time, and the time after that.

Lissy and Mitch started picking out what my father should wear that day, but I didn't feel like helping. I was in the bathroom, studying my eye in the mirror. My eyelid still looked lumpy, red, and purple, a little like a raspberry. But when I touched it, it felt solid beneath my fingertips.

It had only been five days, and even if nothing was changing on the outside, something inside was under way. Until then, I'd never really thought about my eye. I knew there was a problem with it, but it wasn't serious. It was just my eye. But now that I'd found something that could cure it, my eye had started to bother me. And suddenly, what I wanted more than anything was for it to be normal, like everybody else's. I didn't like the way I looked anymore. I decided I needed to be fixed.

Now I understood why my parents had tried to fix me before. I was six weeks old when they first noticed my birthmark. There it was one day, having surfaced out of nowhere like an unexplained bruise. The pediatrician was certain I'd outgrow it. But instead, the hemangioma continued to grow, and by the time I was a year old, my entire right eye was discolored and twice the size of the other one. Before the age of five, I'd undergone four unsuccessful operations. All they did was leave a few tiny scars on my lid where there should have been a fold. After the last surgery, my father started buying thick medical books that he stacked on the floor in his office. He subscribed to half a dozen medical journals, searching for something that could help.

I grew up with strangers staring at me, coming up to my mother in the supermarket, in line at the post office—wherever—asking what had happened to my eye. "Did she fall?" "Was she in an accident?" My mother would wave them off, her voice dismissive. "Yes, yes, she was in an accident."

My father's approach was different. Whenever someone asked about my eye, he'd come back with something like "Aw hell, you should see the other guy." He said this was easier than going into the whole story. Besides, it always got a laugh.

It was almost four o'clock when my father dropped us off at the diner next door to Flip's nightclub. And while he met with Flip, we kids sat at the counter with my mother, sipping Cokes, waiting.

I dug down in the front pocket of my mother's purse for a piece of Juicy Fruit and put the whole stick in my mouth, molding it over my front teeth, like braces. I showed Mitch and then he wanted gum, too. We were both smiling at my mother and Lissy, tilting our heads from side to side, giggling.

The waitress behind the counter looked at me a beat too long, offering what I realized was a pitying smile. I closed my mouth and started working the chewing gum off my front teeth with my tongue. I locked my eyes onto the napkin dispenser, staring at my reflection in the metal holder, looking to see how my eye was doing.

I was still studying my eye when my father came through the door. "Christ, Sandra, you didn't hear me? I've been sitting out there honking!" He thumped his toe on the doorjamb. "C'mon, c'mon . . ." He'd left the car running; he wanted out of there.

My mother paid for our Cokes and then we kids piled into the backseat, silent. We knew my father's moods, and when he got like this, we'd try hard not to give him anything to jump on.

"There's nothing to tell" was what my father said after my mother asked about his meeting. "It doesn't matter." But from the sound of his voice, you could tell it did matter. A lot. And even though my father wouldn't say anything more, we had already figured out he wasn't going to be playing clarinet for Flip.

❋

Back at the hotel room, my father sat on the side of the bed, chewing on the bit of his pipe, sorting through his money, repositioning the twenties on the outside, then the tens, the fives, and, finally, all the singles tucked in the middle. He always carried his money this way, big bills on the outside and never in a wallet. I think it made him feel like he had more that way.

My father still wouldn't speak to us, and my mother was trying to get him to talk, asking where he wanted to go for dinner. He shrugged and finally said he didn't want to go out. My mother lit a cigarette, walked over to the windows and stood there, staring at the ocean. She was smoking fast, one puff right after the other.

We kids didn't know what to do when they got like this other than keep our mouths shut.

It was getting late, and we were hungry. My mother tried again, asking my father if he wanted anything from room service. He just shook his head, and that's when my mother yanked the receiver off its cradle and sent the base of the phone crashing to the floor. "You really know how to spoil it for the rest of us, Artie, don't you!"

It was her rage that finally broke my father's silence. And after she'd placed our order with room service, he made a few groans and moans, and then started letting out phrases like "You try and be a *mensch,* a stand-up guy, and where does it get you?"

I could tell he wanted to talk then, but he didn't know how to get started. This was how he got sometimes, and whenever he did, he'd wait, expecting my mother to coax whatever it was out of him that he couldn't bring himself to say. "Will you please tell me why Flip said he wanted to meet with you?" My mother knew how to handle my father, when to get angry, when to hold back and let him have his moods.

"Oh yeah," he said, "he told me straight out."

"And?"

"Carpeting. The son of a bitch wants me to get him a deal on carpeting."

"But did you tell him you were hoping to play clarinet?"

"He knows—"

"But did you tell him, Artie? How do you know he knows?"

"Sandra, please! The man knows!"

Then he went silent again until after room service arrived.

"The nerve of him, Sandra! Just comes right out and asks what kind of deal I could work out for him. 'It's your shop, Goldman,' he says to me. 'You own the place. So tell me what kind of deal you're gonna give me.' "

"What did you tell him?" my mother asked, checking to make sure our order was right, letting bursts of steam escape each time she peeked under our dome-covered dinners. "Did you agree to help him?" She passed our plates around the room. The rims all looked shiny, peppered with beads of moisture.

"Well, what could I say? I told him I'd see what I could do." My father paused, reaching for one of my mother's french fries. "It's not gonna be a small job. I mean, we're talking something like seventy-five hundred square feet . . . I could make some decent change . . ."

"Uh-huh." My mother set her plate in between them on the bed.

Lissy, Mitch, and I nibbled our food, trying to be invisible.

My father reached for another fry. "I might as well make it worth my while." He opened a packet of salt, shook some into the palm of his hand, and sprinkled the fries. "I could still mark it up, plus the padding—not to mention the labor . . . And believe me, this isn't the end of my music!"

"Of course not, Artie."

"What's to stop me from putting together another band?" He was eating freely off her plate now. "Some damn good musicians back home . . . I could round up some talent."

This kind of talk went on for a while, until my father looked over at us as we sat on the extra bed, empty plates on our laps. He must have felt guilty, because in less than a minute he said he was taking us out for a fancy sit-down dessert, where they made banana splits right at your table. As soon as he said that, the air in our room lifted and I started to breathe again, relieved.

☼

On the morning of our last day, my father had slipped back into a quiet mood. I felt down then, too. We were leaving the next day, and my eye still wasn't normal. But I did have a plan. And while the others were at breakfast, I went up to the room and looked for containers to empty—Lissy's shampoo on the ledge of the shower, all those miniature bottles on the counter, the pill bottles along the sink in my parents' bathroom, whatever I could find.

I'd gotten the idea after seeing bottles of sand in a souvenir shop, stacked next to the canned sunshine and coconut pirate heads. I stuffed the containers inside my beach bag and headed back to the restaurant. And there I sat, back-kicking the leg of my chair while my father settled a dispute with the waiter over the bill. Who cared if we got charged for an extra order of bacon? It was just bacon and I had to hurry back to the ocean.

It didn't start out as much of a beach day. Early on it looked like rain and it was windy and cold. All the hair on my arms was standing straight up and you could see the goose bumps underneath. The waves were rough and the water had turned mossy green, scalloped with whitecaps.

Lissy, Mitch, and I walked along the shoreline, the surf bubbling over our toes, cool and tingly, the sand smooth beneath our feet. I was dragging my beach bag behind me as we walked, the plastic containers clattering around inside. My mother said we couldn't go in the water unless the weather cleared up, and I was feeling cheated, like someone had given me a present and then taken it back.

After lunch, the sun came out and Mitch and I were in the ocean, seeing who could hold their breath the longest. Lissy waded in the surf, eyes closed, her nose pointed to the sun, working on the finishing touches of her tan. I lunged head-on into one wave, and then another and another. I wanted to take in all the salt water I could.

At the end of the day, my mother stood at the top of the deck, waving us in. It was still windy out, and her hair swirled up on top of her head like a soft-serve cone. She wore big sunglasses with black-and-white checkerboard frames. I pretended not to see her and held my breath under the water again, trying to count to one hundred.

When I came up for air, my mother was gone from the railing and Lissy was shaking the sand free from her beach towel, calling for us to come in. Mitch ran ahead of me, scouting the sand one last time for shells. I went to my beach bag, took out the containers, and ran back to the surf to fill my empties. This way I could do my saltwater treatments back home. I'd dab just a bit along my lid every day until my birthmark was gone.

"Jesus Christ, Nina! I could have taken your mother's goddamn thyroid medicine!" My father stormed about the hotel room holding a fistful of pills.

I'd thought it would be okay, since I'd left them on a tissue and not just on the counter. I sat there, frightened by the sound of his voice. It didn't even matter what he was saying. He was yelling and I could feel my heart beating way up inside my eardrums. The tears started trickling down my cheeks.

"Christ . . . so now you're gonna cry about it, huh? Huh!"

"Artie, calm down, would you, please?" My mother gathered the dirty laundry strewn about the room, slung over the chairs and onto the beds. "It's over and done with," she said. "It's not a big deal."

"Well, it sure as hell is a big deal if she thinks she can just go into other people's things. You could have taken my Valium, for chrissakes! What do you have to say for yourself, young lady?"

I couldn't breathe, couldn't say a word. His yelling scared me and that was making me bawl even harder.

"Are you satisfied now, Artie?" my mother said. "You want to make her cry some more?" She leaned over the suitcase on the bed, tucking dirty socks down into the corners.

"Nina, I'm talking to you!"

I stared at my father and found myself giving him the same look I'd given the policeman the day we got pulled over for speeding. I knew it was the same look by the way it made me feel. I had found a way to make myself pathetic and beyond reproach.

My father threw up his hands and shook his head. "Ah, Christ—you want to baby her, Sandra? Go ahead and baby her. I give up!" My father grabbed the ice bucket off the dresser and walked out of the room.

He had backed down. My father had given up and I had won.

And that's when I realized that my father had taught me something that day the cop pulled us over. He'd taught me that I could use my eye to get out of things, too, and make people do things for me. It could maybe even make them go easy on me.

I got up from the bed, snatched my beach bag off the floor, and ran into the bathroom, shutting the door hard behind me. I emptied all the salt water down the sink. Right then and there, I didn't want to be cured. I needed my eye to be just the way it was.

the turkey run

It was the Wednesday before Thanksgiving. We were getting ready to make the turkey run. I was eight that year, and like every other year, Mitch and I were accompanying my father to Willie's Turkey Farm. Lissy used to go when she was little, hating it every time.

It was my father's thing. As a thank-you, he delivered fresh turkeys to his salesmen, his laborers, his people at the bank, the man downtown who let him make demo tapes in his recording studio on weekends.

"My turkey runners almost ready?"

Mitch nodded, climbing into his sweatshirt, the tip of his crew cut poking through the neckline, looking all velvety brown, like carpet brushed the wrong way.

"Thirty seconds before the turkey express shoves off." My father was leaning against the kitchen counter as we plopped down on the floor, jamming our feet inside our snow boots as fast as we could. "Ten more seconds, gang!"

Mitch and I ran to the closet and yanked our parkas and mittens off the rack on the back of the door. My father made the turkey run seem like a big outing for us, but that was just because he didn't want to do it alone. I didn't care why he invited me along, I was just happy to be around him.

Willie was waiting for us when we pulled up to the turkey farm. As he said hello, we could see his breath hanging in the air like puffs of smoke. He was a big red-faced man, wearing a hunting coat and a thick scarf wrapped twice about his neck. There were feathers and bird droppings stuck all over his work boots. His wife, Mildred, came out to greet us, her coat looking like it was two sizes too big for her. I would have bet money that it had probably once belonged to Willie. She was short and thin, but she must have been strong, because she helped run the farm, helped with the killings, the pluckings, the guttings. While Mitch and my father went inside with them, I went over and stood by the fence, watching the live turkeys. I didn't like it inside the slaughterhouse, all those turkeys hanging upside down by their feet. And the smell—so stinky, you had to plug your nose.

I pulled off my mittens and strung my fingers through the chicken wire and watched the turkeys pecking away at corn kernels and grain pellets scattered on the ground like loose bits of gravel. One of the turkeys stopped feeding and looked me, flapping its wings. I couldn't stand thinking that these birds would soon be dead. This was the part of the turkey runs I didn't like at all.

Business was slow that year, so we had only thirteen birds to deliver. The year before we'd had twenty-one. But good times or bad, I don't think anything would have stopped my father from making his turkey runs.

On these Thanksgiving outings, my father took us to parts of Akron we didn't even know existed—long dirt roads, deep stretches of grass, and fenced-in yards with big houses staked out in the middle. We'd pull into the driveway and then Mitch and I would take turns carrying the turkeys up to the front door while my father waited in the car. He thought it was a nice touch, having one of us kids drop off the birds. Either that or else he was just too lazy to do it himself.

I could never tell if the people who answered the door were being nice to me because of the turkey or because of my eye. They always seemed concerned at first, like maybe they'd thought I'd hurt myself and was coming for help. I'd stand there letting them get a good look at my eye before I'd hand them their bird and deliver my line: "Quality Brand Carpets wishes you a quality-brand Thanksgiving."

That's when they'd step out onto their front porches and wave back to my father.

"They know I'm the turkey man," he'd say, smiling, when we'd get back in the car. "Yep"—he'd give off a satisfied laugh—"I'm the turkey man every Thanksgiving!"

Everything nice my father did seemed to have a catch. He was always looking for something in exchange—maybe a better interest rate from the bank, maybe free time at the recording studio, or maybe just in case he needed a favor later on.

❁

When we got home that afternoon, a big green-and-gold Mayflower truck was parked at the end of our street. We knew it was the McFaddens moving onto our block. My family had known their family long before they turned up in our neighborhood. They had five kids, so Lissy, Mitch, and I each had one of them in our grade. My mother knew their mother from the PTA, and Mr. McFadden was in paints and wall coverings, so every now and again, my father's business crossed paths with his.

My mother had already invited the McFaddens for Thanksgiving the next day.

"Now, why in the world would you go and do a thing like that?" my father asked, lifting our turkey out of its cardboard box, setting it on top of the butcher-block table in the kitchen. Pumpkin, our little wiener dog, was up on her hind legs, investigating, wagging her tail.

"I thought it was a nice thing to do, that's why," my mother said, chopping celery so fast, she reduced a whole stalk down to tiny pieces in seconds, like magic.

My father shook his head and reached in his pocket for his Zippo lighter and started singeing pale hairs off the turkey's goose-pimpled skin. "Christ, goddamn bird's got almost as much hair on its arms as you do, Nina."

I glanced down and saw where I'd pushed my sweater up past my elbows. I *was* hairy. Too hairy for a girl. I pulled at my sleeves, tugging on them till they hung down past my wrists.

"Artie, they just moved in—they're not even unpacked. And besides, you're the one who's always complaining we don't have anyone to invite for Thanksgiving. And I'm sorry, but we don't need a twenty-pound turkey just to ourselves—"

"Twenty-two, Sandra. Twenty-two pounds!"

My father always thought the bigger the bird, the better, even if it was just us five and my grandparents for Thanksgiving. And not one of our turkeys, not even the smaller ones, ever fit in the refrigerator. They were always kept out in the garage—where my father said it was cold enough so that they wouldn't spoil—stored overnight on the hood of the car.

"Christ, Sandra . . ." My father gave the bird a rubdown, massaging its pink skin with both hands. Another thing about our turkeys: No one but my father was allowed to touch them. They were his birds. His! He'd be the one to dig down inside the cavity and scoop out the neck, the heart, the fistfuls of stringy fat that he'd deposit on the counter. He'd leave greasy handprints on every spice jar in my mother's cupboard, and by the time he'd finish seasoning the bird, he'd have paprika and garlic stuck in the grooves of his wedding band. Watching the way my father handled a turkey could make you not want to eat it the next day.

"I don't see why you're getting so upset, Artie. If you want, I'll go down to Beverly's and just cancel."

"Well, not now, Sandra! Not after you've already gone and done it. It's just that if you would have asked me, I would have said no—Samuel McFadden is not my idea of good company. He's a typical *goy*!" A Gentile. My father shook his head.

I think the main thing that bugged my father about Mr. McFadden was that up until they started building at the end of our road, we had the biggest house on the block.

"Would you look at how goddamn showy he has to be," my father had said when we drove down the street after construction had gotten under way. "He doesn't need pillars in the front. What's he trying to prove anyway?"

I never thought Mr. McFadden was trying to prove anything. They had more kids than we did, they needed a bigger house.

My father lifted the bird by its drumsticks and carried it over to the kitchen sink and turned on the faucet. He'd let that bird soak for hours while clumps of fat floated to the surface, swimming there in a pool of oily bubbles.

He dried his hands on a dish towel, grabbed his jacket off the closet hook, and took off out the back door without saying a word. My mother blew out a deep breath and went back to chopping celery.

Two and a half hours later we heard a rumbling outside. Pumpkin started barking, bounding for position at the front window, her snout pushing aside the curtains, her tail thrashing against the leaves of my mother's rubber tree plant.

There was a Sears truck idling in the drive, right behind my father's station wagon. Not as big a truck as the McFaddens had earlier, but still, it was a truck. I stood behind my mother at the front door and watched my father get out of the car, motioning to the driver to keep going: *Back it up*.

My father called to us when he saw us coming, zipping our jackets as we ran. "Wait till you see this one, gang! Wait till you see what your Big-Joe-Daddy-O just went out and bought us!"

"Oh, Artie, what in the world!" My mother brought both hands to her mouth when she saw the enormous box being lowered from the platform at the rear of the truck.

"Wait till you see this, Sandra—a brand-new microwave oven, huh! Huh? Twenty bucks extra just to get same-day delivery. How about that!"

"A what kind of oven?" Mr. McFadden asked the next day as we all crowded around the window, watching a glass of ice cubes being microwaved.

"Don't tell me, Samuel, you've never heard of a microwave oven before. It's the latest thing!"

I bet we had one of the first microwave ovens in Akron. It was a huge model, almost as big as our gas stove.

"Now, you just wait and see, gang," my father said, crouched down between the two oldest McFadden boys, Matthew and Greg. Timothy, the baby brother, the youngest of all the kids, was squatted right in front, barely blinking, watching the microwave like it was Saturday-morning cartoons. Patty and Keith were looking over their brother's shoulder. Lissy, Mitch, and I had already seen it do this half a dozen times the night before. Now it was the McFaddens' turn.

"I still don't get it," Mr. McFadden said, leaning one elbow on the counter, taking a sip of beer.

"You will, Samuel, you will. Now, just hang on . . ." The timer went off and my father reached inside for the glass. "Look at that, would ya!" He passed it around. "Go on. Don't be afraid—you can touch it. That glass is cool as a cucumber on the outside, but inside—boiling hot! Isn't that something else, huh?"

Mrs. McFadden dipped her pinkie inside the glass. "My, that is hot! Look, Sam—"

"Uh-huh . . . I see." Mr. McFadden reached in his breast

pocket for a cigarette and just nodded as the glass went from his wife to his daughter. He wouldn't touch it, wouldn't give my father the satisfaction.

"So what do you do with it?" Mr. McFadden asked.

"What do you mean? You cook with it, Samuel!"

"Why aren't you cooking your bird in that gizmo, then?"

"That's exactly what I'm gonna do."

"Oh no, Artie—" my mother said, pulling the dish towel off her shoulder. "Not when we're having company!"

"I'm telling you, that entire bird'll be cooked in under two hours."

"Ah, you're crazy, Artie." Mr. McFadden took another sip of beer.

"Am I really? How much would you like to bet?"

My mother reached over and gave Mrs. McFadden's wrist a squeeze. She smiled back and patted my mother's hand.

"I'm serious, Samuel. How much you wanna bet?"

So a bet was made. Twenty-five bucks said we'd be ready to eat by six o'clock. The bird came out of the regular oven where it had started cooking and went inside the microwave, and we kids went down the street to the McFaddens'.

The McFaddens' new house didn't look ready for company yet. Every room smelled of fresh paint and new carpeting, and I remembered then how my father had said something about Mr. McFadden not giving the business to him. "Would it have killed him, Sandra? We bought goddamn window blinds from him, didn't we?" he'd said.

The McFaddens had boxes stacked up in the hallways and in most of the rooms. Wires stuck out of the walls and some of the outlets didn't have any covers on them yet. They had other things, though, things we didn't have at our house, like intercoms in all the rooms. And upstairs, their parents' bathroom had two toilets sitting side by side.

"How come this one's broken?" Mitch asked, pointing to the toilet that didn't have any water in it.

"It's not broken," Keith said, pushing the lever, causing a fountain of water to spring up. "It's a bidet."

None of us asked the McFadden kids what a bidet was or what in the world you were supposed to do with it.

After that we went out back where they'd started digging for the swimming pool. It was nothing yet but a big hole of clay, sloping downward along the bottom like the hill at the top of our street. We climbed down inside the hole and I wandered about the shallow end with Patty and Keith. Patty was my age. Keith was just a year older, and you could tell that he and Patty liked to pal around, acting more like buddies than brother and sister. Greg, the next oldest one, was the same age as Mitch, but that brother fascinated me. He was the handsomest of the McFadden boys, and I couldn't help but watch him while he and Mitch slid down the side of the deep end, calling for Timothy to come join them. Timothy was too afraid to slide down there, so he stayed on ground level with Lissy and Matthew, who were sitting on a stack of bricks, watching us like they thought they were grown-ups. Matthew even lit a cigarette and smoked it right in the open where anyone could have seen him. Lissy said he was a troublemaker at school and that he spent a lot of time in the principal's office.

Patty started doing a tug-of-war with a tree root she'd found sticking through the wall of clay. Her pudgy cheeks puffed out full and pink as she pulled and pulled, determined. She was the only one of the kids who had their father's red hair and freckles, and his potbelly, too. Her brothers were skinny and took after their mother, all of them blond, good-looking, and athletic, even Matthew, who, despite his reputation, was the star of the basketball team. Inside their house were boxes full of trophies sitting on the living room floor, waiting to be unpacked; each box was stuffed with miniature baseball, basketball, and football players all frozen in gold. Greg had taken first place that summer in the Soap Box Derby and they had a big picture of his handsome face on the cover of the *Akron Beacon Journal*.

About half past five, we heard my mother calling for us, and both Matthew and Greg had to help pull Patty out of the pool because she couldn't heft herself up high enough to climb out on her own.

By the time we made it back, my grandparents had arrived. We saw my grandfather's white Plymouth parked on the street, even though there was plenty of room in the driveway. That way he could just go around the block when it was time to leave. My grandfather never drove in reverse if he could help it.

"Backwards I get *vermisht*—confused," he'd say.

My father was still in the kitchen, where we'd left him earlier, this time trying to explain the microwave to my grandparents. "Dad, did you listen to what I just said? It's *not* a convection oven!" He was saying this to a sixty-six-year-old man who still referred to cars as "machines."

Mr. McFadden came into the kitchen then, tapping the face of his wristwatch. "You got twenty minutes left, Goldman." He had a cigarette between his lips and a long unbroken ash lying on the front of his sweater where his belly served as a ledge, keeping it from dropping to the floor.

I took Patty and Keith upstairs to show them the laundry chute in Lissy's room and then all the way down to the basement to show them my father's pool table. Then it was back up to the family room to show off his pipes—hundreds of them, racked and resting on built-in shelves. After that we went into the living room to see my mother's clown collection. It wasn't like having a bidet, but still, they were things to show and I wanted them to think our house was just as good as theirs. And my mother did have a lot of clowns—on the walls, inside the china cabinet, on the glass tables, the fireplace mantel. She said they watched over our house, brought us good luck.

"Hey, you—you be careful with that," my mother said when she saw me lift her favorite clown off the piano lid.

She and Mrs. McFadden were taking the folding chairs out of the front closet and snapping them open, arranging them around the dining room table. Mrs. McFadden got hold of the bad chair, the one that always came unhinged in the back. My mother stepped in and, with the base of her hand, whacked the chair back into place.

Then Mr. McFadden came over, telling them not to hurry. "No way is that bird gonna be done by six o'clock!"

At six o'clock our turkey came out of the microwave, looking just as pale as it had two hours before. Even the gizzard looked anemic. My mother was embarrassed; I could tell by the way she shook her head, looking over my father's shoulder, watching him carve around the uncooked parts with his electric knife.

"Ah, would you look at that! Huh? What'd I tell ya?" My father marveled at the steam rising from the cavity.

When my mother went to brown the turkey slices under the broiler, my father grabbed her arm. "Sandra, don't you dare—"

"Artie, I can't serve it this way." My mother's lips barely moved as she said this. It was like she was a ventriloquist.

"The hell you can't serve it this way! This is the way it's supposed to be. This is not an ordinary oven, Sandra—in case you haven't heard!"

"Artie, you're shouting!"

"Now listen, Sandra, we're gonna eat this goddamn bird exactly the way it is!"

And we did. When we were all seated, my father explained that this was the way of the future. "Takes some getting used to," he admitted, holding up a pale drumstick, "but you can't say it doesn't taste just as good."

The McFaddens were being polite, even Mr. McFadden. All

he said was, "If this is the way of the future, Goldman, then count me out."

"Tell you what, Sam," my father said, licking his thumb and forefinger. "You can forget about the bet. We've had our fun—I'm not gonna hold you to it."

"You're something else, Artie. I'm telling you." Mr. McFadden shook his head and passed the platter of turkey to my grandmother, who passed it to my grandfather, who passed it to Lissy. I felt bad for my father, so when the platter came to me, I took two pieces.

After that Thanksgiving, Patty McFadden became my best friend. Now that she lived down the street, we walked to school and back together every day. Keith used to walk with us sometimes, but lately he'd made it a point of running on ahead, like he didn't want to be seen with us. I couldn't say I blamed him. His sister was the fattest girl in school, and I was the ugliest. That year, the boys in our third-grade class starting calling her "Patty the Fatty" and me "Big Eye–Little Eye."

They'd corner us on the way home from school, once we were out of the patrol boy's sight. They'd put their faces up close to mine and squint one eye shut, going, "What happened to your eye, Big Eye–Little Eye!" When they were finished with me, they started in on Patty the Fatty, snapping her training bra, trying to cop their first feels. You'd see her looking for her brothers, but they were nowhere to be found, busy with basketball and football, baseball and track, depending on the season.

After we'd made it past the school yard, we always went to Patty's house to play. Both her parents worked at Mr. McFadden's wall-covering store, and her brothers were always at practice, so we usually had the house to ourselves.

We'd play Barbies, listen to *Hair,* and pull out the stack of

Playboys from her father's nightstand, not believing our bodies would ever ripen like those Playmates'. We'd pour Elmer's glue into the palms of our hands and wait for it to dry so we could peel it off like a second skin. We'd have races going down the stairs on our bottoms—something that was forbidden at my house because my father said it was bad for the carpet.

Another thing we'd do at Patty's was play Can't Touch the Floor. We would start at one end of her house and work our way to the other, spider-crawling on all fours over countertops, across the kitchen sink, over the range top, along the coffee tables, anyplace but the floor. I always beat Patty when we played this game, because I was skinny and could move faster. Because of her weight, she was afraid some of the furniture wouldn't hold her, so at certain places she had to take a different route. One time, though, she did break a glass table, cracked it right in the center. She didn't even get grounded for it. She just told her mother it was an accident and that was that. You could get away with things at Patty's that you'd never even try at my house.

At my house it was different. I turned quieter there, even when my father wasn't home. Mostly I spent time alone, upstairs in the kids' bathroom. We had three sinks up there, one for each of us. I'd lock the door, stand in front of the mirror, and study my face, searching for even a hint of beauty. Sometimes I'd take Lissy's retainer out of its plastic dish and put it in my mouth just to see if it could make me look like her.

Other times I thought maybe if I had a pug nose . . . Kara Elberts, one of the kids at school, had one of those and dimples, too, and everyone thought she was pretty. So I'd take a piece of Scotch tape and run it from the tip of my nose to the center of my forehead. Then I'd try to make dimples by grinding eraser ends of pencils into my cheeks, hoping I could drill a pair in. I'd stare in the mirror for the longest time with my face taped up and pencils to my cheeks, trying for an improvement.

Nothing I did ever seemed to help, but I kept trying.

art's creation

One night we were watching *The Wizard of Oz* on TV. My father did a great Cowardly Lion, beating on his chest, singing, "If I were king of the forest—TAH!" He did a good Scarecrow, too, making his arms go all floppy, singing "If I Only Had a Brain." That night, my father acted out the entire movie, from the first bars of "Somewhere Over the Rainbow" to the reprise of "Ding-Dong! The Witch Is Dead." He sang every song, every word. He even chased me around the family room, going, "I'll get you, my pretty."

Even after the movie was over, he went on singing as he walked behind us, turning out lights, checking the back door, climbing the stairs with his shoes tucked under his arm. He was like a kid dodging bedtime, walking up and down the hallway, coming in and out of our rooms, serenading us: "We're off to see the Wizard / The wonderful wizard of Oz . . ."

My mother came out of their bedroom in her bathrobe. "Show's over, Mr. Wizard," she said, looping her arm through his as he broke into another round of "Follow the Yellow Brick Road."

He didn't want to stop and I didn't want him to. I loved it when my father goofed around. When he got silly like that, he made everything fun and he made me giggle till my sides ached. I never tired of my father's good moods. I kept climbing out of bed, running down the hallway, waiting for him to come back out just one more time. Just one more encore.

The next morning, my father made an announcement. We were going to form a family band.

"Why not?" he said after my mother and Lissy had stopped laughing. He was standing in his undershirt and a pair of corduroy slacks, sorting through the dry cleaning hanging from the back of the doorknob. "Sandra, we happen to be a very talented family."

I never thought of us as being very talented, but my father seemed convinced.

"I'm serious," he said, holding up two shirts, both different shades of blue. "Which one?" He brought both hangers to his chin..

"Either one, Artie."

"Really?" He held them at arm's length to study his choices. I noticed then that he had three tiny holes in his undershirt, right in a row, like ticktacktoe.

"You know, it's not such a crazy idea." He set one of the shirts back on the doorknob and tore through the cellophane. "Why the hell have I been paying a fortune in music lessons for the kids? Huh?"

I looked away. My father would be upset if he knew I hadn't practiced my scales all week. I don't think Lissy had picked up her guitar once, either. Mitch was the only one who didn't mind practicing. He was always banging on his drums in the basement, and we'd have to stand at the top of the stairs, flicking the light switch on and off to tell him it was time for dinner or if he had a phone call.

"And you—Sandra, you play piano."

"Oh, Artie, no." She was already shaking her head. "Leave me out of this." My mother actually *was* very talented. She had turned down the chance to study at Juilliard. When she was eighteen, my grandparents had taken her to New York so she could visit the school. She didn't like the city, couldn't picture herself living there. But she did like the talented street musician she'd met on the corner of Eighty-first and Amsterdam. It was love at first sight, and it didn't matter to my mother that this handsome, skinny clarinet player was broke. And it didn't matter to my father that this blue-gray-eyed beauty lived hundreds of miles away in Ohio. Two weeks later, my father turned up in Akron, got a job selling carpet, and that was that.

Unlike my father, my mother never thought about performing after she turned down Juilliard. She wanted nothing from show business. She played for her own pleasure.

"This is perfect, Sandra," my father said, now getting even more excited about his idea for the band. "Don't you see? With the kids and you—and your dad on violin—now, that's an act!"

"Oh Artie—"

"What do you say, gang? Huh?"

I was already Dorothy, doing "Somewhere Over the Rainbow," when my father smiled and started to laugh. That's when Mitch got in on the act, upstaging me with his best "In the Merry Old Land of Oz." He knew what to do to steal my father's attention away from me.

We started rehearsing that night after dinner, upstairs in the living room. Mitch carried his drum set up from the basement while we rearranged the furniture, pushing the glass coffee table flush with the sofa and moving the love seat smack up against the fireplace.

Lissy tuned her guitar while I practiced my breathing exercises. Off in the corner, my grandfather warmed up, a crimson silk handkerchief folded and tucked between his chin and violin. My father took his clarinet case down from the shelf in the front hall closet and assembled its parts, slipping the mouthpiece inside his mouth to warm it up so the reed would be more flexible.

My mother stayed in the kitchen futzing about, coming back into the living room every so often, smiling as she leaned against the banister, her arms folded, a dish towel slung over her shoulder.

Halfway into "Strangers in the Night," my grandmother had gotten out the Super 8 movie camera. And that's when Mitch launched into a drum solo and Lissy set her guitar aside and cut right in front of him, waving her hands and blowing kisses into the lens. As soon as Lissy did that, I ran over, cutting in front of her, blowing kisses just like she was, going, "Gram, Gram—over here! Over here!"

Then my father grabbed Mitch's drumsticks, and in an instant everything went silent, except for the sound of film running through the sprockets. "You think this is all just fun and games! You want to just clown around!" My father slammed the drumsticks down on the snare.

"Oh, for crying out loud, Artie! What's wrong with you? They're just trying to have a little fun."

"She's right, you know, Artie," my grandmother said, turning off the camera.

My father turned his back to them and glared at the rest of us. "If we're gonna do this, damn it, we're gonna do it right. It takes practice. Lots and lots of practice! You want to make records? Get your pictures in the paper? Make movies, make—"

"What records? Movies? Artie, please. Give me a—"

"Sandra, please!"

"Artie—"

"SANDRA!"

"Artie," my grandfather jumped in, "you and your *vershtoonkeneh*"—stinking—"ideas. And you wonder why every time you form a band you have such *tsores.*" Such troubles! "Your own children, Artie—please! *Genug!*" Enough!

Usually, my father listened to my grandfather, even though he was my mother's father and not his own. We never knew my father's father. He had died when my father was a baby, and none of us knew his mother, either. She passed away just two years later. That's when my great-aunt Fanny and great-uncle Stanley stepped in and raised my father and my aunt Flo, along with their son, Cousin Ricky.

My father said the only family he really had was my mother's and he looked to her parents as he would have his own. Only this time, my father wasn't listening to my grandfather. After my father had kicked Lissy's guitar case in the middle of "Hello, Dolly," my grandfather called him *"mishugeh,"* crazy, and he quit the band.

As soon as we heard my grandfather's Plymouth drive off, my father was back into rehearsal. My mother stormed into the kitchen and started running the garbage disposal, slapping cupboard doors, muttering to herself, going, "For crying out loud . . ."

My father stood in front of us, conducting while we played "I've Got You Under My Skin," calling out commands: "Concentrate! Watch your phrasing! Okay, hold it—HOLD IT—everybody just STOP!" He ran his hand over his face and I braced myself for whatever was coming next. "Mitch, for chrissakes, where the hell are you racing to? Melissa, why don't you try looking at the sheet music, huh? And you," he said pointing to me, shaking his head, "you need to focus on what you're doing." We all slumped before him, bruised. "Now, we're gonna do this again. And this time I need you people to concentrate. Mitch"—he turned to my brother—"from the top!"

Mitch sighed, still hunched over his snare.

"Mitchell?" My father was waiting, his toe tapping the carpet.

Mitch forced himself to sit up straight, raised his drumsticks above his head, and clacked them together, going, "A one, a two—a one-two-three!"

And then we were back to rehearsing, this time getting it right.

❋

In the fall, my father got us booked on *The Phil Moran Show,* a local amateur variety hour taped in Cleveland. He'd sent in the demo tape we'd made—all of us huddled together in the family room, performing "Cracklin' Rosie" into Mitch's cassette recorder.

After they'd heard our tape, Phil Moran's producer invited us up to Cleveland for a live audition. The next week, they called to say we'd been selected for the show, and by then my father had convinced my mother that we needed her on piano. She wasn't happy about this, but she did it for him, for us. Even though she said it was nonsense, she knew we believed my father when he said we could get discovered. According to him, we could be like the Jackson Five or the Osmonds. We could be famous, and since I was the youngest and I could sing, there was a chance I might be soloed out like Donny or Michael, and who wouldn't love me then?

We were at my grandparents' house getting measured for our TV costumes and having dinner. My grandfather was having a good time, teaching us the right way to eat spaghetti—how to hold our big spoons at an angle so we could twirl the noodles around our forks. Then my father showed up and my grandfather turned quiet. I could tell he was still mad at my father, because he set his spoon down and left the table. He said he was going to mow the lawn, and it was already dark outside.

My grandfather was nothing like my father. A retired lawyer, someone who had worn a suit and tie to work every day, he was a perfectionist. He read Yiddish poetry, English literature, and loved the opera. When they were little, he used to take my mother and Uncle Irwin to the ballet and the art museum in Cleveland. Not that my grandfather didn't love my father, but I think he always thought his daughter should have married a professional man.

While my grandfather was still outside, my grandmother brought out her sewing basket, packed full with scissors, spools of thread, and a tomato-shaped pincushion so full, it looked more silver than red. My father stood in the middle of the dining room with his feet set far apart while my grandmother knelt in front of him, measuring his inseam, her legs tucked beneath her bottom.

I went in the kitchen to help my mother and Lissy with the dishes. While we wiped down the countertops and dried pots and lids, I watched my father and Mitch sitting around the dining room table with my grandmother, looking at the swatch of fabric she'd selected for our costumes.

"I don't know, Mom—you sure that color's loud enough?" my father asked, packing his pipe with tobacco. "I was thinking something, I don't know, something loud, flashy."

My grandmother pulled the fabric out from under his fingers. "*Oy gevalt!* You're driving me nuts, Artie! You want you should glow in the dark now? It's plenty loud. Trust me."

"I just want it to be the right color, that's all." He struck a match and, with one puff, filled the air with a cloud of sweet smoke.

"Mr. Color-Blind—the maven! What difference does it make? It's in the blue family."

"But it's got to be flashy. I don't know. Mitch, girls—what do you think?"

Lissy and I came back in from the kitchen. We liked it.

My father bit down hard on his pipe and kept his hand over the bowl as he puffed. "It looks a little bland to me."

"*Oy veh is mir!* Give me a break!" My grandmother rubbed her fingers together like she was working in hand cream. "It's a nice periwinkle blue!"

"What's periwinkle look like?"

"Flashy, Artie. Very flashy."

❋

The big day arrived. We were in the car, on our way to Cleveland for our taping of *The Phil Moran Show.* We were dressed in our costumes: sequined vests and periwinkle bell-bottoms with sequined bands running down the legs.

As my father backed down the drive, Lissy complained that I was crowding her, so she lifted her foot and shoved me into Mitch, who pushed me back onto Lissy's side.

"No shoving!" my mother called out from the front seat without even turning around. The woman didn't miss a thing. "Now behave back there, you three."

"Say, gang"—my father lowered the radio—"what are we gonna call ourselves, huh? We gotta have a name. Every band has a name."

We kids started shouted out things like the Grand Goldmans and the Goldman Family Singers, and it went downhill from there. Just as we got to the Cleveland exit, Mitch came up with the winner: Art's Creation, named after my father. We all liked it. It was only fitting. After all, what other father could get his children booked on TV? What other father could dream as big as ours?

My father had a way of believing in something, and once his mind was set, he'd pull you right along with him. Once on board, you were with him all the way. He'd have you convinced that whatever he wanted was the very thing you'd always wanted, too. That was my father. He could persuade anyone of anything. He was a salesman, a salesman of carpets, a salesman of dreams.

. . .

And then Art's Creation was at *The Phil Moran Show.* We were standing in the wings backstage, anxious as we watched the act they were taping ahead of us. It was another family of five, spinning plates and playing harmonicas at the same time.

"Would you look at that!" my father said. "You call that talent? That's not talent. That's a circus act." He thought he was whispering, but a tall, skinny man with a clipboard and a pencil tucked behind his ear shushed him twice.

When it was our turn, we took our places on the stage. The set looked so much bigger when you saw it on TV. We were waiting for the go-ahead when the skinny man with the clipboard came over to arrange us. "Tell you what we're gonna do," he said, grabbing the pencil from behind his ear, scratching down a note on his clipboard. "We're just gonna move you all around a little." He shuffled Lissy an inch or two to the left, scooted my father closer to her. "Piano's fine. Drums are fine. And now for you," he said, placing an open hand over my head, contemplating, "let's see where we're gonna put you . . . How about right back here—right behind your mother?"

My father shook his head, laughed. "Wrong! No—Nina's in front. She's one of our singers. Can't even see her back there."

"Ah . . ." The man paused and consulted his clipboard. "Ah, Mr. Goldman . . ." He looked up and beckoned my father with his index finger and then placed a hand on his shoulder. His voice dropped to a whisper, but we could still hear every word. "You see, when we brought you all into the studio last month for your audition, well, we didn't understand—"

"What didn't you understand?" My father's smile was beginning to slip.

"Mr. Goldman, at the time of your audition, we thought the eye was only a temporary thing. Kids' stuff—you know . . . a real shiner." The skinny man shook his head, forcing a laugh. "We didn't realize, see, that it was a permanent sort of thing."

"So what are you trying to say here, huh?" My father broke away from the skinny man's hand.

My mother rose from her piano bench.

I realized then that this was about me: I was the problem. I turned to Lissy, who had her pinkie tucked under the sequins on her vest. She was pulling so hard on the threads, I could see her finger turning white. She wouldn't look at me. Neither would Mitch.

The man with the clipboard rocked back on his heels and shook his head. "It's just that this sort of thing doesn't make for what we call 'good TV,' if you know what I mean. And after all, this is a family show—a lot of young children watching. You understand . . . We'd hate to upset anyone."

"Well, you know what? You're upsetting me!"

I still wanted to be famous, and I knew all about my father's temper. I was afraid he was going to get so mad that we'd get thrown off the show. I inched closer to him. I didn't care where they wanted me to stand. I didn't want that to be the reason we weren't going to be on TV. "Dad, it's okay, I—"

He gave the back of my neck a squeeze to quiet me. It was a hard squeeze and it hurt. "Let me tell you something," my father said, "this little girl can sing circles around half the kids you put on here. I've seen. I know!"

I looked up at my father and he gave me a wink. When he did that, I felt like I was on his side. It was just the two of us against this tall, skinny man. I felt myself smiling and it didn't matter that my father had just hurt the back of my neck. He and I were in this together.

The skinny man looked at me and slid his pencil back behind his ear and tucked his clipboard under his arm. He mumbled something to one of the cameramen and then disappeared through a side door.

A few minutes passed and then another man wearing a headset came onto the stage and stood next to my father. "Mr. Goldman, sir, my apologies. If it's okay with you, we can proceed as planned. We'll just put the little girl right here. Right here in front." The man with the headset squared my shoulders and pointed to a camera, telling me where to look. "Big smiles now, everyone!"

I was giddy. We were on TV and on our way to becoming famous.

The following Sunday night, we were gathered around the television to watch *The Phil Moran Show.* I was already in my pajamas, lying on the floor in front, my chin resting on my knuckles. Mitch was stretched out beside me. Lissy sat with Pumpkin in her lap, her fuzzy slippers crisscrossed on top of the coffee table. My parents were side by side on the couch, my father with his pipe, my mother with her cigarettes. My grandparents were in the two chairs, angled along the side, so they could see the TV.

My grandfather didn't seem all that interested in the show, and I wasn't sure if that was because he was still upset with my father or because he was getting antsy about having to drive home in the dark. He kept getting up and peeling back the drapes, looking out the back window, checking what he called "the elements."

After the plate twirlers were finished, it was our turn. On television we looked small, boxy, and nervous. Mitch never looked into the camera, not once. All you saw was the top of his head—his face turned to the side, his ear close to the snare, as if it were whispering something back. They did a fancy camera move where you saw my mother's face on half the screen and then just her fingers playing piano on the other half. They did the same thing with my father and the keypads of his clarinet. It was Lissy, though, who got the longest, tightest close-ups.

"Gross me out!" Lissy moaned through splayed hands each time they showed her. "I look horrible!"

She didn't look horrible. She wasn't capable of horrible. My sister looked beautiful and she knew it. She just said that so the rest of us would deny it and tell her what she wanted to hear.

I kept waiting to see myself, but the camera just went from close-ups of Lissy and my father to wide shots of us all, then to close-ups of Mitch, then to my mother and back to Lissy. Then it was over. Finished. That was it. We were gone and the boys with the Chihuahuas were on. I didn't even get one close-up. Not one!

As soon as the show was over, I marched upstairs to the kids' bathroom and slammed the door shut. I hated the way I looked. I was gross. Too gross for TV. I reached for my Scotch tape and ran a piece from my nose to my forehead. I grabbed two pencils and started working the eraser ends into my cheeks. I was going at it when my grandmother walked in. I dropped the pencils and whirled around, but it was too late—she'd already seen.

My grandmother closed the door behind her. "What are you doing to yourself, Ninaleh?"

"I hate my face, I hate my eye," I mumbled, looking down at my toes. "I just wanna change it all."

She walked over to me and peeled the tape off my nose and forehead. "Ah, Nina, such a *shayne punim*. A pretty, pretty face." She led me away from the mirror, put the toilet lid down, and then gave it a pat.

I went and sat on the furry cover, tugging at the sleeve of my flannel pajamas. "Why can't I look like Lissy?"

"Because you look like Nina!" She smiled and touched her finger to the tip of my nose. "And there's nothing wrong with that."

"But I didn't even get a close-up. I'm the only one who didn't. I'm never gonna be famous." I lowered my head and started to cry.

"Is that what you want? To be famous?"

I nodded, still crying.

"And why is that, Nina? Tell me?"

I shrugged. "At least then I'd be popular."

"And you can't be popular now?" My grandmother made a

face, like she was eating something rotten. "You have to be famous to be popular?"

"Either famous or pretty. And I'm not pretty."

"Oy, Nina, you know what makes a person pretty? It's what's inside. When you're happy on the inside," she said, "that's what makes all of you pretty on the outside. Not pencils, not tape—that won't change a thing." She raised my chin and smoothed the hair away from my eyes. "And believe me, just because someone has a pretty face doesn't mean they're happy. And it doesn't make them popular."

After I wiped my nose on my pajama sleeve, my grandmother handed me a tissue that was tucked inside the cuff of her dress. I sniffled as she leaned over, pressed her forehead against mine, and whispered, "Ninaleh, I'm going to tell you something. Everybody has a gift inside them. Something special that no one else in this whole wide world has. It's your gift and no one else has the same one. And do you know why it's a gift?"

I shook my head.

"It's a gift because once you discover what it is, then that's the part of yourself that you can give to other people. You give them your gift and that's what will make you popular." She leaned back and tilted her head to the side. "Don't worry about pencils and tape—or who's popular and who's pretty. Go find your gift, Nina. That's what you need to do."

every crooked pot

When I was ten, my father met a woman named Bobbie Novak. He was excited about this. So was my mother. Bobbie Novak had a hemangioma, and a special doctor in Chicago with an experimental drug. My father had read all about her in one of those medical journals that kept arriving month after month. As it turned out, this woman lived in Canton, less than thirty miles from us, and my father had arranged a meeting.

Her house was small, with dented siding and a rusted-out mailbox in the yard. When we pulled into the drive, the front door opened and a middle-aged woman stepped outside, clutching a beige sweater to her chest. As soon as I saw her, I wanted to go home.

I wanted Bobbie Novak to be beautiful, but she wasn't. Not exactly ugly, but not beautiful, either. When we got up close, I could see patches of her scalp showing through her thin brown hair. The skin on the side of her face and neck was just like the skin I had around my eye, all raised and lumpy, purple and red.

Her house was dark inside and smelled like cheese. She left us alone in the living room for a moment, and in her absence, my father walked the perimeter of the room, tapping the toe of his loafers to the corners.

"Carpet's shot," he said to my mother.

"Artie, sit down and behave yourself, will you please?"

"Shame," he said, "makes the whole room look like hell."

"Artie, will you please!" My mother grabbed hold of his back pocket and he winked at me as she yanked him onto the sofa next to her.

Bobbie Novak came back into the living room carrying a tray of lemonade and fancy green leaf cookies, the kind lined with chocolate that you get from the bakery. They were my favorite, so I took two.

Bobbie Novak was telling us how much worse her hemangioma had been before her treatments with Dr. Waxler.

"And how often do you see the doctor?" my father asked, leaning forward, placing his elbows on his knees.

"Oh, now, that depends . . . See, before my husband retired, I went to Chicago twice a month. But it's expensive—and you can forget about insurance covering the treatments. So we've had to cut back now on the injections."

Injections? Did she say injections? Like shots! As in needles! I put my cookies down. I wanted to run out to the car and hide and pretend I'd never heard any of this. I wished we'd never met Bobbie Novak. I wanted to go home.

"Injections?" My mother lifted her glass of lemonade and then set it back down without taking a sip.

"But really"—Bobbie Novak smiled—"it's not as bad as it sounds."

"What sort of injections?" my father asked, still leaning forward, now lacing his fingers together.

My head felt weird, like it wasn't attached to the rest of me anymore.

"It's a shot—a special agent he uses. See? I get my injections in my cheek and right here, in my neck." She ran her hand along her throat. "Now, in Nina's case, I'd imagine the injections would be given along the eyelid itself . . ."

In my eye! I couldn't sit still. I started picking at an ugly plastic button sewn to the seat cushion.

"I see . . ." My mother was fidgeting with her necklace. "I didn't realize there'd be injections . . . Are they painful?"

I couldn't listen. Even a shot of Novocain made me flinch. I felt dizzy and clammy, like I might throw up. I was yanking hard on that button and didn't care if I pulled it off and ruined the whole chair. I didn't want to think about the shots, and tried to make everything inside my head turn to white static, like television snow.

Later, after my parents were done talking about needles, Bobbie Novak turned to me and asked if I had any questions for her, anything I might want to know. I did have a question, but it had nothing to do with this doctor in Chicago. I'd been looking at that blotchy skin on her face and then at her wedding band, and what I wanted to know more than anything was how she met her husband and if there was something wrong with him, too.

I asked my parents about that on the drive home. I asked how a woman who looked like Bobbie Novak could find a husband.

"Tootsie," my father said, glancing back at me through the rearview mirror, "every crooked pot has a crooked cover."

☼

The next thing I knew, the three of us were in Chicago, sitting in the doctor's office. After Dr. Waxler explained everything, my father said it was the right thing to do. He said it wouldn't even hurt. "Just a pinch, Neen. That's all."

So once a month, from the time I was ten until I was thirteen, my mother took me to Chicago to see Dr. Waxler. And at least I got to miss school each time I had a treatment. That was the good part. My mother and I would fly up in the morning and come back that same day, usually on a Friday, so that I'd have the weekend to recuperate. My father would drive us to the Akron/ Canton Airport, the carpet sample books shifting in the way back of the station wagon.

Walking us to the gate, my father would put his arm around me, lean in close, and say there was nothing to worry about. "Everything's gonna go just fine, sweet pea." Then he'd hand my mother an extra twenty-dollar bill—just in case—get us all checked in, and then give us both a kiss good-bye.

As soon as my father left us at the gate, I could see the change wash over my mother's face. Her brow would wrinkle, her lips would tighten, and she'd grab hold of my hand. We were on our own and my mother always looked as though she wasn't ready. She'd never been anywhere outside of Akron without my father or my grandparents.

At home she was just the opposite, always in command—of herself, of us, and of everything in her domain. There wasn't a bicycle chain she couldn't fix, a channel she couldn't get in on the portable TV. No spider was too big, no splinter too deep, no fever too high, and no zipper she couldn't unstick. When we were running late for school, she always knew where we'd left our shoes the night before. In Akron, my mother was so sure of herself, but in Chicago, her uncertainty showed like fingerprints on the lid of her baby grand.

Even after we'd made that trip a good twenty times or more, she'd still look around the terminal, studying the overhead signs at O'Hare as if seeing them for the first time. "Now, let me just get my bearings here," she'd say, more to herself than to me. "Okay, ready?" Then off we'd go.

We'd get into a cab and I'd press my face to the window, waiting for the skyline to break through in the distance, like airplane wings cutting through the clouds. Sitting in traffic, miles before we'd entered the Loop, my mother was already getting the cab fare from her pocketbook. I'd be pointing out the hot dog and ice-cream vendors, or the elevated train running on ahead, and she'd nod, going, "Uh-huh." But she wasn't looking. I could tell she was mentally figuring the meter, adding on the appropriate tip according to my father's instructions. I just kept babbling, pointing out skyscrapers and the policemen on horseback and other things you'd never see in Akron.

Each time my mother and I went to Chicago, we did exactly the same thing. The whole day we'd never leave this one block of State Street. We'd eat huge hand-carved roast beef sandwiches for lunch at the Blackhawk, and afterward, we'd go to Dr. Waxler's office. His nurse would take me into a room and have me lie flat on an examination table. My mother always crowded into the corner, near the door.

The nurse would dab a cotton swab over my eye. It was soaked in something that was supposed to numb my lid, but I could still feel everything. I'd see the needle and hear Dr. Waxler telling me to stay still while his nurse held my head in place, her fingers positioned on either side of my temples. The antiseptic smell in the room was so strong, I could taste it.

"Hang on now . . . we're almost finished, Nina." Dr. Waxler would say this even though he'd just gotten started.

First, there was the prick of the needle going into my eyelid, breaking the skin, then the burn of the sclerosing agent being fed to my blood vessels. The skin would begin to tighten around the needle, and it would start to sting, like when you get soap in your eyes. I couldn't see my mother standing in the corner anymore. I was alone and everything turned cold inside me. I could feel Dr. Waxler weaving the needle across my lid, like he was hemming a piece of fabric. The nurse would tighten her grip around my temples while I'd bear down harder, trying to push my shoulder blades flat against the table.

The worst surge of pain came when Dr. Waxler pulled out

the needle. And by then, my eyes would be tearing, my fingers white from gripping the sides of the table. His nurse would always press a wad of cotton over my eyelid, trying to keep the swelling down.

The whole procedure, start to finish, took less than thirty minutes. And by the time we'd leave Dr. Waxler's office, the broken blood vessels around my eye would be rushing to the surface, turning the skin even more red and purple than normal—you could see it happening right in front of you. This was a good sign. They said it meant the sclerosing agent was working; the sort of thing that had to get worse before it got better.

The next stop on our routine, even with my eye bugging out, was Marshall Field's, located right across the street from Dr. Waxler's office. My mother would pull lacy dresses and smock tops off the racks, hold them up beneath my chin, and say, "Oh Nina, now that's just darling. Let's try it on. Want to?" I never felt like trying on clothes after my shot, but at least it gave us something to do until it was time to leave for the airport. My mother always came inside the dressing rooms with me, even the tiniest ones, where she'd stand half in and half out, the pull curtain draped around her body.

In Chicago my mother would buy me things like the elephant bell-bottoms and gaucho pants she'd denied me back in Akron. Without asking how much we'd spent, my father would make a big deal out of wanting to see everything. He'd sit back in his chair with his *Wall Street Journal* folded on his lap, whistling as I'd model each new purchase.

My parents did their best to disguise my doctor visits as shopping sprees, but no matter how many new outfits we bought, I still knew that in another month, I'd have to go back to Dr. Waxler's and go through the whole thing all over again.

The hardest part about Dr. Waxler's treatments was going back to school the following Monday. I always looked like I'd been hit with a line drive—my eye all swollen, the red and purple skin darker than normal. And it hurt. My eye stung like a bee had gotten to it, and aspirin didn't help. The only thing that made it feel better were tea bags. Something about the acid took away the stinging and burning.

At home I'd just wander around holding a paper towel to my eye with a damp tea bag inside. But at school it was different. You had to have both hands free, so my mother would take one of my father's handkerchiefs, wrap a wet tea bag inside, and stick it across my forehead with thick white tape.

At first I thought I'd get the same treatment Audrey Weber got after she flipped over the handlebars on her ten-speed and broke her jaw. She came back to school all wired up and everybody thought it was cool. They fought over who got to sit with her at lunchtime just so they could watch her suck her soup through a straw, loving it when she'd get a noodle or a carrot stuck in the middle.

I hoped that they'd think my eye was cool, too, but they just stared at the handkerchief and asked why I had that thing taped on my face, so I told them all about the shots. "And the needles are *this* big!" I said, holding my index fingers eight or nine inches apart. I wished I'd come up with something better to say about the tea bags, because those kids blabbed it to the whole school. The next day a group of boys circled me in the hallway, going, "Nina's a little teapot—arf, arf, arf."

I didn't mind them teasing me because these were the boys who had never paid attention to me before. So I would hang around outside the gymnasium door, pretending I was reading the bulletin board, waiting for those boys to come by. But when Mike Smithers, the boy I liked most, started in with the others, it wasn't fun. I started crying right in front of him, hoping I could make him feel sorry for me and be nice to me. And that way, maybe he'd start to like me. But he never did.

And after that day when the boy I liked most started arf, arf, arfing at me, I stopped wearing the tea bags. The stinging and burning I could take. It was all the rest that I couldn't. I didn't want to be stared at, didn't want anyone barking at me. I wanted to be normal.

But no matter what I did, every time I came back from the doctor's, the other kids teased me worse than ever. This went on once a month, every month for three years. And that's why I started feeling sick on Sunday nights following a treatment. It was my head, or else I was dizzy—afraid I'd throw up. It was always something.

"Like hell she's sick! Every goddamn time, Sandra . . ."

I overheard my parents arguing about me one morning as I stiffened under my covers.

"Well, what can I do, Artie? It's hard on her."

"You can quit babying her, Sandra. That's what you can do! You want her to use her eye as a crutch? 'Cause that's exactly what you're doing every time you give in. She's gonna use that eye to get out of anything she doesn't want to do. And I'm not gonna stand for it anymore. We've tried it your way long enough. Now we're gonna do it my way."

I heard his chair push out from the table, followed by the sound of him climbing the stairs, taking them two at a time. I could feel him getting closer and I couldn't move, couldn't even swallow. I was bracing myself.

My father barged into my room, snapped on the overhead light, and went to my closet. "Get up NOW! You're going to school!" He started sorting through my clothes and flung a tartan kilt onto my bed. "You're going to school and don't you dare start crying about it! You want to feel sorry for yourself, Nina? You don't like this hand you've been dealt? Well, then you'd better toughen up. You better learn how to survive and just be grateful for what you've got!"

His words clobbered me.

"Take a look at the kid who has no eyes, no arms, no legs! You have your sight, don't you, huh?"

He didn't know it, but I would have given up the sight in that eye just to have it look normal. I was hating him then. Why was he making me go to school? Didn't he know what it was like there for me?

By now my father had worked himself into a rage. He was rifling through my drawers and pulled out an orange Danskin turtleneck that was two sizes too small for me. He threw it onto the bed next to the red plaid skirt.

"I see you're not too sick to stay up here and play with all your toys," he said, stepping over a set of checkers and a heap of Barbies lying in the center of the floor. "You know, I didn't even have toys when I was growing up. I had it tough—not like you, kid. Thank God you don't know from tough! I didn't have a mother and father who loved me. No, I had an aunt who used to lock me in my room for hours at a time. And I didn't have a father, either! No, I had an uncle who came after me with his belt—and he used the end with the buckle. No, you don't know from tough, kid. Thank God you don't know from tough."

Now I was feeling guilty, because, compared to my father, I didn't have it so bad, even with my eye. He was still talking and it was hard to keep listening to him just then. I had to turn my face into my pillow so he wouldn't see me crying.

According to him, I was a bad daughter. I was "goddamn spoiled rotten!" That's what he was saying to me now. "And if you think you're gonna sit around and pout—well, I'm not gonna have it!" He reached into my top drawer and tossed a pair of pink tights onto the bed. "Now hurry up and get dressed!"

I rolled over and looked down at the outfit my color-blind father had selected for me. I was too afraid to tell him that nothing he'd picked went together.

"I'm dropping you off at school on my way to the store. You're late as it is! Now hurry it up!" My father had almost reached the door when he heard me sobbing. "I said don't cry about it, Nina!"

He slammed my bedroom door and I dragged my knuckles across my eyes to clear the tears. But still, I couldn't stop crying. I pulled on the pink tights and then tugged my way into the orange turtleneck and stepped into the plaid skirt. I looked at myself in the mirror on the back of my door and started to bawl.

I couldn't go to school dressed like this. It was bad enough that my eye was all bruised and swollen, but now my father had dressed me like a clown. I stared at my reflection in the mirror and all I saw was a blur of pink, orange, and red plaid running together, mixing with my tears, a pool of watercolors gone bad.

I know I could have changed my clothes, but I didn't dare. I was too afraid that would have made my father even angrier.

When I went downstairs, my mother was at the kitchen table, smoking a cigarette, rolling the tip against the side of the ashtray, making it into a point, like a sharpened pencil. I stood there hoping she would look up and see what I was wearing. If she did, I knew she would have saved me, would have made me change my clothes. But she wouldn't look up. She just kept her eyes on the ashtray.

I stomped over to the front closet and yanked my coat off the hook as hard as I could. I went and sat on the rug in the foyer and laced up my shoes, wiping my nose on the sleeve of my jacket. I stared back at my mother one last time, willing her to look. If she had given me even one glance, just one, I would have ran to be coddled, to be protected from my father, to be saved from having to go to school dressed like that. But she wouldn't look my way. Pumpkin jumped on me to lick my tears and I swatted her away so hard, she almost snapped at me.

"Hurry it up, young lady." My father stood over me, car keys jangling in his hand. "You're going to school."

the ballroom

When we were growing up, my sister and brother always had their friends over to our house. Everybody got a kick out of my father, knowing that just poking their heads into the family room for a quick hello could start an hour-long discussion on everything from what they thought of George McGovern to how the Cleveland Indians were doing that season. My father had a way with these kids. He could get them to confess if they'd ever been drunk, smoked marijuana, popped any pills. According to my father, nothing was beyond asking, and for some reason, they always answered.

He could get them to do all kinds of things, too. Like the night he got my sister's friends to try Limburger cheese. Lissy's boyfriend, Rob, and maybe four or five others were lined up in the kitchen. All of them, boys and girls, looked exactly the same—long hair, tie-dyed T-shirts, patched-up bell-bottoms trailing on the floor. They watched my father slice the cheese, squaring it just so on thin crackers, capping them off with slices of Bermuda onion.

Lissy was back-kicking the cupboards, going, "Da-ad, do we have to? That stuff stinks."

"Ah, now, here we go!" my father said, ignoring her. "Doesn't that look good? Don't be bashful, gang!" He held out a platter, the crackers all arranged at angles.

"You guys don't have to," Lissy said, but her friends each took a cracker anyway.

Rob went first, cramming the whole thing in his mouth.

"Not bad now, huh? Huh? Didn't I tell you?"

I'll never forget the look on Barbie Sinclair's face as she chewed. Her eyes were tearing and you just knew she wanted to spit it out.

Then there was the time my father performed yo-yo tricks for Mitch's friends.

"You've seen Around the World, you've seen Rock the Cradle, but none of you," my father said, slipping the loophole onto his middle finger, casting the yo-yo to get the feel, "none of you have ever seen Goldman's famous Bite the *Tochas* trick!"

My father spread his feet far apart and started throwing the yo-yo down between his legs. "Ready, gang? On three. One, two—and three!" This time he threw the yo-yo through his legs with such force, it caught on the seat of his pants. "Ta-da! Isn't that something, huh? Eh!" He tugged on the string to prove the yo-yo had a firm grip on his backside.

My father spent the rest of the evening teaching that trick to my brother's friends.

While my father entertained everyone, my mother would slip upstairs with whatever paperback she was into at the time and run the bath. Sometimes, when I was feeling left out, I'd go up after her and just walk right into the bathroom. My mother's silver hair would be tucked inside a pink shower cap and she'd have a cigarette burning in a seashell ashtray on the ledge of the tub, the pages of her paperback wavy from water.

I'd sit on the area rug cross-legged, telling her about a new way the girls were wearing their hair, or what Patty talked about on the way home from school, or what happened during recess, or at lunchtime. On and on I'd go. "Uh-huh," she'd say every few minutes or so, the whole time keeping her eyes on her book.

Then there'd be a big burst of laughter coming from the family room. What was my father doing this time? Without a word to my mother, I'd spring up off the bathroom rug and race downstairs to see what I was missing.

I'd been waiting for my turn, my chance to have my friends gather at our house, but it never happened. So I felt cheated, because when I entered the sixth grade and Kara Elberts and her gang started hanging around us—well, around Patty really—I knew these girls would never rally around my house or my father.

These were girls who had barely spoken to us the year before, but they had now befriended Patty because she had what every girl our age wanted: four cute brothers and a house full of all their friends. My father was no match for the crowd that gathered night after night at Patty's house.

☼

The McFadden kids had turned their basement into the Ballroom. At first glance, the Ballroom didn't look all that sinister, just a typical finished basement with wood paneling and linoleum floors. Occasionally, you might even find a basket of laundry folded and waiting to be carried upstairs. But for those of us who knew what went on in that room, we understood the Ballroom was something you didn't tell your parents about. It was called the Ballroom for a reason and that's because it was home to nightly make-out sessions for some, and even going all the way for others.

Keith was the mastermind behind the Ballroom, but the rest of the McFadden kids had their hand in transforming their basement. Matthew, being the oldest, made sure they always had a reliable source for pot and beer. Greg was in charge of the music and used his looks to get the prettiest girls down there. Patty organized all the parties, getting the word out to everyone, and poor Timothy was usually put on cleanup detail.

The McFadden kids moved all the old furniture that had once been the good stuff upstairs, down to the basement. In less than a month, every piece had developed a new scar or blemish. They had Greg's big hi-fi system in the corner, and you could always find an album cover lying around with pot seeds still in the fold from where someone had cleaned their weed. In the Ballroom, the McFadden kids burned candles, smoked cigarettes, and blew bong hits in their dog's face. You could do that sort of thing at the McFaddens'—smoke right in front of their parents, reach inside their refrigerator for a beer.

Mrs. McFadden always said, "If you kids are going to drink and smoke and carry on, then I'd rather you do it under my roof than out on the street." This only added to the allure of the Ballroom.

And at my house—even if I'd let those girls smoke cigarettes in the garage and even if my brother was just as cute as Keith or Greg McFadden—it was never going to be as much fun, and I was never going to be as popular as Patty.

But even before the other girls came along, back when it was just Patty and me—even then, there was always something going on at the McFaddens' house. Patty's brothers' friends were forever sleeping over in the Ballroom, crashing on the mattress in the back. There were mornings when I'd stop by to pick Patty up on our way to school and there would be one of Keith's or Greg's friends with their hand stuffed inside a box of Lucky

Charms, or else they'd be standing in front of the opened refrigerator, drinking orange juice straight from the carton.

Evenings, while her parents worked late at their store, Patty made dinner for whoever happened to be there. At twelve, she was already a better cook than her mother, and I'd sit on the kitchen counter, watching her shape ground beef into a meat loaf, season a roast, or stuff Cornish hens, both of us pretending we were making dinner for our husbands.

Patty was always married to a football or baseball hero, and my husband was a rock star—someone like Eric Clapton, or maybe one of the Beatles. It would be love at first sight—just like it had been for my parents—the greatest compliment anyone could have paid me. To have someone love me on sight alone, without needing to know who I was on the inside first, would have been just fine by me—even preferred. And even though the shots were starting to help and my eye was beginning to look a little more open, people still thought I'd been punched out. Strangers still came up to me, asking what happened to my eye. I knew it was the first thing people noticed about me, but that wouldn't have mattered at all if I had the love of a rock star.

Making dinners for our famous husbands stopped once Kara Elberts and the others started coming around. That's when everything changed for Patty and me. These girls were beautiful, and luckily for Patty, they were friends with her because she had the Ballroom and all the boys who went with it. I had nothing that could compare. Patty didn't call me anymore unless I called her first. She wouldn't wait for me after school, either, and if the others invited her to the mall or the movies, she never asked me along.

"I don't like the way those girls treat you," my mother said, looking up from the piano one day when I came home pouting. Her fingers were poised, feeling for their next notes. "They can be so mean. They just go out of their way to do hurtful things."

I started to cry and then my mother stopped playing and slid over on the piano bench, making room for me beside her. The spot where she'd been was warm beneath my bottom, already making me feel better.

"I think it's time you made some new friends, Nina," she said.

But I didn't want new friends. Patty had been my first and only friend. If she found other friends, there'd be no one for me. I would rather have tagged along with Patty and her new best friends than have been left alone, so in exchange for being allowed to hang around them, I did crazy things trying to fit in.

Sometimes after school, waiting for the boys to show up, we girls would take turns riding around inside the McFaddens' dryer. Theirs was a huge industrial-size model, the kind you found in Laundromats. One by one, they'd put you inside, shut the door, and start you up. You'd curl up like a potato bug and try to find something to hold on to. And as you'd go round and round, you'd stare out the porthole at the others, hunkered together, staring back at you. And somewhere, someplace off in the distance, you'd hear them counting: "One . . . two . . . three . . ."

Patty was the hardest one to fit inside, and Emily would start pounding on the door after just one or two times around. But I held the record—one hundred revolutions. I'd stumble out of the dryer so dizzy I couldn't focus. I'd have to lie down on the concrete floor, staring up at the heating duct while the others stood over me, clapping and laughing. It would always take a long time before I could stand. But I was the Queen of the Dryer Runs and no one ever broke my record.

Sometimes I did things for Patty just so she'd keep me around. These were things I wouldn't even do for myself, like clean her bedroom, acting like it was all a big joke, all in fun. Everyone, especially Mrs. McFadden, would get such a kick out of me picking Patty's dirty socks and underwear off the floor.

"Burn these," I'd say, plugging my nose with one hand, carrying the laundry to the hamper at arm's length with the other.

I'd change her sheets, make her bed, rearrange the shoes in her closet.

Keith would stand in the doorway, laughing. "My room's next, right, Neen?" Then Greg would sneak up behind him and get Keith in a half nelson, going, "No way! Come do my room next." "What about me?" Matthew would chime in. "I've got three cases of empty beer bottles lying around that need pitching!" Timothy, feeling left out, would stand in the middle of Patty's room, whining, saying, "My room needs it, too, you know."

I loved it when Patty's brothers fought over me. It was important for me to be liked by the McFadden brothers and their friends. When I could make them laugh, it made me feel like I fit in, and then it didn't matter so much how I looked. And besides, I told myself that being pretty was just a matter of chance. Born lucky, that's all that was. But being funny—now, that was something you had to cultivate on your own. It wasn't a given. You had to work at it and I went out of my way to make people laugh.

I knew I could always make Mrs. McFadden laugh. She was easy. While other kids were helping themselves to unopened boxes of cookies, not thinking twice about finishing off a half gallon of ice cream, I'd tell her how someday I'd write a book about everything that went on inside her house. "Even things you don't know about," I'd say. "Oh, if only these walls could talk!"

She'd giggle whenever I said something like that. The thing about Mrs. McFadden was that she wasn't like a real parent. Sometimes she acted more like one of us kids. Everyone started calling her by her first name, Bev, and she loved it.

For her birthday one year, Mr. McFadden had a terra-cotta bust made of Bev that looked exactly like her from the shoulders up. When we first saw it sitting on the coffee table, I pointed and said, "Look, everybody! It's Bev's Bust!" That's what everyone started calling it, and they all gave me credit for coming up with the name.

And oh, the things we would do with Bev's Bust! Bev would

come home and find her bust in the refrigerator, sitting on the top shelf, right between the Smucker's preserves and the jar of Miracle Whip, with a slice of rolled bologna tucked in the parting of her lips. Other times, she'd come home and see it sitting on her glass coffee table with a cigarette burning in its mouth. She'd shriek, laughing so hard, her shoulders shook.

Mr. McFadden didn't always find us so amusing. Every now and again, he'd blow, surprising us all. He'd snap and kick everyone out. "Matthew, Gregory, Keith, Patricia—Timothy! Everyone is to leave—NOW!"

Two days later, we'd all be back, like we'd never been asked to get out in the first place. And those were the only times Mr. McFadden ever ventured down to the Ballroom. He'd stay just long enough to smoke a cigarette, make a little small talk, have a look around and make sure nothing too offensive was going on. Then he'd smile and head for the stairs, saying something like "Well then, you kids have fun down here, okay?"

I always had fun in the Ballroom. Except for one time. Patty was throwing one of her parties, only this time it was just for the kids in our grade. Kara and the others had talked her into letting the boys make up the list of girls to invite. I wasn't supposed to know about the party because my name wasn't on the list. They tried to keep it from me. Patty and Kara, Anna and Emily all passed notes back and forth, whispering around me in study hall. In the girls' bathroom they huddled together, giggling about the party.

"Why can't I go?" I protested one day on our way home from school, when I couldn't handle any more of their pretend secrecy.

"Because you just can't, OKAY!" Kara barked at me. "The boys decided who can go and who can't."

"But it's Patty's house! C'mon, you guys," I whimpered, dragging my windbreaker behind me, the hood and sleeves collecting dirt as I walked.

"Don't be such a baby, Nina!" Kara snapped. "If we could invite you we would—but it's not up to us."

The next day, details about the party started to leak and all that secrecy began to make sense. Word traveled all over school—they were going to play kissing games at Patty's party. So that was it. They were going to play kissing games and that's why the boys didn't put my name on the list. Nobody wanted to kiss me.

On the night of the party, despite my best efforts to stay away—I had baked cookies with my mother, watched *The Mary Tyler Moore Show*, tried to do my algebra homework—nothing helped. I caved, and soon found myself standing outside the McFaddens' house, hiding behind one of their front pillars. I caught a glimpse inside the bay window of Bev and Mr. McFadden slumped down on the sofa in the family room. Their Irish setter, Buster, was jumping around, trying to get Mr. McFadden's attention.

I moved around to the back of the house, circled around the pool, and crawled in between the bushes and the air-conditioning unit, rumbling in my ear. Patty and I would always go to that spot to spy on her older brothers. Keith would gather in the Ballroom with his buddies and do his scheming, always coming up with wacky ideas, like the time he decided to plant a row of marijuana behind the tennis courts at the Akron Swim & Tennis Club. Matthew was no fun to spy on. He and his friends just got drunk and stretched out on the furniture, listening to music. But Greg was the best. He always invited girls down to the Ballroom. Once, I remember we saw him down there with two girls at the same time, both of them taking turns kissing his handsome face. From this one spot, you could see everything that went on inside the Ballroom. Only that night, all the lights were off down there and it was dark. I couldn't see a thing. Then the air-conditioning unit cut off and I heard "Bennie and the Jets" playing.

I was sandwiched in between the air conditioner and the

bushes, dying to know what was going on down there. Were they playing Truth or Dare, or Five Minutes in Heaven? I was wondering all this when the McFadden's dog sneaked up on me. I heard the tags on his collar jangling, and before I could move, Buster had me cornered. His cold snout was pressed up against my cheek.

"Oh, Nina—that you?" Mr. McFadden crouched down, yanking on Buster's leash. "Well, come on out of there, Nina. For goodness sakes . . . what are you doing in there?"

I crawled out of the bushes, pretending to brush peat moss off the front of my jeans where I'd been kneeling. I didn't want to look at him. I could feel my face flushing red, all the way to my ears.

"Why aren't you inside with the others?" he asked.

I didn't want to admit that I hadn't been invited. So I said I got locked out and as soon as I'd said it, I looked to see if he could tell I was lying.

"Oh well, c'mon now," he said, not suspecting a thing. He was laughing as he started walking me in through the back way with an arm around my shoulder. I braced myself as he opened the basement door and called down, "Hey, Patty—"

There was a rumbling of hushes and giggles and then Patty came to the foot of the stairs. She poked her head around the corner and saw me standing there with her father. Her face drooped and her red hair fell over her eyes. I shrugged, trying to give her some sort of inside sign, like I had no idea what her father was doing with me.

"Poor Nina got locked out. Found her out back." Mr. McFadden's hand was still on my shoulder, only now he was prodding me toward the first step.

Patty didn't say anything; she couldn't, not with her father standing there.

When I reached the bottom of the stairs, I saw how the Ballroom had been rearranged for the party; the beanbag chairs, the old sofa and recliner—all had been pushed into a circle. Girls on one side, boys on the other. I sat on the floor near Patty's chair with my ankles crossed and my arms circled around my knees. Kara looked over at me, and I was sure she was going to make me leave, but she didn't say a thing. And no one else did, either. They were all too caught up in Spin the Bottle to care if I was there or not.

They used an empty Rolling Rock bottle and with a flick of the wrist, they set off a wave of anticipation. I was so anxious, I could hardly breathe. My eyes were locked on that bottle's every move. As it spiraled round and round, everyone grew quiet, watching and waiting to see where it would land. Once the bottle came to a stop, there was an explosion of laughter as the others sat there clapping, chanting, "Go-go-go" while the boy and girl made out, both of them on their knees, leaning forward, arms wrapped around each other for balance.

Patty got picked twice in a row, and the second time, she gave the boy such a long kiss, the others had to yell at them to break it up.

Another spin and the neck of the bottle pointed at Danny Myers. The opposite end stared my way. I noticed no one was howling. Instead, they all fell silent and turned toward Danny, who looked at me but said nothing. I didn't know what to do, so I smiled, and that's when he demanded a respin.

"It hit Bruce's shoe" was what he said, but his friends weren't buying it.

They started teasing him, going, "Go get her, Danny Boy! Go-go-go!"

And that's when Danny Myers stood up and brushed the back of his jeans. I thought he was coming over to kiss me. So this would be a stand-up kiss, not just a lean-in one. That's what I thought. But instead he said, "Forget it, man. I'm not gonna kiss her."

the birthday surprise

My father always said, "Tootsie, the day you were born, the whole world celebrated." That was New Year's Eve, just two hours and some odd minutes shy of having my picture taken for the *Akron Beacon Journal*; the first baby of the New Year.

Thirteen years later, on New Year's Eve day, I sat downstairs with my family gathered around me, all of them watching me open my birthday presents. The first one was from Lissy: a large flat box, wrapped in pretty blue paper with a white button of a bow on top. After I tore off the wrapping paper and saw what was inside, I didn't know what to say. I sat for a moment with the box in my lap and one magical word running across the lid: Maybelline. The whole family watched as I kept my eyes locked on the lettering. I could feel my face flushing red.

"Aren't you gonna open it up? It's a whole kit. Look at all you got, Neen!" Lissy pointed to the drawing on the lid. "Look, there's three different lipsticks, and see all these eye shadows!"

I didn't want to open it just then because I didn't want them to see how much this meant to me. Up until that moment, I was sure my mother and Lissy never knew that I played with their makeup. When no one was home, I'd slip into the bathroom and steal pressed powder from their compacts, dusting it on my cheeks. I'd untwist their lipsticks and paint my lips bright red, hiding the stained Kleenex in the bottom of the wastebasket after I'd rubbed it off my mouth. I used to take my mother's eyebrow pencil and darken the mole on my cheek, telling myself it was a beauty mark. I loved the rouges and the cold creams, but it was the eye shadows that were my favorites. I'd dab the brightest shades I could find on top of my lid just to see how they'd make my eye look.

I was sure no one even knew I wanted to wear makeup or cared about how I looked, and here Lissy had gone and given me this kit in front of everybody. It was like they'd all been let in on my greatest wish to look pretty, or at least prettier.

I'd just come back from having my twelfth injection that year with Dr. Waxler, and I was beginning to see a little bit of a difference. A fold was trying to form along my upper lid and some of the red and purple in the corner had faded to more of a pink color. Even the skin didn't seem as bumpy anymore. I couldn't wait to see what I would look like now with eye shadow on. More than anything, I wanted to leave the rest of my presents unopened and just run upstairs and put this makeup on for real, but I couldn't let on.

Later that night it was just Lissy and me upstairs in the bathroom with my new makeup kit. For some reason, I was afraid this was all a big joke to my sister. I started to worry that she thought all the eye shadows and lipsticks in the world couldn't make me look beautiful, not with an eye like mine. I decided that if I started making fun of myself first, she couldn't take anything away from me.

So I reached for Lissy's hairbrush and started singing in a

high, squeaky voice, "I feel pretty/Oh so pretty . . ." I got Lissy laughing then and that made me feel better, safer.

I watched her blot her lipstick on a square of toilet paper. She finished her makeup before she did mine, racing around, getting ready for her boyfriend. She and Rob had been together all through high school. My father wasn't happy about this, but at least he was a Jewish boy. He had that much going for him.

I put the lid down on the toilet and sat while Lissy tacked my hair off my face with bobby pins. She leaned over me, humming "I Feel Pretty" while she blended blush onto my cheeks. She held my chin in her hand and tilted my face toward her. "Okay . . . Look up, Neen."

She went to line my eyes and I jerked away. I couldn't help it. Any objects near my eye reminded me of Dr. Waxler's injections.

"Shit—nice going!" Lissy stuck a Q-tip in her mouth, gave it a twist, and then wiped the smear clean from my eye. "Now hold still this time," she said.

While Lissy was working on me, I looked at my sister, noticing how pretty she was. I was hoping she could make me look like her with this makeup. I wanted her to make my eyeliner curve up at the outer corners the way hers did. I wanted my lashes to look long like hers and fan out, almost reaching to my brows, too. I pictured myself with the same shimmering green eye shadow as hers brushed along my lids, the same hint of rouge on my cheeks. "Can I look now?" I asked.

"Not yet." Lissy went over what she'd just done with a fresh Q-Tip. "Go like this," she said, puckering out her lips, uncapping a white frosted lipstick. "Let's see now . . ." She stood back, contemplating. "Okay, Neen—what do you think? Huh?"

I went to the mirror and looked. Everything sank inside me. There it was: the same big puffy lid, but now with green eye shadow and too much liner. You could still see all the red-and-purple skin showing through, so the eye shadow looked more gray than green. My eye wasn't any different. I still hated it. It ruined the rest of me.

"You like it, Neen?" she asked.

I didn't know what to say. I couldn't answer.

"Well? Don't you like it?"

"Do you think I look okay like this?" I asked, biting the inside of my cheek. I didn't want to hurt her feelings. She seemed so proud of what she'd done to me.

Lissy looked at my reflection in the mirror, cocked her head to the side, and smiled. "You look fine. You just have to get used to seeing yourself in makeup, that's all."

I stared back in the mirror. I tilted my face to the left, then the right. My chin went north and south. I looked at myself from every possible angle. I wasn't sure . . . Maybe I didn't look that awful. Maybe Lissy was right. Maybe I just had to get used to seeing myself in makeup.

"Well, what do you think, girls? Pretty sharp, huh? Huh!" My father stood in the hallway, futzing with his cummerbund.

I reached up and brought my hair all down in front of my face. I didn't want my father seeing me all made up. I was afraid he'd tease me.

"Sandra," he yelled down the hallway, "would you hurry it up? Please? Today already!" He turned back to us. "I'm telling you girls, your mother . . ." He shook his head, still looking for her over his shoulder.

The Art Goldman Jazz Quartet was playing Burton's Lounge out in Cuyahoga Falls that night. My father was antsy. This was a newly formed band and they'd played out only once before, at the Holiday Inn on Market Street. Over the past few years, my father had organized a couple other bands, but somehow they never seemed to gel beyond a few performances. There were rehearsal and scheduling problems, bickering among the players, and soon the bands would fold. But my father was optimistic about the Art Goldman Jazz Quartet, and because this gig was on New Year's Eve, it was special.

Another thing about being a New Year's Eve baby was knowing my mother had gone into labor just in time to make my father miss the one gig that could have launched his career. At least that's what it did for the clarinetist who took his place at the last minute. That man got discovered that night and went on to land a big recording deal. My father always said he would have taken me over that gig any day, but still, I had to wonder.

Lissy stood behind me now, doing the presenting. "What do you think of Nina, Dad?"

There was no getting away then. I held my breath, watching him adjust his cummerbund.

"Dad?" Lissy nudged me from behind.

My father looked up. "Well, well, well, and who might this grown-up lady be? Huh?" He reached out to shake my hand. "I don't believe I've had the pleasure, madam." I was still shaking my father's hand, when he turned toward the door and said, "What in the world is keeping her? SANDRA!"

"I hear you, Artie! You don't have to SHOUT!"

"We're running late, you know!"

"Okay, okay! Don't get so excited." My mother stopped in our bathroom and checked her hair one last time in the mirror. "Lissy, not too late tonight, huh?"

"Ma! It's New Year's Eve, in case you haven't heard."

"Oh, is that what tonight is?" She looked at me and winked. "You look very pretty, snookums," she said, leaning over to kiss my forehead, blending the rouge on my cheek with the ball of her thumb. "Now you have fun tonight with your friends. There's extra pillows and blankets in the linen closet if anyone needs anything."

This New Year's Eve I didn't mind that everyone was leaving me at home. Friends were coming to take their place. It would be the first New Year's Eve that belonged to me, an entire night wrapped around my birthday, like a bow around a present.

I was having a slumber party that night with Patty and Kara, Emily and Anna. They were starting to take me in and I was slowly becoming one of the gang. Me, crazy, zany Nina. Emily and Anna would call and invite me to go to the mall, or to the movies. They knew I'd instigate us going into Claire's Boutique, where we'd stuff fistfuls of cheapo rings from the display baskets in our pockets. Later we'd huddle at the opposite end of the mall, by O'Neils Department Store, and compare what we'd gotten away with. I did this only because I thought it would make the others like me more, but I could never bring myself to wear any of the rings I stole. Usually I just threw them down the sewer at the end of our street whenever the coast was clear. I did good stuff, too, though. Honest stuff. I knew how to shoot pool from watching my father, so I taught them how to play eight ball. No matter what, I made sure they had fun with me, and I wanted them to have a blast at my slumber party.

My mother had stocked the pantry with chips and cookies and soda pop. I figured we'd make popcorn later and have backgammon tournaments. I thought they'd want to see my Maybelline kit and take turns making one another up. But really, they couldn't have cared less about playing with makeup. All they said when I answered the door all done up was, "Look at you." That was it.

What they wanted to do was sit outside on the front porch, smoke cigarettes in the freezing cold, and keep watch on the McFaddens' house, waiting to see if the boys were there yet. That year Keith McFadden and his friends started calling themselves "the Mad Marauders." These boys were a year ahead of us and they were the cutest, most popular boys in the whole school. Sometimes, when they were bored, they'd let us hang out with them. Other times, though, we girls would plant ourselves downstairs in the Ballroom until Keith would yell at Patty, "Get outta here!" To the Mad Marauders we were just a bunch of little girls, but to us, those boys were everything.

It was getting cold and we were about to go inside when Kara spotted two of the Mad Marauders, Alex Korbington and Eric Slater, walking in the middle of the road. They were stepping inside the tire tracks left in the snow-blanketed street, heading toward the Ballroom, the Mad Marauders' official headquarters.

Kara waved them over to the front porch, and for a few minutes everyone stood around with their hands stuffed down in their pockets, making stupid small talk. Emily and Kara turned all giggly.

Patty told them it was my birthday and that's when Alex Korbington's eyes locked in place with mine. I was standing there, stunned that he was staring at me. All I could think was, *It's the makeup! I really do look good this way!* Everything inside me brightened. I bit down on my lip and tucked all the hair behind my ears, away from my face so he could get a really good look at me in my makeup. Then, I saw the corner of his mouth curl up in a smile. When he did that, a million sunbeams danced inside my chest and a warmth like I'd never known spread throughout my body. All I could think was, *This must be love!* This must be what it feels like! I knew I was staring at him, but I couldn't help myself.

And then Eric nudged him, saying it was time to take off. Before I knew it, Eric and Alex were gone, heading down the street. I was still glowing inside just thinking of his smile.

Later on, the five of us huddled around the television set, waiting for the ball to drop on Times Square and give us all a fresh start. We'd made our resolutions. Patty was going to make her bed every day and lose forty pounds. For Emily, it was getting straight *A*'s, making the cheerleading squad, and going to tennis camp in the summer. Anna wanted to be on the squad, too, and get two boyfriends. I was going to try out for the school musical and get a boyfriend. I knew my boyfriend would be Alex Korbington, but I kept that to myself. Kara had a crush on him and I knew she'd be jealous now that he liked me. Besides, Kara's New Year's resolution involved giving her first hand job to Alex. She seemed so certain that this would happen. But I knew Alex Korbington hadn't given Kara the kind of smile he'd given me when we were standing on the porch. He hadn't looked at any of the other girls the way he'd looked at me.

At four minutes till midnight, the telephone rang. I thought it might be my mother calling from the club. Instead, it was Alex Korbington! I couldn't believe it. He was calling from the Ballroom to talk to me! He said he'd forgotten to wish me a happy birthday. He wanted to know what I was doing to celebrate, wanted to know if I got any good presents. There was something weird in his voice, like maybe he was being shy, or maybe that was just the way he sounded on the telephone. I didn't know because this was only our first call, ever.

I stood with the receiver still pressed to my ear, feeling prettier than every girl in my family room, even Kara Elberts. Alex Korbington was calling me! Me and Alex Korbington! What would kids at school say? I could sit with him in the cafeteria, cheer for him at his wrestling matches, and ride double on his bicycle down Burlington Road with my arms hugging his waist. This was even better than makeup.

Then other voices splintered the line and I couldn't hear Alex anymore. His voice drifted off, overpowered by the rest of the Mad Marauders, who were shouting into the phone, all at one time. They were howling and laughing, and the only part I heard in the clear was "Happy birthday, Big Eye–Little Eye—arf, arf, arf!"

I stood still for a minute, not believing what I'd heard. Then it hit me. I dropped the phone. Patty asked what was wrong, but I couldn't answer. A trickle of tears ran down my cheeks and I fell to the floor. I was sobbing so hard that all of a sudden giant clots of blood started shooting out my nose and onto the good carpet.

Anna ran out of the room yelling. Emily stood back with both hands to her mouth, her cheeks drained white. I wouldn't talk to any of them, not even Patty, who kept asking if I needed a doctor. Strings of spittle drizzled off my lips. Mascara was streaked across my eyes and cheeks. I couldn't stop crying and my nose was still bleeding. Those boys had humiliated me and now I was making it worse. I couldn't recover, and that upset me even more.

Patty and Emily, Kara and Anna thought I'd gone insane. But they couldn't begin to understand. No one had ever barked at them. Besides, if they had understood, they never would have left me alone, even after I yelled at them to get out. They just didn't get it.

They didn't get that what I wanted was for them to stay overnight and play backgammon and make popcorn. I wanted everyone to lie around in their sleeping bags and stay up late telling ghost stories. I just wanted to have a fun birthday. That was what I wanted, but instead I told them to leave me alone. "Just go AWAY!"

And they did. They went down the street to the McFaddens'.

I stood watching them from the far window in the dining room. They were carrying their sleeping bags and overnight cases, stepping between the snowdrifts, going on without me, going to the Ballroom, to where the boys were. Alex Korbington was going to get that hand job after all.

Then it was just me, alone. When I looked down at the carpet, I saw what I'd done. Splatters of blood were everywhere and I began to panic. I ran and filled a bucket with hot water and soap and started scrubbing the bloodstains. I was on my hands and knees, going over the same spot again and again till my knuckles stung, turning red. Fresh tears quivered from the tip of my nose. I was afraid my father would be angry because I'd ruined the carpet.

After that night, my father and I started fighting over my hair. I'd taken to parting it on the extreme left, letting it fall so it hid the right half of my face. I thought it looked good like that and I spent a lot of time every morning spraying it in place so it laid just right.

"I can't stand that goddamn hair in your face," my father would say. "You're such a pretty girl if you'd just get that hair of yours cut—get it out of your eyes. You're only calling more attention to it. And once people get to know you, Nina, they don't even notice your eye anymore."

I wanted to believe my father, but if what he said was true, why was he the one subscribing to all those journals, so set on finding doctors who could fix me?

And besides, I knew the boys noticed my eye. Obviously, they didn't like me, and it didn't matter that I could dance and sing and had a spiral notebook of poems I'd written. I was thirteen years old and so far the only person who had ever kissed me, really kissed me, was Joyce Tauben.

I was ten when that had happened. Joyce was four years older, baby-sitting for me on a Friday night when everyone else was gone; my parents off to another one of my father's gigs, Lissy off with her boyfriend, and Mitch out with his buddies, probably sitting outside a drug store trying to get someone to buy them cigarettes.

Joyce Tauben had frizzy hair and reminded me of Big Ethel in the *Archie* comic books. The night of our kiss, we were lying in the dark on my parents' bed, feet facing the headboard. We were watching the Friday-night lineup on television, going from *The Brady Bunch* to *The Partridge Family* to *Love, American Style.*

Whenever they'd show a kissing scene during *Love, American Style,* Joyce and I would giggle and roll toward the center of the bed until our bodies bumped into each other, then bounced off, heading in opposite directions. We kept doing this, rolling back and forth, each time moving a little closer together. By the time the eleven o'clock news came on, Joyce and I were side by side on our stomachs, touching shoulder-to-shoulder, hip-to-hip.

Later that night I wrote in my diary that it was Joyce who had started it. She kissed me. I wrote that she made me do it. That she threatened to tell on me if I didn't do it. She had forced me into it. But even as I wrote those words, I knew I was the one who had started it. I had kissed her first.

the lotus blossom

My father was making me nervous. I was afraid he'd break something. We were in Chicago, in an examination room, waiting for Dr. Waxler. My father was scooting around on the doctor's little black stool, rolling over to a tray of shiny instruments, holding each one up. "These would make great ice tongs, huh? Open your purse, Sandra—they'll never notice 'em missing."

My mother reached over and jiggled my knee. "Just ignore him, snookums."

My father had already helped himself to one of the doctor's tongue depressors and had come over to me and crossed his eyes, going, "Open wide." I knew he was trying to make me laugh, trying to take my mind off the visit. He knew I was worried because Dr. Waxler's nurse had called and requested that my father come with us this time. My father said it probably meant good news.

When Dr. Waxler finally came into the exam room, my father stopped fooling around and got down to business. He shook the doctor's hand, agreeing that, "Yes, yes, we sure have come a long way . . . Yes, she's doing just terrific."

"Well, let's have a look, shall we?" Dr. Waxler took a seat on his little black stool, and with one good push, he glided across the room until he was just inches away from me. He leaned forward slowly and moved the tips of his fingers over the surface of my eye. I looked down at his feet—polished loafers with pennies winking back at me. He told me to raise my chin and look straight at him while he used his thumb to prop my eyelid open.

My father was right there, leaning over him, saying, "Yup, looks good, Neen."

Dr. Waxler didn't seem to mind my father's interference, or the fact that he answered every question Dr. Waxler asked me. "Would you say you're experiencing any burning from the injections after the swelling's gone down?"

"No, not after her swelling's gone down."

"Any blurred vision or headaches?"

"Nope! She's fine on those counts, too."

Dr. Waxler checked with me to make sure this was true, then went on asking questions, marking my file. Afterward he placed my head in a machine that butted my chin and forehead up against two wide bands. Sitting opposite me, he looked through the eyepiece, instructing me to look left, then right, up, then down.

When he finished, Dr. Waxler tapped me on the shoulder, said I could go ahead and relax, and with one more push of his heels, he was back on the other side of the room. I went and sat over by my mother, who was dog-earring the paperback she'd brought along.

"Well," Dr. Waxler said, standing up, palming the front of his lab coat, "let me preface what I'm about to say with this." He folded his arms and blew out a deep breath. "When Nina first came to see me, we didn't know how she'd react to the injections, or if she would at all. Given this, I'd say we've made tremendous progress. The fold is much more pronounced now. We're also starting to get a nice almond shape to the lid. I had hoped that we'd get a little better fading on the pigmentation, but still, there's been some improvement there as well." Dr. Waxler paused again, then glanced at the floor. "Now that we've reached this degree of success, it's time to reconsider our form of treatment."

"Meaning?" My father ran a finger along the inside of his shirt collar.

"Basically, what I'm saying is that for right now—given the state of the eye and its response—there's no point in our continuing with the injections."

From the corner of my eye, I saw my father nod and I thought this meant they had something even better for me.

"I'd simply be injecting into scar tissue at this point. And then we run the risk of creating even more scar tissue in the ptosis. And of course, in addition to the residual ptosis, I'm concerned about the long-term side effects of the sclerosing agent. In dealing with a vascular abnormality like Nina's, we could do more harm than good if we continue. Half the science of this sort of thing is knowing when to quit."

I looked over at my father, who was still nodding, still giving hope. All I could think was, *No more shots!* I hoped the next treatment, whatever it was, wouldn't hurt.

"And really," the doctor went on, "with the exception of the enlarged bulbar conjunctiva and what we call the venous blood in the skin tissues"—he walked over and ran his finger across my brow—"she has virtually no ocular complications. Her visual fields are quite normal. And I just don't feel that at this point it would be advantageous to risk further injections."

"So what's our next step?" my father wanted to know.

"Now we have to be patient and see how she does. It is possible," Dr. Waxler added, folding his arms again, "that the injections she's had will continue to work for anywhere from a month up to a year. And who knows"—he undid his arms, holding them out like a showman—"maybe in another year or so we'll come up with something new that can help. The eye may even be operable at some point. Unfortunately, there's no way of knowing that ahead of time."

It wasn't until Dr. Waxler's nurse gave me a hug good-bye that I realized we were leaving, and this time for good. There wasn't going to be another appointment.

I looked at my mother. She was stuffing her paperback inside her pocketbook. Then I looked at my father. He was shaking the doctor's hand. They weren't going to challenge this? They were just going to accept my eye? They were satisfied with it the way it was?

I didn't care that it looked better than it did three years ago. I wasn't looking for better. I wanted perfect. I'd been planning on perfect. My whole future depended on my eye being perfect. They could keep injecting me. I didn't care if Dr. Waxler didn't think that would work. At least if they were injecting me, they'd be doing something to try to help me!

I burst into tears. I was never going to be normal. What boy would ever want a Big Eye–Little Eye for a girlfriend? No one would ever see me and fall in love with me at first sight. Or ever. I felt it in my gut—I knew this one thing about myself more than I knew anything else: I was going to be alone forever.

"Oh Nina," my mother said, reaching in her purse for a tissue. "C'mon now . . ."

"Hey, lady," my father said to me later, at O'Hare, when I couldn't keep from crying, "pull yourself together." We were waiting to board our flight for Akron. Other passengers were staring. One of the airline employees came up and asked my mother if there was anything she could do.

I kept apologizing to my father, knowing how he hated it when I cried, even though he cried all the time. It was okay for him, but somehow I wasn't entitled to my sorrows. It was so backward—I was the kid here, not him. I was supposed to cry about stuff like this. And so my tears kept coming and I didn't even try to fight them off.

"C'mon now, Nina," he said, trying to be patient with me. "There was a time when we didn't think you'd look this good, remember? Huh? Huh!"

That made me wail; my bottom lip quivered as a thread of spittle oozed out, running down the front of my shirt.

My father looked at my mother, then back at me, shaking his head. "Oh for crying out loud, Nina! It's not the end of the goddamn world—and you're not a baby! Now, I know you're disappointed, but that's life kid. Get used to it! You'll survive. And it's about time you learned to be grateful for what you've got!"

I glared at him through my tears. I was screaming on the inside. At times, I swore I hated him.

During the flight home, I tried to do my homework, but I couldn't think about anything other than my eye. My biology book sat open and neglected in my lap. The more I thought about my eye, the more questions I had. The big one was, *Why me?* Why not Lissy or Mitch? Why hadn't either of them been born this way? What had I done to be punished like this? And why was it that now, when the eye looked better, it bothered me even more than before?

The captain's voice came on, crackling over the loudspeaker, something about reaching our cruising altitude. I looked out the window. City lights were growing tiny below us, like stars turned upside down, now twinkling from the ground up. Everything looked different from so high up.

I glanced back at my biology book. The page was turned to the lesson on lotus flowers. It said that they blossomed in muddy ponds and that the muddier the water, the more beautiful the flowers became. I went back to staring out the window. Our plane was climbing higher and the lights on the ground were growing dimmer. I realized then that the look of things always changed when you changed where you were at. That was just the way the universe worked. So if that was true, then maybe if I took myself to a very high place, I could change the way I saw my eye.

Maybe I was like one of those lotus flowers. Maybe because I'd started out looking so terrible, I'd end up blossoming into a beauty. Maybe someday soon they'd find a way to fix me and when they were done, my eyes would be even more beautiful than the eyes of someone who'd never had a problem at all.

All this was going on inside my head as the city lights vanished outside my window. Everything had turned dark now and endless, as far as I could see. Such a stretch of nothingness, or maybe of possibilities. The world was full of mysteries, things we might never understand for sure. But if this theory about the lotus flowers was right, then there was nothing for me to be sad about. I was starting out ugly, but I'd end up pretty. I was a lotus flower growing in a pond filled with mud.

I tried to explain all this to my father, thinking it would please him. At least I'd stopped crying and I was trying to find something positive in it all. But when I got to that part about the lotus blossoms, that's when my father sighed, creased his *Wall Street Journal,* and looked at me, exasperated. I think he would have liked to have shoved me in the overhead compartment.

All he said was, "Don't be so goddamn heavy about everything, Nina. It's been a long enough day as it is."

hope certificates

After my last visit to Dr. Waxler, Cousin Ricky came to stay with us. He arrived in late September and lived with us until Christmastime. I was fourteen, and since Lissy was away at college, I had moved into her room so Cousin Ricky could have mine.

We always called him "Cousin Ricky." He was my father's age—they'd grown up together—and it sounded disrespectful calling him just Ricky, and he wasn't our uncle, so always it was Cousin Ricky.

It had been about two years since we'd last seen him. He and Cousin Doris and their two daughters had stopped for a visit on their way to Cincinnati. Back then, Cousin Ricky was just like my father. He wore things like dress slacks and wing-tip shoes. But this time, Cousin Ricky was in our family room, sitting in a half-lotus, his hair nearly touching his shoulders. He was wearing faded blue jeans, a T-shirt, and a braided macramé bracelet made of rope.

Cousin Ricky had once owned a chain of dry cleaners in West Orange, New Jersey. All was fine until he got caught with his seamstress in the back room. Cousin Doris threatened to divorce him if he didn't agree to go into couple's counseling. After a few sessions, their therapist suggested they attend a spiritual retreat in Eureka, California. They shipped their kids off to Cousin Doris's sister and headed west, where they devoted themselves to studying meditation.

According to Cousin Ricky, meditation had done wonders for him. After less than a month, he told Cousin Doris he wanted a divorce. Cousin Doris meditated on it, then decided to pack up and go back to New Jersey and be a mother again.

Cousin Ricky stayed in Eureka for about a year and a half, until he turned up in Akron. He'd gotten rid of his wife and the dry-cleaning business and his daughters weren't speaking to him, but he was sure that would pass. He claimed to be happier than he ever imagined possible. Only now his money was running out and Cousin Ricky didn't know what to do. My father offered him a job and a place to stay until he got back on his feet.

"For the last time, Art, it wasn't a commune," Cousin Ricky was saying, trying to explain the retreat to my father. "And I gotta tell you, meditating has made everything in my life better."

"So meditating made you get a divorce and abandon your children? That's beautiful, Ricky." My father banged his pipe on the side of the ashtray, clearing out a clump of burnt tobacco.

"You can't make me feel guilty, Art. I'm perfectly at peace with all this. In fact, I've made peace with all my old baggage. While I was out there, I discovered this energy inside my life. It's electrifying. This is *pow-er-ful* stuff." He pounded his fist to each syllable.

"No kidding . . ." My father nodded and went back to packing his pipe. "That sounds *pow-er-ful* all right." He was scooping tobacco from his pouch, pushing it into the bowl with the ball of his thumb.

Mitch and I were sitting on the floor near the fireplace, playing Scrabble. It was rare that we were both home in the evening, but Mitch was grounded for having set off an M-80 in the school parking lot, and I was in the middle of a fight with Patty over who didn't call who back the night before.

"C'mon already." Mitch got impatient whenever I was winning. "Jeez, Neen—I don't got all day you know."

Just for that, I took my time picking my next four wooden tiles out of the box lid.

My mother looked up from the afghan she was crocheting. She didn't have to say a word. I'd picked my last two tiles and had already started arranging the letters on my tray.

"I realized," Cousin Ricky was saying, "I couldn't just be concerned with Doris and the kids anymore—I had my own needs."

My father was lighting his pipe, nodding at everything Cousin Ricky said. The pipe was all aflame then and he let it burn like that until he snuffed it out with the flat side of his Zippo.

"Until I started meditating, I never realized what an angry person I was."

My father puffed on his pipe and nodded some more.

I had just finished spelling *phlegm* and already Mitch was challenging me, going, "There's no such word as *fa-leg-em.*"

"I had no idea how much pain I carried around inside. You know, Art, I could teach you just a few quick meditations—open up your whole world."

My father thought for a moment, resettled in his chair, and pulled the pipe from the corner of his mouth. "Ricky, I've known you for what, thirty-six, thirty-seven years now—we don't need to stand on ceremony with each other, am I right?" My father paused here, took a tiny puff off his pipe. "So I know you'll understand when I tell you I think you are so completely full of shit—"

"Ah-ha!" Cousin Ricky clapped his hands. "I knew you were

gonna say that! I said the same thing at first. But then I learned more about it. I was open to it. See, that's the thing, Art. You gotta be open to—"

"Listen, Ricky, I'm offering you a job and a chance to pull your life back together. I'm not looking to be converted."

"Who's trying to convert you? I'm trying to give you a chance at happiness."

"I'm plenty happy."

I told Mitch that *fa-leg-em* was another word for mucus and so, thinking it was spelled the way it sounded, he was now looking up *flem* in the dictionary.

"All I'm saying is that you need a spiritual outlet. You've got your family. You've got your work. But what about your spirituality?"

"Oh, Jesus Christ!" My father shook his head and puffed away on his pipe.

"Told you so," I said, grinning, after Mitch finally looked up the right spelling, closed the dictionary, and took his turn.

"And what about your music?"

My father yanked the pipe out of his mouth. "What about my music! Where the hell have you been, Ricky, huh! I've been playing music all my life. I'm in the musicians' union. I've been in more than a dozen bands!"

"Artie," my mother said, "you're shouting."

"Yeah, but are you where you wanna be? Art, you were talking albums, concerts. You were gonna sing and dance. The next Sinatra. The whole shot."

"Nice try," I said to Mitch, who had tacked on *ing* and was now trying to convince me that *phlegming* was so a real word.

"You know, Art," Cousin Ricky was saying, "if you'd let me, I could show you how to remove the blocks to your music career."

"Ricky, forget it!"

"Art—"

"Rick—"

"Arthur, you are so stubborn."

"Ricky, I said FORGET IT!"

Mitch forfeited his next turn and I came back with *phlegmatic* and a triple word score.

My father and Cousin Ricky were still going at it when I went up to bed. I could hear them through the laundry chute opening on the wall above my head. The next morning, everything seemed quiet. I was in the bathroom getting ready for school, combing my hair down in place, covering my eye and half my face. I was spraying my hair stiff with Aqua Net when I noticed the door to my parents' bedroom was open. Their bed was empty.

My father was almost never up before us kids. He usually stayed up late at night, slept in late in the mornings. Once when I was in first grade, I had to fill out a form, and when it asked, "What is your father doing now?" I looked at the clock. It was nine-thirty, so I answered, "Sleeping."

After I brushed my teeth and sprayed my hair in place one last time, I went downstairs and found my mother and father standing in the kitchen, looking out the window, their backs to me, shoulders heaving like when you're crying really hard.

I was sure something bad had happened, probably something to do with my grandfather. Ever since the day he got his cane caught under his brake and over his gas pedal and plowed into the side of the Acme grocery store, I'd been worried about him.

Suddenly, there was this *OMMMMMMMmmmmmmmmmmmmm* noise coming from the basement vent, and my parents covered their mouths and laughed.

"Ma?" I whispered. "What's going on?"

"Shssssh." She turned and smiled, her shoulders still shaking. "That's Cousin Ricky—med-it-ta-ting." Just saying that made them start to laugh all over again.

After his last *OMMMMMMMmmmmmmmmmmm,* everything below us turned quiet and then we heard the light panel snap off and the sound of Cousin Ricky coming up the basement steps.

He seemed transformed that morning, wearing dress slacks with lace-up shoes. His hair was combed back, slathered with Brylcreem. He wore a thin tie and a crisp button-down shirt, with a hint of his rope bracelet peeking out below his cuff.

"Well," Cousin Ricky said, smiling at my father, "do I clean up okay, boss?"

My father was still in his bathrobe and Cousin Ricky was ready for work.

❋

After just a few weeks, Cousin Ricky had made a big carpet sale, got a company car and a haircut. I don't know if Cousin Ricky had anything to do with my father forming another band, but something tells me he did. This was the first band my father had put together since the Art Goldman Jazz Quartet dissolved the year before. He found real studio musicians this time who wrote their own music and pushed themselves, rehearsing five nights a week and playing out nights six and seven. They talked about the four of them going to New York after the first of the year to shop their tape around.

I think my father was trying to prove something to Cousin Ricky. He wanted to show him that all it took was focus and hard work to get his music career going—he didn't need to meditate, didn't need "hope certificates," as he liked to call them. Anything that wasn't grounded in reality, my father regarded as wishful thinking, daydreams, nothing but hope certificates.

I'd listened to my father poke fun at Cousin Ricky's meditating, but I wondered if maybe there wasn't something to it. Cousin Ricky said there were lots of people who did it. I figured they couldn't all be crazy, so I decided to become one of his disciples.

I got the idea after I heard Cousin Ricky say he'd cured himself of backaches. That's when I went to him in my old room and asked if he thought meditating could cure my eye.

"If you want to cure something, you first have to understand that whatever the problem is, it comes from inside of you. Inside of your life, see?" Cousin Ricky explained as he rifled through the top dresser drawer. I stood off to the side, pretending not to notice his jockstrap resting among his balled-up socks and boxer shorts. He picked up his hairbrush and tapped it against his palm. "The body is made up of four elements, see. There's water"—tap—"earth"—tap—"fire and air"—tap, tap. "When you have a problem of any kind—physical, emotional, even financial—it means that one, or maybe all your elements are out of harmony."

"But I was born this way, Cousin Ricky."

"You can be born with too much of one element, not enough of the other three. And that's what meditation will do for you—bring your elements back into balance."

"And that's all there is to it? When I do that, my eye will look normal?"

Cousin Ricky didn't answer. Instead, he brushed his hair. I watched it fill with electricity, long strands standing straight up. "Let me put it this way Nina," he said eventually. "Once I started meditating about my backaches, I realized that all the negativity inside my life was centered here." He indicated the small of his back with the tip of his brush. "After I realized that, I meditated to purify my life and get rid of all this negativity. And the next day, the back pain was gone."

A self-made miracle. I was sold.

When Cousin Ricky said to meditate ten minutes twice a day, I did thirty minutes three times a day. And I did my meditating upstairs in the big bedroom that used to belong to Lissy. I still felt her presence everywhere, felt as if I'd never be enough to fill that room. Staring at me from the back wall of her closet was her name, spelled out in psychedelic letters. I got up and closed the closet doors, then went back and sat like Cousin Ricky—lotus-style. My open hands rested on my thighs, palms facing up. I *OMMMMMmmmmmmmmed* softly, privately. I wanted to believe in meditation the way I'd once believed in Herbert Wensley, the local televangelist my father and brother liked to imitate.

"Evil spirits come OUT!" My father would shout this, placing a hand on Mitch's forehead, forcing him to his knees.

Mitch would get back up, shaking his head, going, "Hallelujah! Praise be to God! I can walk! I can walk!"

My family watched Herbert Wensley's broadcast every Sunday morning just so they could make fun of it. But how could they be so sure it was all a hoax? Right from our living room, we'd seen Herbert Wensley cure the blind and the deaf. We had watched people rise from their wheelchairs and walk the stage. If God could make cataracts disappear and straighten crippled limbs, why couldn't He fix my eye?

I was sure there was something to it. So when Herbert Wensley said, "You people at home—I want you to pray for the miracle of Christ our Lord," I was praying, asking with all my heart for Christ our Lord to come down from wherever He was and cure my eye.

Well, He never did answer my prayer, so now it was up to Cousin Ricky's meditations. Cousin Ricky told me to travel deep inside and picture the extra blood vessels in my eye drying up, growing smaller and smaller till they disappeared. I'd focus on that image for as long as I could, hold it like a still life in my mind, until the most ordinary things distracted me—the sounds of heels walking across the kitchen floor, the thermostat kicking on, the drip of the showerhead, one drop at a time. Life had called me back, and by then, there was only one thing left to do: go to the mirror and check my progress.

Each time, I was a little surprised that my eye didn't look any different.

❋

In the middle of December, Patty and I had a big fight. She had promised to write me a note in English class, but she never did. She swore she passed it to me in history class, but I would have remembered if she had. I lived for notes and I didn't get that many, not like other girls. So when I got one, it was special. I even saved them. Patty and I were still mad at each other, and by day two of our fight, she had started lording Ben Stewart over me. He was the Mad Marauder I was loving at the time. He was best friends with Keith McFadden and Patty kept threatening that she'd tell Ben that I had a crush on him.

"She's gonna ruin everything!" I said to Cousin Ricky when it was just us two alone, sitting side by side on the couch in the family room.

"Can't let that get to you," Cousin Ricky warned. "Anger will only work against you—it'll hold you back from purifying your soul and bringing your four elements back in line."

That must have been important because so far, no matter how hard I meditated, my eye stayed the same. "So that can really slow things down?" I asked.

"Absolutely. Look at me, see? I have no anger—no rage inside my life." He brought a cigarette to his lips and lit it with my father's Zippo. "It's like me and your old man, Nina. I've spent hours meditating for that man's soul, trying to find a way to forgive him."

"For what? Were you mad at him?"

"It wasn't really a matter of being mad, Nina. It was more a matter of coming to understand him. You know your dad was only about three or four when he came to live with us." Cousin Ricky took another drag off his cigarette, smoking it like you would a cigar, overhand-style. "My mother told me I had to be extra nice to my cousin Artie because he didn't have a father or mother anymore.

"And I felt bad for your dad. Everybody did. And man, did he know how to play that one. I'm telling you, your father always needed an audience! I remember he used to blow out the flames on the burners on the stove and sing 'Happy Birthday' to himself." He looked at me and shook his head. "Your father was the fair-haired boy—I don't care what he says." Cousin Ricky raised a hand of protest. "I know, according to your father, he got beaten all the time. And sure, my dad was strict. But he was that way with me and Flo, too. He got that belt out a few times—we all got it sooner or later. But no one ever got *beaten*. Especially not your father. He could talk his way out of anything, even my dad's belt. I'm telling you, everybody favored your father. For as long as I can remember, your dad wanted to be a musician, or a movie star, always something big," Cousin Ricky said with a light laugh.

"He was always hounding my dad about wanting to take music lessons. My father lost everything during the Depression, but still, somehow he managed to find the money to buy your father his first clarinet."

I looked at Cousin Ricky, not sure of what to say. I knew my father was a complicated man, full of distortions and embellishments. But knowing he had grown up with love and kindness after all—knowing he hadn't been that abused, abandoned little boy—surprised me. I couldn't understand why he wanted us all to think he'd had such an awful childhood. What was to be gained by that? Just when I thought I understood my father, another layer showed itself to me. There was so much about what made him tick that I didn't understand.

"Your father pulled a bunch of crazy stunts, like running away to New York City. Scared my parents half to death. They had the whole neighborhood out looking for him. But that was your dad. Once he got something into his crazy head, there was no stopping him.

"But you see," Cousin Ricky said, "none of that matters anymore. Nope. I feel no anger or envy toward your father." He took a final drag off his cigarette and stubbed it out in the ashtray, sending a ribbon of smoke curling upward. "Nope," he said on the exhale, "I'm happy for his success. He's done well for himself. And he loves being a father. More than anything, he loves that—even though he keeps you all on a short leash," he said, shaking his head. "He's the closest I'll ever come to having a brother. And I'm proud to say I do love your father. I really do."

❂

On Christmas Eve, Lissy came home from college with her new boyfriend, Stephen. They'd just arrived—their bags were still in the front hallway—and already my father had taken to calling him *Boychik*. That was how you said "young man" in Yiddish.

"Oh, Lissy," my father said, "I thought you told me he was short—*Boychik* here isn't all that short." My father gave him a wink and you could see Stephen shrink beneath his gaze. I could tell my father liked this boy as much as he was ever going to like one of Lissy's boyfriends. He wouldn't have teased him like that if he hadn't.

Later we were sitting around the dining room table; an extra leaf had been dropped in to make room for Lissy's boyfriend, Cousin Ricky, and my grandparents.

We had just sat down and already Lissy was annoyed. "Who's shaking the table? Mitchell!"

"What?" Mitch looked up.

"Would you quit shaking the table!"

"I'm not shaking the table."

"Mitch!"

We all knew it was him. Mitch was the one who'd sit there bouncing his leg up and down, sending a tremor down the table.

"That's all you're eating, young lady?" My mother stared at the spoonful of green beans and the sliver of roast turkey on my plate.

I shrugged, said I wasn't that hungry. I was too excited to eat, because I was going to see Ben Stewart later that night. "There'll be tons of food at Patty's," I told her, and that seemed to settle it. After dinner we were going to the McFaddens'. Every Christmas Eve, we were the token Jews invited to their place for their big open house. I wanted everyone to hurry so we could go over there. Ben Stewart was at the McFaddens' and I worried someone else would get there first and claim him.

My father was in no hurry. He sat next to Lissy's boyfriend, giving him grief for majoring in art history.

"People don't realize what all you can do with a degree in art history," said *Boychik*. I think he was trying to impress my father, because suddenly he had become a hand talker. Sweeping gestures seemed to punctuate everything he said. "I could be a curator . . . or teach art therapy!" He smiled, proud, and then, with all the zest of a conductor, he flung his hands out to the side and clipped the edge of my father's wineglass, sending a tidal wave of red onto my mother's favorite tablecloth.

There was a moment of disbelief. *Boychik*'s face was turning the shade of the spilled wine. Lissy didn't look too good, either. This was followed by rounds of apologies, offers to have the tablecloth dry-cleaned, which Cousin Ricky weighed in on with his expertise, saying red wine would never come out.

"Don't worry about it," my mother said, trying to reassure *Boychik*. "It's no big deal," she said, blotting the stain with a dish towel as a deep crease formed between her eyebrows. Everyone was silent then, watching the edges of the stain crawling out from under the towel, inching its way to the center of the table.

And then my father did a kind thing. He shifted the focus

away from *Boychik* and turned it on Cousin Ricky. "Did you hear," my father said, "Cousin Ricky here came in number one—the number-one carpet salesman for the month! Little *pisher* even topped me in commissions."

"And you say meditating doesn't work, Art!" Cousin Ricky breathed on his fingernails and gave them a quick buffing on his lapel, his rope bracelet sliding up his wrist.

"Oh, c'mon now, Ricky. You expect me to believe you had this kind of a month because you sat in a corner and said a bunch of nonsense words?" My father stabbed a piece of turkey and shook it over his plate until it dropped from the fork. "Would you like to know why you had such a good month, Cousin? Because you went out and knocked on a few doors, you made the calls."

My father passed the platter to *Boychik,* who handed it to Lissy, careful-like, using both hands. I still felt embarrassed for him, especially when my grandmother started dabbing at the stain that had now reached the edge of her plate. "Do you have club soda, Sandy?" she asked a little too loudly. "That might take it out. You should do it before it sets."

"But what you're missing, Art," Cousin Ricky said, "what you just don't get is that I would have never knocked on those doors in the first place if it weren't for meditation."

"Aw *schlecht!* That's a bunch of crap!" My father's fork clanked down hard on his plate. "Ricky, for chrissakes, you can't take a piss without saying 'if it weren't for meditation.' "

"Oh Artie, please—" My mother made a face.

I looked around the table. No one else was talking. My grandmother's eyes shifted between my father and Cousin Ricky as she frowned. Mitch was sawing at his turkey and Lissy was scooting a green bean about on her plate while her boyfriend kept his eyes low, his head bent forward as he chewed.

"Ricky, you're turning into a goddamn fanatic," my father said, pouring salt into his hand, then sprinkling what he had over his plate. "And you want to know why? Because deep down inside, you know it's nothing but bullshit! That's why you have to preach it! You're trying to convince yourself more than anybody else, 'cause you don't believe it yourself."

If this was true, did that mean my eye wouldn't be cured? I pushed my plate away.

My grandfather got up from the table and took his plate back into the kitchen. My grandmother called after him to stay away from the *gribbenes,* the pan drippings. "You don't need it, Sy," she said, leaning back in her chair, watching him to make sure.

"Mitch!" Lissy set her water glass down hard.

"What?"

"Stop shaking!"

"Shssssh, shssssh . . ." My grandmother reached over and squeezed Lissy's wrist. "I mean it, Sy," she said, still straining toward the kitchen, "stay away from that. It's all fat—and you don't need it!"

"And you know what your problem is, Art?" Cousin Ricky was saying now. "You're so narrow-minded, you don't even let yourself imagine what could be."

"What you mean, Ricky, is that I'm not blessed with the kind of ignorance that lets me believe in hope certificates. You're kidding yourself. You think everything's going to work itself out magically. You don't have to take responsibility for a goddamn thing. You're counting on magic, Ricky. Nothing but goddamn hope certificates."

"HOPE CERTIFICATES! I've cashed in on every one of them!"

"Yeah, by selling out on your wife and kids. Admit it," my father pressed on, "just admit you walked out on your family!"

"Let's just drop it, Artie, will you do that for me, please?" My mother tried keeping peace.

"You know what that does to me, Ricky? It makes me sick! It makes me absolutely sick to my goddamn stomach!"

"Oh Artie, please..." My mother was shaking her head. "Can't we just for once all sit down and have a nice simple dinner together?"

"Nothing's nice and simple with this guy, Sandra," Cousin Ricky said. "That's 'cause he's so insecure he has to *control* everything, has to *overpower* everyone. He gets so—so—so . . ." As Cousin Ricky's voice trailed off, I noticed he was rubbing his lower back with both hands.

"I don't have to listen to this kind of crap in my own house, Ricky!"

"You can't stand how good I'm doing right now, can you, Artie! That's the truth, isn't it? It's killing you! You son of a bitch! You think you're fooling anyone with all your talk about your music! Going on and on about moving to New York, shopping your tape around! You know what you are? You're nothing but a joke! A big, pathetic joke!"

"Why, you . . ." My father threw down his napkin and suddenly Cousin Ricky and my father were both out of their chairs, rushing toward each other.

"Ricky! Artie!" My mother was on her feet now, too, knuckles ground into the tablecloth. "Will the two of you just stop! Will you, please!"

But it was too late. They were already going at it. Their arms were wrapped around each other, and if I hadn't known better, I would have thought they were hugging. Either one of them could have easily taken a swing at the other, but neither one even tried. They were mad, though, and you could hear them both grunting, calling each other names. They even used the *f* word.

My brother and *Boychik* were trying to pull them apart, and who knows how long this would have gone on had it not been for the crash coming from the kitchen.

That broke up the fight. We all rushed to the kitchen and saw where my grandfather had dropped a glass and apparently knocked the roasting pan and a bunch of forks onto the floor. He whirled around, glared at us, and suddenly started rambling, speaking more Yiddish than English. He began arguing with an imaginary person, calling him a *kunni lemml,* a loser! My grandmother tried to calm him down, but that only agitated him more. He was yelling now in a voice I'd never heard him use before. My grandmother backed away from him, her hand covering her mouth, her eyes wide in alarm. It took both my mother and father to settle him down so they could walk him over to the couch. After they had convinced him to lie down, the rest of us gathered round him, listening to his mutterings, hoping he would be okay.

I didn't want to be there anymore. It frightened me to see my grandfather like that. I was still trying to get over seeing my father and Cousin Ricky going at it. But more than anything, I wanted to go to Patty's house and see Ben Stewart. I knew it was selfish of me, but I went to the McFaddens' house anyway and left my family behind.

❋

The McFaddens' house was lit up inside and out. A string of Christmas lights snaked around each of their front pillars from top to bottom, and each window ledge burned with a plug-in candle. Cars spilled out of the driveway onto both sides of the street.

A giant Christmas tree stood in their foyer as you walked in, trimmed with twinkling lights and ornaments that had been in their family for generations. A huge gold star was at the very top, its pointy tip practically touching the ceiling. Garlands of holly were hung from the walls and red velvet bows graced the banister. Mr. McFadden was wearing a Santa's hat, greeting people. Every once in a while, he'd pull a sprig of mistletoe from his pocket, holding it above a couple's head until they'd kiss, usually just giving each other a quick peck. The adults stayed upstairs, balancing cocktails and appetizers, making small talk, while all the kids were already downstairs in the Ballroom.

From the top of the stairs I could hear "Jungle Boogie" playing, and when I got down to the Ballroom, Keith, Eric Slater, and Larry Tennin were piled on top of Kara, trying to tear off the little red Levi's tag on the back pocket of her jeans. Stealing Levi's tags was the latest thing at school. Only the kids no one liked were safe to walk the halls wearing a new pair of jeans. The rest got tackled and pinned down until someone held up the tag—victory.

I remember the time they stole my tag. All those boys on top of me; Eric Slater holding my head down, blades of crabgrass tickling my face. I kicked and screamed, not wanting them to stop. It happened only that one time. After that, I cut off all the other Levi's tags myself, not trusting it would ever happen to me again.

All the guys were back on their feet now. Alex reached down and helped Kara up. She was laughing, raking her hair away from her face. Ben Stewart stood next to Keith, who was holding up her Levi's tag. When Ben saw me watching him, I turned away and stood on the far side of Emily. I was afraid of giving myself away.

Later, when most everyone went upstairs for food, I couldn't go. I was hungry then, but I couldn't go because Ben Stewart went upstairs and I didn't want him to think I was following him. But by the time he came back down, carrying a plate of cookies, I had worked up the nerve to say something to him.

"Hey, Ben—" My voice was shaky. "It's cool, huh, that we don't have school for two weeks?"

"Yeah, it's cool." He set the plate of cookies down and hooked his thumbs inside his front pockets. There was a streak of powdered sugar on his cheek.

"So, um, what are you gonna do for the next two weeks?" My voice was still weird-sounding and I was so nervous, I didn't even hear his response. I just kept thinking how much I wanted him to like me. He was standing there looking at me, then looking around the room. I was trying to think of something to say to fill the silence, when Patty came over to us. At first I was relieved, thinking it wouldn't be as awkward with her there. But then she leaned over and brushed the streak of sugar off his face and tapped the toe of her shoe twice against the tip of his boot. *Why did she do that?* It was the way she had touched his face and then touched her shoe to his—it was the combination that got to me.

I couldn't believe it—Ben Stewart and Patty! But she was fat! Her fat had to be worse than my eye. It had to be. But there she was, gloating. Standing just inches from me, she watched for my reaction each time she tugged on his sleeve, cupping her mouth, whispering in his ear before pulling away, laughing. I was sure she was laughing at me. How could she do that? She knew that I loved Ben Stewart. I had told her all about it and made her swear she'd never tell.

I glared at her, but it did no good. Ben Stewart had completely abandoned me and was now just talking to Patty. I felt so stupid. I was just standing there staring at them. I had to get her away from him, so I made a big show of leaving, pushing Larry Tennin out of my way.

A few minutes later Patty came after me, which was exactly what I wanted. She called my name three, maybe four times before she caught up with me in the foyer, right in front of the Christmas tree.

"What's the matter, Nina? C'mon." She grabbed my arm.

I shook myself loose. "He was talking to me, Patty! And then you came over and hogged the whole conversation!" I looked right at her so she couldn't miss the tears spilling down my cheeks. I was trying hard to make her feel guilty, but it wasn't working.

"You are such a baby, Nina!" She shook her head. "How do you expect him to like you when you act like this!"

"Shut up! Just shut up!"

"You know, I wasn't gonna say anything, but Ben Stewart didn't even want to talk to you!"

I told her to shut up again and gave her shoulder a shove. She looked wounded, rubbing her shoulder like I'd really hurt her. I was thinking maybe I should apologize when Patty got a mean look on her face and shoved me back as hard as she could—much harder than I'd shoved her. It almost knocked the wind out of me. A second later, I gathered everything I had inside me and charged into her. I pushed and pushed and Patty lost her balance. She went straight back into the Christmas tree, landing on her rear end and knocking the tree off its stand, shifting it to an angle, so that it was slanted now, leaning against the back wall. Some of the ornaments and trinkets that were their family heirlooms had crashed to the floor, shattering on contact. The rest of the ornaments were swaying back and forth and you could see where the star on top had etched a deep scratch in the ceiling.

I knew it was bad, but I'd gone ahead and done it and now Patty was making a big show of it all, sobbing and everything. I tried helping her up, but she pushed me away. "Just leave me alone!" she said, her chubby arms reaching out for someone else to help her up. The adults gathered in close to see what had happened, and before the pieces had time to fit together, and just before Patty could point the blame at me, I ran for home.

❋

The next day, Christmas Day, Cousin Ricky left us. He came downstairs with his bags packed, his business cards slapped facedown on the kitchen table, like a deck of cards waiting to be cut. He was going back to West Orange, back to spend what was left of the holidays with Cousin Doris and his daughters.

He didn't have to say it, didn't have to admit my father was right. He was going back to face up to his responsibilities. No one tried to stop him and no one asked if he'd be coming back.

And about a week after Cousin Ricky left, my father's quartet went on to New York without him. They had picked up another clarinetist and left town after New Year's. Other than explaining that he didn't want to be away from his wife and children, my father didn't say a word about it after they left. It was almost like he'd never planned on going with them at all.

As for me, after Cousin Ricky left, I apologized to Patty and then she apologized to me about the whole Ben Stewart thing. She promised she'd never let a boy come between us, but I knew that wasn't true. Patty wanted a boyfriend just as much as I did. And as it turned out, Ben Stewart didn't really like her any more than he liked me. There was another girl he *like*-liked. But if he had *like*-liked Patty, I knew what she would have done.

Once Cousin Ricky was gone, I stopped meditating and started negotiating with myself. I'd gone from expecting my eye would be normal someday to adapting my hopes once again around its imperfections. I couldn't buy into Cousin Ricky's theories anymore. There was nothing left of my faith in the powers of meditation. I decided that the next time I was going to believe in something, it had better be real. I was through waiting on miracles. I was done with hope certificates.

fathers, lost and found

It's true what they say about death. It comes in threes. I had just turned fifteen and there they were, three in a row. First was Perry Stevens, a kid from school. He had jumped in front of a freight car at the railroad tracks behind the athletic field. The *Akron Beacon Journal* said his body had been dragged for more than a quarter of a mile. Then it was my grandfather. One night, he passed away in his sleep. After they told me, I stayed up in my room and cried all day, even though everyone said it was a blessing. They said he was old and he'd had a good life. They said he didn't suffer, and I loved him and was grateful for that.

So the first death was violent, the second peaceful, and the third one was too unreal to believe.

That time it was Mr. McFadden. A heart attack on the back nine at the Fairlawn Country Club and suddenly he was gone. He was forty-four years old.

The news traveled through school the next day like notes

being passed in study hall. And when Kara showed up in homeroom with a brand-new pair of tennis shoes, nobody bothered to scuff them up. Everybody talked. They bunched together in the halls by open lockers, saying how awful it was. Because I was such good friends with Patty, kids who normally wouldn't even say hello were coming up to me, asking if I knew things they didn't. In the cafeteria, everyone picked at their sandwiches and talked about whether or not they'd go to the wake.

By the time I'd made it back to our neighborhood that afternoon, cars were already lined up and down the street near the McFaddens' house. It was an Indian summer day and the leaves were changing colors, spiraling dead to the ground. There was a heaviness in the air. Everything was somber. I couldn't get myself to go to Patty's house just then. I didn't know what to say, how to act, so I turned for home instead.

As I stood in the doorway, I was struck by the silence and emptiness inside our house. Now that Lissy and Mitch were away at college, I was the only kid left at home. You used to have to step over a mountain of shoes piled on the floor when you came through the back way, and now there were only two pairs—mine and my father's. The key rack with everyone's house keys and car keys had thinned out and the cases of Pepsi that once sat on the floor in the pantry had been replaced with six-packs. As a family, we seemed to be shrinking. But my father couldn't accept this. I listened as he made long-distance calls to my siblings and airline reservations for them, casting his net even farther, trying to keep his young from straying.

It was working on Mitch. Every other weekend my father's guilt trips brought him home. He wasn't happy at the University of Cincinnati anyway. His classes were too hard, the workload too intense. He couldn't keep up. Mitch didn't want to stay in school, but he didn't want to come home, either.

I took out a carton of orange juice and gave it a shake. Then Pumpkin started barking just as I heard the garage door going up, followed by the quiet rumble of my mother's Cadillac pulling in.

As soon as she walked in, I could tell by the look on her face that she'd heard the news. She set her purse down on the kitchen table and came over and hugged me hard. Pumpkin was on her hind legs, yelping, wanting in. And it was in my mother's arms where grief shattered me. I was crying hard, but not because of Mr. McFadden. I was scared. Nothing felt solid anymore. Security had been yanked out from under me. I wanted to tell her how much I loved her. She just had to know how much. My grandfather had been old; he was supposed to die. Parents weren't. It was in my mother's arms when it hit me. Every day brought you that much closer to losing the ones you loved. Death would always find you, and there was nothing you could do about it.

My mother dried my eyes with the tips of her fingers and told me that I really ought to go see Patty. "Dad and I will stop by later, but you really ought to be there for her. Right now, she needs you . . ."

My mother watched me from the front door as I left. So did Pumpkin, her little snout peeking out the bottom pane of glass. I didn't make eye contact with anyone as I headed for the McFaddens'. I walked slowly, concentrating on what to say.

The McFaddens' front door was unlocked, so I walked in, like I always did, and right away I saw Bev. She looked at me and broke into a nervous laugh. I'd forgotten what I had planned to say to her, but then she pulled me close and patted me on my back, saying, "It's okay. It's all gonna be okay."

Keith came downstairs in the middle of this to let her know he'd finally gotten in touch with Matthew. Bev nodded and Keith reached over and gave his mother's shoulder a squeeze. I felt like this was something private, something I shouldn't have been a part of, and so I drifted away, heading toward the kitchen to find Patty.

She was sitting at the table smoking a cigarette. She looked up at me when I called her name. Neither one of us knew what to say, so I just leaned down and hugged her, my hand rubbing circles along her back. It felt like the same kind of hug her mother had just given me, only I couldn't bring myself to tell her everything was going to be okay. Patty just sat there. She seemed distant, far away. Something in her had changed. She had lost her anchor, that fatherly weight that grounded a daughter and kept her from going astray. She'd lost all that and now she was free-floating, aimless and unguided.

I straightened up and looked at her face. She wasn't crying or anything. When I sat down beside her, she stood up. She went to the cabinet, took down a mixing bowl, and pulled a package of ground beef and a couple of eggs from the refrigerator. Patty asked me what she'd missed at school that day as she cracked the eggs and dug her hands in the bowl, kneading the ground beef.

I started telling her about an assembly we'd had that morning. It felt wrong talking to her about something so insignificant, but nothingness was what she seemed to want or need from me just then. And if that was all I could do for her, then that's what I would do.

I was still babbling on about things that didn't matter when I happened to look out the back sliding glass doors and saw Anna on the pool deck with her arms around Gorgeous Greg, as we'd taken to calling him several years back. Just the sight of them irritated me. They had been boyfriend and girlfriend the summer before, up until Greg had left for Ohio State. Anna must have just come from school, and it bothered me that she had gone straight to Greg. Why didn't she come see Patty first? She and Greg had already broken up! And besides, when Patty first found out about the two of them, it had started a big fight. The rest of us girls had all taken Patty's side. Probably because we were jealous that Anna had gotten Gorgeous Greg. After all, he was gorgeous and three years older. Kara, Emily, and I would have killed to have had a boyfriend like that. But Patty had felt rejected, questioning all the times Anna had come over to the Ballroom all prettied up, or turned up on the McFaddens' pool deck in her skimpiest bikini.

That had been just a few months ago. Now everything had changed. An entire season had passed. The cover over the top of the McFaddens' pool was sprinkled with dead leaves shed from the surrounding trees. I could see that Greg was still crying, his tears falling onto Anna's shoulder.

So Anna was out back with Greg. What about Emily and Kara! Where were they at a time like this! I was sitting there, feeling smug, thinking that I was the only one who was really Patty's friend, when I realized with shame that I was just as bad as the rest of them. All I cared about was myself—and at a time when I should have been concerned about Patty.

Timothy came into the kitchen, carrying empty glasses and a stack of used paper plates. He set them on the counter and looked at what Patty was mixing in the bowl.

"That's disgusting!" he said.

"Then you don't have to eat it." Patty went back to kneading the ground beef.

Timothy came and sat down with me at the table. He was quiet and pale. His wristwatch was on upside down. There was a notepad on the table with a big TODAY'S THE DAY going across the top. Timothy picked up a Magic Marker and began sketching me.

He was always doing quick caricatures in his notebooks. You could say, "Do Keith!," "Do Matthew!" and within seconds, he'd nail them, grabbing that one feature and just the right detail or two that seemed to define them. For Keith, it was a big grin and a lightbulb or a thought bubble above his head; for Matthew, it was all captured in his sneer with a cigarette or joint dangling from his lips. Patty always had the chubby cheeks and something like a mixing bowl or a wooden spoon in her hands, and Gorgeous Greg had the long lashes and some pretty girl in the background looking adoringly at him. Timothy may have been the baby, a year younger than Patty and me, but already he'd found his gift, the one thing he did best.

I kept looking over to see how he was drawing me, how he was drawing my eye. Was he making it look normal? I craned my neck to see, but I couldn't really tell because he had drawn all my hair down, covering half my face. I supposed that made sense, since that was the way I always wore my hair. So to other people, that must have been my defining feature. It wasn't much of one, but at least it wasn't my eye.

When Timothy finished drawing me, he looked up and asked when Matthew was getting home. Patty didn't answer him and I didn't know. She was busy shaping her meat loaf. Timothy asked again.

"How the fuck should I know, Timothy! I haven't even talked to Matthew yet!" Patty glared at her brother as she wiped her hands on a dish towel hanging from a hook off a cupboard.

"Jesus, I just asked a question. What the fuck's your problem?"

"What the fuck's my problem?" Patty opened the oven, slid the meat loaf inside, and slammed the door shut.

No one said anything after that. No one even tried breaking the silence. And in those quiet moments, I wasn't thinking about my most defining feature anymore. All I was thinking was how death was bigger than everything else. What difference did it make if my eyes weren't identical? Death was so final, so unrelenting. It neutralized everything around it. It had the final say.

Later, when my parents stopped by, the McFaddens' house was still full of people. My father leaned over and whispered something to Bev. Whatever it was, it brought a real smile out of her and a hug that under different circumstances wouldn't have looked right.

Then he turned to Patty and butted his forehead up against hers, draped his arms over her shoulders, and said, "You're not alone."

Three words. Three simple words and he had her bawling. A houseful of people trying all day to comfort her, and my father was the one who reached her. He stood in the living room, holding her while she cried, telling her he'd be there for her—anytime. He knew what she was going through, having lost his father at a young age, and then his mother, too.

After a moment, my father walked her out the back way and sat with her on the pool deck, where Anna and Greg had been earlier. The rest of us were watching them through the sliding glass doors. Patty was sitting alongside my father, her legs dangling down, their knees touching. They were both talking, their heads nodding. I saw my father reach in his back pocket for his handkerchief and hand it to Patty, using the heel of his hand to dry his own tears. Then Patty rested her head on my father's shoulder and started crying all over again.

Everyone in the living room was still watching, admiring the way he was comforting her. "Isn't he wonderful!" I heard someone say. And he was. He was my wonderful father, and in some way, that made me wonderful by association. I sat on the arm of my mother's chair, gazing out the window, watching my father in action.

After the funeral, after the fruit baskets stopped arriving and people stopped dropping by or calling, after Matthew and Greg had gone back to college and Bev had gone back to work, the McFaddens tried getting back to whatever normal was going to be for them from that point on.

Of all the McFaddens, Timothy was the only one who showed his grief. We'd hear him crying in his room, behind his closed door. Even with a houseful of kids, he'd slip off by himself to smoke a cigarette, sketch something in the spiral notebook that he always carried with him.

Bev was just the opposite. She couldn't get enough of us kids. She'd sit around the kitchen table with us, drinking a bottle of beer, listening to our stories. We told her about the time we ate all the nutmeg in her spice rack because we had heard it would get you high, and about the night we got this guy from school down to his boxers in a rigged game of strip poker.

"Oh, you kids are just awful," she'd say, laughing, taking another sip from her beer. Then she'd point to me and say, "I want this all in the book, Nina!"

Patty was a lot like her mother. She never mentioned her father. I supposed she mourned in her own way, and after Mr. McFadden died, Patty went to extremes. She cut her hair short, wore tighter clothes and higher heels. And the parties she threw were bigger, with more beer, more pot, and more boys.

It seemed like nowadays, Patty was always with one of the Mad Marauders, and what puzzled me was how she got so many boys being as big as she was. Keith and Greg weren't all that crazy about her fooling around with their friends, but Greg couldn't say anything about it, ever since he'd started seeing Anna. But I do remember one time Keith told Eric Slater, "Listen, man, whatever you're doing with my sister, I don't want to hear about it!"

So Patty was playing with the boys and I was jealous, ugly jealous, because it seemed she had her pick. I couldn't get a boy to kiss me, and here she was, kissing them all! And she just went from one to the next. None of those boys seemed to mean much to her. It didn't faze her when it was over. Maybe after you lose your father, losing boyfriends just didn't matter that much.

little darling

When I was sixteen my mother took me to see a makeup artist in Cleveland who specialized in burn scars and skin grafts. My father was the one who discovered her. He'd seen this woman on a local TV talk show, but because it dealt with makeup, he had turned the task over to my mother.

At first I didn't want to go. My last experience with makeup, the night of my thirteenth birthday, had ended in disaster, and ever since then, even the thought of wearing makeup made me anxious. I pictured the Maybelline kit from Lissy, tucked away in the bottom of my sock drawer. I couldn't even bring myself to wear blush or lipstick. But all that changed the day my mother and I visited the makeup artist.

The makeup she used was thick and had to be set with a sealing powder that made it waterproof. It came with a special remover, an oily-based lotion that smelled like wet dog. She spent a long time blending ingredients, trying to get the shade and texture right.

It seemed like a lot to go through to cover the bad parts of my eye where the skin was all different colors. Before the injections, my eye was so much more discolored, and I wondered how much more foundation it would have taken to have covered that mess. She was using so much on me as it was.

While she worked on my eye, I worried that the kids at school would make fun of me the way Alex Korbington had done on the night of my birthday. I couldn't handle being mortified like that again. I couldn't handle any more disappointments.

But then, after I saw that she had hidden all the reds and pinks and purples, I began to see possibilities. I started to relax.

"Now, Nina," she said, "we're going to use light shades to make this eye look bigger." She leaned over me and brushed an almost white shadow over the lid of my one eye. "And then darker shades to make the other eye appear smaller."

I thought I'd look two-toned, especially when she lined one eye so much heavier than the other. But she said to trust her. "We're building an illusion . . . Now, the thing to remember with mascara," she said, "is to point it this way." She pulled the wand free from the tube, demonstrating. It smelled strong, like shoe polish. "And stroke the lashes on this eye toward your nose . . . And on the other eye, go like this"—she tilted the wand in the opposite direction—"toward your ears."

"Let's see, Neen." My mother sat in a stylist's chair that swiveled all the way around. She studied my face for a moment, then nodded with a smile. "Amazing what the right makeup can do, isn't it?"

I looked at myself in the mirror. I had two eyes now that looked like they belonged on the same face. I stared at myself for the longest time. I could have cried. Even though the one lid was still thicker, it wasn't as noticeable as before. It looked more like I had a drooping lid, like I had a sty. And all the purple, red, and pink was gone for the moment, hidden. For once when I looked in a mirror, I saw my whole face. For once my eye was not the first thing I saw staring back at me.

❋

At first I thought my special makeup had saved me. That's because I was wearing it when Mike Farling started to like me. He was the first boy who ever did. His family had just moved from Toronto to Akron the summer before. His father was a big shot with Goodyear. I guess it made sense that Mike would be the one to like me; he didn't know me as Big Eye–Little Eye. I was starting to look normal by then and I'd been working hard at reinventing myself.

Instead of being known as the girl with the eye, I wanted people to think of me as the girl who could roll a pencil-thin joint, the one who could hold her beer better than most of the boys—though they never suspected that my cans were usually still half-full when I pitched them. I was never half as cool as I pretended to be, but nobody knew that.

And I had fooled Mike Farling. His friends told my friends that he thought I was funny and smart, and then my friends told his friends that I thought he was, too. I thought about him all the time. He was the star in all my daydreams. He was in only one of my classes, but I could never bring myself to sit near him, let alone talk to him. We were both shy, so our romance progressed slowly. If it hadn't been for our friends forcing us to sit across from each other one day in the cafeteria, we might never have worked up the nerve to even say hi.

The day it all came together and then fell apart for Mike Farling and me was the day a group of us cut eighth-period study hall and went to Dairy Queen. I was in a booth, sitting on the same side as Mike. I was sure he was wishing he'd sat next to Kara instead, who was sprawled out on the other side.

Then Mike pressed his leg to mine and I pressed my leg back against his. I knew we both were where we wanted to be. He looked over at my book and asked what I was reading.

I held up *The Bell Jar.*

Then Kara bummed a cigarette off him and asked for a light.

"You want me to smoke it for you, too?" he said, but she didn't respond.

Emily, Anna, and Patty were at another booth, squeezed in with Larry Tennin and Eric Slater. They were smoking cigarettes, laughing at every little thing, having more fun than we were. At our table nobody said anything. I turned shy and self-conscious. I fingered the spine of my book and Mike just sat there watching Kara rub her cigarette ashes into her Levi's, trying to fade them faster.

The radio was tuned to WMMS. The Beatles were singing "Here Comes the Sun," and Mike joined in. You could tell he knew he had a good voice, and something about the way he sang, the way he tilted his head just so, reminded me of my father on that stage at Flipper's all those years ago. He started really hamming it up then, using the pepper shaker as a microphone. And then, when he got to the part that goes "Little darling, it's been a long cold lonely winter / Little darling . . ." what I heard—what I swore I heard him sing to me—was "Little doggie."

I looked around and saw everyone laughing at Mike. At me. I felt cornered. I shot back in time and there I was again, in the hallway, in grade school, with a tea bag taped to my forehead and the boys all arf, arf, arfing at me. I felt like such a fool. Even with my special makeup, everyone still thought I was ugly as a dog. I was certain Mike Farling had never liked me, and that the others were all in on it. I felt tricked. He was sitting there making fun of me.

I looked at him singing into the pepper shaker and my face must have given me away, because suddenly Mike stopped, put down the shaker, and asked what was wrong.

I couldn't answer. I couldn't even look at him. My eyes were beginning to tear up and I knew I shouldn't cry. But it was too late. The tears were already flowing. I made sure that Mike saw me crying, and when he didn't say anything more, I glared at him. "Everything's just a big joke to you, isn't it!" I got up, grabbed my book, and tore out of the Dairy Queen. I slowed my pace once I got past the doors, thinking someone, hopefully Mike, would come after me. But he didn't. No one did. I knew I had just humiliated myself and I started to sob even harder.

It was like the time I ran crying out of McDonald's after a high school football game just because Emily said she didn't have room for me in her booth. I made a scene, thinking she was trying to ditch me. No one came after me then, either, and it wasn't until the next day that I found out she'd said the same thing to Anna and Patty because she wanted to be alone with Eric Slater.

I looked back through the window, catching the corner of the booth where Patty, Anna, and Emily were sitting. They were exactly the way I'd left them, smoking cigarettes, goofing around. It didn't even matter to them that I'd left.

Later that night, Patty called to find out what had happened. After I'd cried into the phone and told her everything, she said, "What are you talking about? You're crazy, Nina. Mike was singing 'Little darling.' And he was singing it to you!" She said he couldn't understand why I got so upset. No one could. "They were all asking why you got so mad and left like that."

The next day, I didn't wait for Mike after first period like I usually did. I just couldn't face him.

And by the time I could, almost two weeks later, it was too late. Mike Farling had already found another girlfriend. She wasn't even popular. She was just a regular girl, someone no one even noticed or thought about until he'd found her. Now she was someone you paid attention to, or maybe it was just me who was so aware of her. But each time I saw the two of them huddled together on the bleachers at homecoming or sitting by the railroad tracks behind school sharing a cigarette, I always thought it should have been, could have been, me.

☼

Then one day Jack Bruin started passing me notes. We sat across from each other in history. The first time, I thought he meant for me to pass the note to the girl one row over. But my initials were on top and that meant the note was for me. It was just one simple line about all the peace-sign stickers I had on my notebook. After that, I loaded up all my book covers with stickers and passed notes to Jack every day. And that's how that one started.

Jack's nickname was "Buzz." He was a six-foot-two burnout, who wore a jean jacket all year-round and checkered high-top sneakers with red laces. He'd smoked so much pot that his eyes were almost the same shade as his laces, even with all the Visine drops he'd used.

The first time Jack called our house, my father got a hold of him. "You say you're calling for Nina?" My father switched the receiver to his other ear and gave me a wink. "Nina Goldman? Really . . . Could you describe her?"

I was pacing back and forth, my arms folded tight. He thought he was being funny, but I didn't like him teasing me just because a boy was calling for me. He never teased Lissy about boys calling for her. I wanted to yell at him. I was so mad.

". . . long brown hair . . . kinda tall . . ."

My mother looked up from her needlepoint, shaking her head. "Artie—be nice."

Finally my father held out the receiver, yelling for me like I was in another part of the house, going, "Nina—oh Nina—there's a Mr. Jack Bruin calling for you. Do you want to take the call or should I take a message?"

I stormed upstairs, and after I picked up the extension, I could tell my father was still on the line. I heard the TV in the background and shouted down to him, "Hang up, Dad!" I had to hear the receiver click before it felt safe to say hi.

After that, I always raced to the phone on the first ring. And whenever Jack was coming over, I'd watch for him from the upstairs window and then rush down the steps and out the front door.

It got easier to see Jack once Patty started seeing his friend Todd Angelos. We'd just meet over at the McFaddens', down in the Ballroom and my father never had to know about it.

Everyone—Kara, Emily, and Anna—always brought their boyfriends to Patty's. But Jack was the only one I ever took there. It was a boy-girl thing. We'd flip a coin or draw straws to see which couple got the water bed in the back room, which pair got the good couch, who'd get the other couch, and, at worst, which two would end up on the beanbag chairs.

Lights out and we got busy. At first the Ballroom was pitch-black. You could hardly even see the boy you were with. But then your eyes would adjust to the dark. Gradually you could see the face before you and the shadows of other couples across the room. And whatever you couldn't see, you heard—heavy moaning and sighing, couch springs squeaking along with groaning and gasping. Nothing escaped us. Nothing was private. After Marc Harris had given Anna a hickey, she had to wear turtlenecks for a week, and it was summertime. We knew when Eric Slater had gone to second base with Emily, because first of all, she had told us girls ahead of time that she planned to do it, and secondly, when the lights came on, her bra was on the other side of the room.

We girls usually cleared our sexual adventures with one another first. That's why I told them when I finally agreed to let Jack go to third base. I was way behind the others. They'd gone there long before me. And I'd only just let him go to second with me the week before.

The day we decided to go to third, Jack and I got the water

bed. It was in the McFaddens' back room, where the basement wasn't finished, wasn't paneled like in the Ballroom. Their giant dryer was back there, along with cobwebs, and dried-out pill bugs in the corners. Bruce Springsteen was coming from the other room: " 'Cause tramps like us / Baby we were born to run . . ." Jack and I started kissing. At one point we opened our eyes at exactly the same time, looked at each other, and then shut them fast.

I felt Jack wrestling with my zipper, feeling his way toward me. My stomach tensed up as he reached his hand inside my underpants. His fingers were busy, wandering around down there like he was lost or something. He'd told the others he'd done this—gone to third—lots of times before, so I assumed he was doing whatever he was supposed to.

After a while, I just couldn't help it: My hips started moving. I didn't know if it was okay to wiggle like I was, but I couldn't keep still. So I guess maybe he'd found his way after all. I was pressing myself against his fingers, harder and harder, rubbing myself against him. I almost forgot Jack was there with me at all. But then suddenly he stopped what he was doing and pulled his hand away. "God, what'd you do?"

What did I do? What did I do! I couldn't look at him. I didn't know what I did.

"Gross, your underpants are all wet!"

The next day in homeroom, three people came up to me to say Jack told them I'd wet my pants.

accidents will happen

The day after Patty got her driver's license, she got a new car. A new-used car. It was a little green Honda, bought with her own money saved from the evenings and weekends she'd put in at the family store. Beeping from half a block away, she finally pulled into our drive. I went outside and saw Kara sitting in the passenger seat. "C'mon!" Kara said. "We're gonna go get Anna and Emily!"

I ran inside to tell my mother I was leaving, and by the time I came back out, I saw my father's station wagon parked next to Patty's Honda in the drive. She was walking him around the car, showing him the tires, the rear bumper, opening the hatchback, the sunroof.

"Do you like it, Mr. Goldman?"

"Aw, Patty, this is terrific. No kidding. I think this is just great. Really and truly—a great little car."

"Really?" Sometimes, especially since Mr. McFadden died, Patty needed my father's approval almost as much as I did.

"What do you think, Patty?" My father smiled. "Let me take you gals for a spin, show you how to open her up. What do you say, huh? Huh!"

Patty looked back at her car and bit down hard on her lip. Her car was less than two hours old. She didn't want to give up her keys, not even to him. I glanced at Kara, who was still waiting in the front seat with a sour look on her face, pounding her arm against the side-view mirror. She was restless. She wanted to go get the others. Kara was making me feel edgy. If it had just been Patty and me, I probably wouldn't have minded my father's intrusion.

"Da-ad—we gotta get going!" The tone of my own voice surprised me. I sounded every bit as annoyed as Kara felt. But the look my father shot back at me, a perfect combination of hurt and resentment, was enough to make me back down. I started to climb into the backseat, and that's when my father asked again.

"C'mon Patty—one quick time around the block. Gotta make sure my gals are traveling in good equipment, right? Eh?"

I knew Patty couldn't say no to him. No one could. She finally gave him her keys and Kara moved in back with me so Patty could ride up front with my father. He adjusted the driver's seat and the mirrors before giving himself a spritz of windshield washer fluid.

"All right, gals," he said, turning up the stereo, "hold on tight . . ."

Actually, it was fun. With my father at the wheel, we were flying, going sixty down the same back roads we'd once walked to grade school. My hair was catching in the wind, snapping before my eyes. I looked over at Kara who had both her fists raised above her, like someone going no-hands down a roller coaster. "All right, Mr. G!"

I could feel the smile growing, stretching across my face. Now even Kara Elberts would know how special my father was. I couldn't believe I'd questioned his wanting to drive Patty's car.

But then my father took that one turn too fast, ran over something, and we went flying up onto the curb. There was a loud thud just before the car skidded to a stop and jolted us halfway out of our seats. The AAA manual and the tiny ice scraper that were stored inside the glove compartment had landed in Patty's lap. The rearview mirror was knocked cockeyed, and in its reflection, I could see the worried look on my father's face as he asked if everyone was okay. Patty looked back at me and Kara, her face stone white.

I was afraid to look when we got out of the car. The bumper was hanging there like a loose tooth; the rear hubcap was lying in the middle of the street. I went over to pick it up. It was dented, ruined.

That's when I first heard my father laughing. *Laughing!* And in between his laughter, he was reassuring Patty that he'd get it fixed. "I'll even make sure you have another car to drive in the meantime." He could barely get the words out, he was laughing so hard. Tears streamed down his cheeks.

I couldn't look at him. It wasn't funny.

Kara went to the back of the Honda and lifted the bumper. It came off in her hands, and when she walked it back around to the front, Patty looked shocked. She was just then realizing what had happened to her car.

"Oh my God!" Patty squealed. "What am I gonna tell my mom? She told me not to let anyone else drive it. She made me promise."

My father had his handkerchief out, still laughing, wiping his eyes, going, "Don't you worry, sweet pea. I'm taking the rap for this one. I'm gonna take you home and explain it all to your mother."

Patty went over and hugged him, her eyes squeezed tight. She was relieved that he was going to make everything all better.

I couldn't believe it. I was more upset with my father than Patty was. In fact, it didn't seem like she was mad at all and that infuriated me. I was embarrassed but she seemed almost grateful that he was going to talk to her mother and take the blame for something he'd caused in the first place. How did he always come out looking like the good guy?

After we drove back to the McFaddens', I waited out front with Kara while my father and Patty went inside to tell Bev.

"Shit . . ." Kara was cracking her gum, throwing pebbles onto the drive. "I can't fuckin' believe your old man totaled her car."

"It's not 'totaled,' Kara!"

"Yeah, well—looks totaled to me."

"He said he'd fix it, didn't he? He didn't do it on purpose, you know. Ever heard of an accident, Kara?" I stood up and brushed the back of my jeans. I couldn't look at Patty's car. It seemed like the dents were getting worse now, all on their own. The next day, it would be all over school that Nina Goldman's father totaled Patty McFadden's new car.

Kara snapped her gum and shook her head. "That car is totally fucked up!"

"It was an accident," I said again. "An ACCIDENT! OKAY! It could have happened to anybody—ANYBODY'S FATHER COULD HAVE DONE IT!"

I started heading for home then, ignoring Kara when she called after me. Keeping my head down and my hands stuffed deep inside my pockets, I kicked an old Coke can in front of me again and again. I was mortified—Patty's car was less than two hours old.

When I got home, my mother was in the family room dusting my father's pipe collection. My father had more than four hundred pipes and he'd boast that each one had been smoked at least once. Cleaning those pipes was a big job, so my mother did it only once a year.

I told my mother what my father had done to Patty's car and she told me to calm down. "Your father will fix everything. If he was stupid enough to have pulled a stunt like that, then believe me, he'll take care of it. Here—" She tossed me a fresh Handi-Wipe and told me to get busy.

"But Ma! You should have heard him—he was laughing! I was so embarrassed, I wanted to die."

"Nina, there's nothing you can do about it now. It's over and done with."

"He just makes me so mad sometimes. He doesn't care what he does or who he does it to. And he always manages to get away with it. It drives me crazy!"

My mother pressed her lips tight together and shook her head. "You kids always complain to me about your father. He's *your* father. If you're so upset with him, then you tell him! It won't do any good if I do it for you."

She made it sound so easy. Just tell my father that I was upset with him. So simple, yet I couldn't do it.

"What is it about you kids and your father?"

If only I had an answer for her. I didn't know what it was about my father and why we were so afraid of hurting his feelings. He had certainly hurt ours. I took a rack of pipes off the top shelf and started pulling the stems apart from the bowls.

My mother had taken to smoking a pipe herself in those days. She'd quit cigarettes the year before during a bout of bronchitis, and instead of going back to her Silva Thins, my father bought her a pipe. A lady's pipe. She smoked it exactly the way he did, adopting all his gestures and habits. One day I saw her leaning over an ashtray, tapping the bowl against her palm, just like he did, to loosen up the dead tobacco.

We kids were used to my mother's pipe, but sometimes friends who didn't know about it would come in the house and see her puffing away. After a while, they'd tease her, going, "You aren't smoking any pot in there now, are you, Mrs. Goldman?"

While we were cleaning the pipes, Pumpkin started yelping,

and a few seconds later, I heard my father's footsteps coming up the walk.

He was still laughing when he told my mother what he'd done. "Sixty miles an hour and that curb—Sandra, I swear to God—that goddamn curb came up out of nowhere! Little pisher of a car is fun as hell to drive. Really!"

"I hope you're proud of yourself, Artie." My mother gave a laugh and backhanded him across the stomach. She was starting to piss me off, too.

"Cute little car," my father said. Then he cracked himself up all over again. "Cheap as hell, though. Made like a tin can. One good knock and the bumper's gone!"

That's when I threw down my Handi-Wipe. "You know it's not funny!"

"Sweetheart," my father said, "thank God it's not such a big deal."

"It's not a big deal to you, but what about Patty? What about *me*?"

"Ah for chrissakes, Nina!" My father wiped his eyes with the butt of both hands. "Let this be the worst thing your father ever does, huh? Don't make it into a federal case."

"I know it was an accident—you didn't do it on purpose. I know that! But you just stood there laughing!"

My father folded his arms and started tapping his foot. "So you're embarrassed, is that it? You're telling me I embarrassed you today? Is that what I'm hearing?"

I sat there for a moment, looking at him, contemplating. I'd picked up one of the pipe cleaners and was twisting the wired ends together, just as he twisted every situation to make it come out his way. None of us ever told my father the simple truth if we thought it would wound him. We only knew how to tell him what he wanted to hear. We were afraid of him and afraid for him. I didn't know which controlled us more.

"Well? Is that what you're trying to say—that your terrible, awful father embarrassed you? Ah, poor little Nina!"

It was his sarcasm that decided it for me. "What do you think?" I practically spit the words at him.

He looked sucker punched. He hadn't expected that to be my response. It took a moment, but he recovered quickly and shot back at me, "What do I think, Nina? I'll tell you what I think. I think you're acting like a goddamn spoiled brat!"

I glared at him and heard myself laugh in a mean, spiteful way. "You know, you always think you're being so cute, so funny. Why can't you just admit that this time you went too far? Your little fun and games backfired on you! Just admit it, Dad—you screwed up today! You ruined Patty's car. And just cuz you can afford to buy her a new one doesn't matter. You ruined it!"

"First of all, young lady, it's not ruined. Secondly, I'm getting it fixed. And last of all, I'm still your father and don't you ever speak to me like that again!"

I was fuming. I dropped the pipe cleaner, leaped up off the floor, and headed up the stairs to my room, slamming the door hard behind me. I was shaking and my eyes were full of tears as I paced back and forth between the bed and my closet. I'd never done that to my father before—talked back to him like that and then just stormed away. Usually, the farthest I'd get would be to the foot of the stairs before I'd hear him say, "Young lady, you get your butt back over here!" But this time, I'd made it all the way to my room. Only now that I was there, I didn't know what to do with myself.

I did know one thing, though: As furious as I was with him, in my heart I had already forgiven him.

the best little girl

I think if it had been up to my father, he would have kept us little forever. It was hard for him to watch us grow up and make choices he wouldn't have made for us. And it seemed that we were failing him in our attempts at independence, one kid at a time.

First it was Lissy, who had thrilled my father when she moved home after college but then disappointed him so by announcing that she'd fallen in love with a man who wore his name on his belt buckle. *Jim* was tall and skinny and had a lot of blond hair that reached down to the center of his back. He wore a red bandanna knotted at his neck and cowboy boots.

When he first came to pick Lissy up, my mother and father said they smelled liquor on his breath. Lissy came home drunk that night, stumbling in sometime after three o'clock in the morning, and after that, my parents didn't want her to go out with him ever again.

And that's when all the trouble started.

Lissy snuck off to be with Jim every chance she could. But my parents weren't stupid. They knew who called her late at night and they knew whose car was parked out front and who it was running across the lawn when they came home earlier than expected. And they let Lissy know that they knew. And over this, my sister slammed doors, threw dishes across the dinner table, and cried. Mostly she cried.

I could see Lissy's point. She was twenty-three, too old to be told what she could and couldn't do, who she could and couldn't see. But then again, I could see my parents' side of it. Jim wasn't the kind of guy you wanted your daughter to date, and the fact that he wasn't Jewish was only part of the problem. None of us could figure out what she saw in him.

One night, after a particularly bad fight over Jim, Lissy marched into my room, sobbing, saying she had to get out of my father's house. "I hate it here. I need my own place. I'm moving out—I have to."

And she did. One month later, Lissy moved into a studio apartment on Highland Square. But even though she was out of his house, she still couldn't let him go.

"He's driving me crazy!" she said one night as we stood in the tiny bathroom of her new apartment.

"I wish you guys would just make up already."

"I have no intention of ever making up with that man. He's insane." Lissy sat on the edge of the tub with one of my mother's old bath towels draped over her shoulders, held together by a giant clip under her chin. I was helping her frost her hair that night with a kit we'd gotten from Woolworth's. She wanted blond streaks, just a few.

"I can't even stand being in the same room with him." Lissy fit the plastic bonnet over her head and tied the ends in a bow beneath her chin.

"He's not that bad!" I told her.

Lissy ignored me and reached in the box, handing me

something that looked like a crochet hook. "Remember, not too much on top. It has to look natural." She tucked a few strays inside the bonnet. "I honestly don't know how Mom puts up with him."

"He's not that bad, Lissy!" I said again as I hooked and pulled strands of her hair through the holes in the cap.

"He's selfish and self-absorbed . . ."

I didn't like her talking about my father like that, and so I dug down too hard with the hook and scraped her scalp.

"Shit, Neen! Take it easy!" She reached up to inspect my work with her fingertips.

"Why are you so down on him?"

"Because, Nina, he's a total control freak."

I grabbed hold of way too much hair then and pulled it through the cap. "What's that supposed to mean?"

"Everything's on his terms. He doesn't care what he says or what he does to you. And then we're all expected to walk around on eggshells with him, never say anything that might offend him! The water doesn't run both ways with him. Never has. Never will."

Even though I knew that some of what Lissy was saying about my father was true, I still felt protective of him. He wasn't as terrible as she was making him out to be. And the more things she said against him, the angrier I became.

"He's the most selfish, arrogant person I've ever known."

Just for that, I hooked more hair and then still more, until half the cap was full of sprouted strands and the other half, barely woven through. Before she had time to reach up, I had the plastic gloves on and the tip of the nozzle snipped off the solution. Fumes rose up and made my eyes water, but I kept applying the solution, catching the spillover with a wad of cotton before it inched down the sides of the cap and reached her skin.

We set the timer, and I quick-like put the plastic baggy over her hair. Then we went into the other room and shared a smoke, passing the cigarette back and forth between us. Actually, I waited for Lissy to hand the cigarette my way. I knew it was something I couldn't just reach for. I had to be invited first. That was Lissy's way of sharing. Always her way. She didn't realize that she was just like my father.

"Just like Dad"—that was code talk among my siblings. "You sound just like Dad." "You're doing the same thing Dad always does." "My God, you're acting just like him!" Whenever we heard something like that, it would bring us back in line, make us deny it, while we checked ourselves to make sure it wasn't so. We were so afraid of picking up his traits, and yet Mitch and I would get on a roll, taking turns mimicking my father, going, " 'Huh! Eh? Huh, sweet pea! Tootsie! You bet your bippie!' " There was hurt there, but there was also love.

Even before Lissy finished her cigarette, I was antsy to get out of there. I was angry with her, but more than that, I was afraid to stick around much longer. I was afraid because I knew—even before the timer went off and she had shampooed out the dye—I knew I had ruined her hair.

I dashed home, hung the car keys on the hook in the kitchen, and went to my room to hide. When the phone rang, I wouldn't answer it. I knew it was Lissy. I huddled by the opened laundry chute, listening to my mother's half of the conversation.

"Now just calm down . . . No, you're not going to have to cut it all off . . . Just calm down. Melissa, I'll talk to her . . . You need to just calm down . . ."

The next day, my mother made me go with her and Lissy to the beauty shop and watch while they reversed the frosting in my sister's hair. Lissy didn't speak to me for almost a week after that.

❋

I felt bad about ruining Lissy's hair, but that was nothing compared to how I felt the time Mitch failed my father, making him cry like someone had gone and died on him. I was standing in the kitchen, stirring a pot of spaghetti sauce, when I heard two car doors slam. My father was shouting at my brother as they came through the front door. "For chrissakes," my father snapped at Mitch, "you've got no business even thinking about going to New York in your financial condition."

"Hello?" My mother lifted a cheek for my father to kiss, which he did, just like any other day. Seated at the kitchen table, she was casually leafing through an upholstery book, looking for a fabric for a couple of chairs she wanted to have recovered. "What are you two doing home so early?" She asked this as if they'd just come through the door skipping.

"Your son here thinks he's moving to New York to become an actor! A big, big Broadway star."

"Really . . ." My mother marked her place on a swatch, then looked at them both, first Mitch, then my father.

Mitch had dropped out of the University of Cincinnati the year before and had been installing carpeting for QBC ever since. The whole time he'd been home, he'd been threatening to quit and move to New York or L.A. He wanted to pursue theater or maybe music. All he knew was that he had to get out of Akron and away from my father.

"Neen," he had said to me the night he stumbled into my room, drunk, knocking some folded laundry off my bed and onto the floor, "you gotta get outta here, too." I was seventeen, but I wasn't ready to think about leaving home. "Next year, after you graduate, get as far away as you can. And don't do what I did—don't come back. That man'll warp your mind."

I said I didn't believe him. It killed me that my brother and sister were suddenly so against my father. I got angry with him, too, but I didn't feel this need to get away from him like they did. No matter what my father did or said to me, I couldn't stay mad at him—at least not for very long.

"So Mitch is gonna become a big goddamn city boy," my father said, now standing by the counter, shuffling through the day's mail. "Sandra, our son here wants to go to New York and wait tables. Isn't that nice?"

"Other people do it, Dad. You did it!"

"And that's exactly why you're not gonna do it!"

"Oh, Artie, don't be so hard on him." My mother got up from the table and moved in on me, taking over the wooden spoon, giving her sauce a stir.

"Our son's gonna grow up to become a bartender. Is that what you want for him, Sandra?"

"Artie, would you just hear him out?" My mother gestured to Mitch with her wooden spoon.

"Dad, I'm not gonna be a bartender. I just don't wanna be a sellout."

"Oh, so now you're saying I sold out?" My father threw down the mail and it fanned out across the counter.

"No, I'm—"

"Listen here, I had a family to support. If wanting to be a good provider—if giving your children everything they ever wanted—giving them a college education—even if they piss it away—if that's what you call selling out"—he raised his hands in surrender—"then I'm afraid I'm guilty. I'm guilty as hell."

"You know, you always tell your friends how we can talk about anything. We don't talk. You talk. And you never listen. I've been telling you for almost a year now that I don't want to sell carpeting, I don't wanna install it. I don't want to be in Akron."

My father sunk down in a chair at the table. "Well, I guess I must be a despicable father. I only spent twenty-five years building a business, making a name for myself in this town, so I'd have something to pass down to my son—my only son." The mean edge in my father's voice softened, and then, right on cue, the waterworks started up. He pulled a handkerchief from his back pocket to catch the tears. "I swore if I ever had a son . . . well"—he sighed—"obviously you don't want my help . . ."

Mitch grabbed both sides of his head. "Why do you always

do this, Dad? How does everything always end up being about you?"

The next thing I knew, Mitch had started to crack. There were no tears from him, but his voice was on the verge. "Dad, I gotta do this. It's nothing against you. But I can't stay here. I just have to do this."

❂

And then it was my turn. I did it to him. I let my father down, too. It was the night of my junior prom. I had a date, my first real date ever. Well, sort of. Nobody knew it, but I had asked Chris Gaynard to the prom. We were both *G*'s and sat kitty-corner from each other in homeroom. I asked him because my friends all had dates and because I knew he'd said yes the year before when a pimply-face girl with thick glasses and buck teeth asked him to the Sadie Hawkins dance. I was a beauty queen compared to her and I figured since he went with her, he'd say yes to me, too.

Chris looked older than other seventeen-year-old guys, mostly because he was taller than his classmates and because he had a full beard, not just fuzz. My friends and I thought Chris looked a little like Cat Stevens and that he could pass for cute until he opened his mouth. It was his teeth: They were bad, crooked and with brown stains on the two in front.

I wore a long peach dress that night, with spaghetti straps that tied above my bony shoulders and a neckline that dipped down, hovering right above my bra. When I first tried it on in the fitting room, I could tell that my mother and Lissy were surprised by how it made my body look. The dress showed off things they didn't know I had: a tiny waist, sloping hips, and then there were the breasts. I had ripened overnight, like a tomato on a window ledge. Mine wasn't a little girl's body anymore. It wasn't even a teenager's body. My body had gone womanly on me. I liked what was happening, I just didn't like everyone else watching it happen. One day I wore a T-shirt to school and some of the boys accused me of stuffing. It was embarrassing.

I know my father wasn't happy about these changes in me. He hated my prom dress and it took an hour of persuading on my mother's part to make him accept that I was old enough to wear it. "She's not a little girl anymore, Artie," I heard my mother saying after I'd stormed out of the room, still in my gown, the price tags hanging from a gold safety pin fastened under my arm.

"But does she have to flaunt it in a dress like that?"

My father was worried about the neckline, but I was worried about my hairy arms showing in that dress. So on the night of the prom, while I was getting ready, I grabbed a razor and shaved them right in the bathroom sink. After that, I put my special makeup on extra thick and let Lissy set my hair in her hot rollers.

"Trust me, Neen," she said, "this is gonna look great. I know what guys like."

Fifteen minutes later, my sister took down the rollers and unleashed the big brown curls that bounced softly against my shoulders. "See? Look how good you look." Lissy was standing behind me as I faced the mirror.

I hardly noticed my new curls or my eye. Instead, I was struck by our reflections, Lissy's and mine; there was something similar about our faces, the angle of our noses, the way our cheekbones were set, the definition of our chins. You could tell we were sisters, but Lissy was the prettier one—much prettier. There was a reason why she never sat home on Saturday nights. There was a reason why she never had to ask a guy to take her to the prom. There was a reason why she'd always had a boyfriend. It was all because she was the pretty sister and I wasn't.

"You should get your hair permed," I heard Lissy saying. "This is a good change for you. You look nice this way."

I wasn't convinced, so after Lissy left the bathroom, I reached inside the bottom drawer for my Aqua Net and sprayed a section of curls down over half my face, covering my eye.

While we waited for Chris to pick me up, my mother and Lissy were sitting beside me on the sofa in the living room, offering last-minute dating tips. My father walked by on his way to the kitchen and paused for a moment, his gaze traveling from my bare shoulders down to my high-heeled shoes. "I got no babies anymore now, do I, huh?" My father's eyes found mine as he pursed his lips, nodding.

I hunched my shoulders forward and hugged myself across the middle. I didn't like looking so grown-up in front of him.

"C'mon now." Lissy stood up and looped her arm through his. "We're having girl talk in here. Scram!"

"I'm going, I'm going," my father said, backing out of the room, his hands raised in surrender.

Lissy and my father had pretty much made up by then, even though she refused to move back home, and my father refused to drop the subject. That guy Jim was out of the picture.

"Now, remember," Lissy said after my father was out of earshot, "wait for Chris to open the car door. And whatever you do, don't reach over to open his side for him. It'll only emasculate him."

My mother lifted her pipe from the ashtray and looked at my sister with her eyebrows arched.

"It's true," Lissy said. "Guys like to prove to you that they're perfectly capable."

"Hmmm." My mother nodded like she'd just learned something new, and went on lighting her pipe. "Well, it's been a few years since I've been on a date," she said between puffs, "but I do remember you have to look him in the eyes when he's talking to you. And you have to act like whatever he says is positively fascinating."

We heard a car coming down the street and I held my breath,

feeling scared, feeling excited—I didn't know which. I didn't even know why I was feeling anything at all. It wasn't as if I liked Chris or had a crush on him. I just needed a date. The car kept rolling past our house, and I was relieved. A part of me was sort of hoping Chris wouldn't show.

Lissy was now telling me what to do if I wanted to make him kiss me good night. I didn't even know you could make a boy kiss you, but she was saying it had to do with staring at their mouths. That only made me think about Chris's mouth and his bad teeth. I was going to ask Lissy about that when my father called for her to join him in his study.

My mother and I were still in the living room. She had just noticed that I'd shaved my arms and was telling me they were going to grow back even hairier than before, when we heard a car pull into the drive. I rubbed my smooth arms, picturing what they'd look like in a week or two, bristly and nappy as a truck driver's. I was thinking how I'd have to shave my arms for the rest of my life when I heard the doorbell ring. I was just sitting there with my arms folded, my hand cradling both elbows, until my mother leaned over and gave me a nudge. "Don't you think you ought to let him in?"

I felt light-headed when I first saw Chris standing there in a white tuxedo with a blue ruffled shirt, a florist box in his hands. "Here," he said, offering me the box, "this is—it's for you."

Inside was a beautiful orchid corsage on a bed of greens, with baby's breath all around it. At first I just looked at it, wondering if his mother had picked it out and made him bring it or if Chris was thinking this was a real date, even though I was the one who'd asked him to the dance.

My mother was pinning the corsage to my dress when my father came out of his study, his hands behind his back, all smiles, going, "Look at what I got for you, tootsie!" He didn't even say hello to Chris; he just brought his hands back around and held up a peach-colored sweater with gold buttons running down the front. "How about that, huh? It even matches your dress."

I looked at the sweater. It was bad. I wouldn't have worn it to my prom. I wouldn't have worn it anywhere. Besides, it was too hot that night for a sweater.

My father held it out to me, like you'd hold up a coat, waiting for someone to slip it on.

"Da-ad . . ." I looked at my mother when I said this.

"What's the matter?" My father was still holding out the sweater. "You gotta wear something over that dress."

"Artie, please . . ."

"Well, she does!"

"Artie, we discussed all this. Remember?"

I stood there with my eyes shifting from my father to Chris, who was watching Lissy as she came into the room. He asked if she remembered him from some party three or four years back.

"Sorry." She looked at him and smiled the way she smiled at boys who whistled at her from their cars. And when she looked at him like that, Chris closed his mouth fast so that she couldn't see his teeth. That was the first I ever guessed that he was self-conscious about them. I felt sorry for him then. He'd never get a girl like my sister. Ever. He'd get girls like me, but not like her.

"Wouldn't you wear this, Lissy?" My father held the sweater out to her.

"No," she said, shaking her head. "I told you that at the store, Dad. It's ugly."

"But you helped pick it out!"

"I did *not* pick that out!" Lissy rolled her eyes. "I just told you that one would at least match her dress." Lissy crossed the room and slumped onto a chair, tossing her legs over the arm. "I did not pick that out!"

"But it's the right color, Neen!"

"Oh Artie—"

My father glared at my mother. "What's with the 'Oh Artie' business? You know I didn't have to go out and do this, Sandra!" My father turned and shook the sweater at me like a toreador taunting a bull with his cape. "Well?"

I didn't say anything. I couldn't.

"Do you want it or not? Cuz if you don't, I'm just gonna take it back. What a goddamn waste."

"It's too hot to wear a sweater, Dad." I couldn't say the whole truth.

"So you're telling me you're not gonna wear it?"

"I'll roast in that," I said, stealing a glimpse at Chris. He was looking at Lissy's legs still dangling over the arm of her chair.

"So what you're saying is that you won't wear it. Is that it?"

All I could do was bite my lip and nod.

"Is that a yes, you want to wear it? Or yes, you don't want to wear it? Cuz if you don't want it—"

"Da-ad! I don't wanna wear it! Okay! Jesus!" I folded my arms and glared at him.

My father let out one staccato "Ha!" and dropped the sweater to his side, looking at me like he hadn't heard correctly. "You go out of your way to do a nice thing for your daughter and what do you get? Nothing. Not even a goddamn thank-you. No appreciation whatsoever . . ."

"Oh God!" I sighed, watching him pull his handkerchief from his back pocket, his eyes full and glassy.

"Don't mind him," my mother said to Chris. "Allergies." She winked at me. "Go on now—scoot, you two, before you miss the prom."

☼

"Your old man was totally ob, man." Chris said this as we walked out to his car. That was his expression, "ob," as in obnoxious.

"He just gets weird sometimes," I said, looking back over my shoulder, watching my father through a parting in the drapes as he stood in front of my mother, his arms flailing about. I could only imagine what he was saying at that moment.

Then Chris reached in front of me and opened the car door on my side. I wondered if that officially made this a date. I slipped into the front seat and pulled the door shut before he could close it for me. I kept my eyes on the eight-track tapes on the floor near my feet. I didn't say another word to Chris the rest of the way. I was mentally apologizing to my father because I'd knew I'd just hurt his feelings.

When we got to the prom, Kara was already too drunk to go inside. Alex Korbington had to hold her up against the bicycle racks. Patty and her date were parked just beyond that, making out in the front seat of her Honda. I stood off to the side with Emily, who was waiting for Eric Slater, who had slipped into the bushes to take a leak. Meanwhile, Chris and Larry Tennin were shooting beers, foam trickling down their necks and onto their ruffled shirts. Then Anna and her date came out of the side gymnasium door, saying the dance was a big drag. Chris said that was "totally ob" and that we should all get a hotel room at the Ramada.

I was disappointed that we never even went inside the dance. I sort of wanted to walk in with Chris so that the other kids at school would at least see I had a date.

There was a dozen or so of us in a single room. Kara was passed out on the bathroom floor, where she'd gotten sick moments after we arrived. The guys just stepped over her and started filling the tub with ice and beer. The party played on in the outer room.

The place was instantly a mess, with the bedspreads pulled back and pillows thrown onto the floor, empty beer cans pitched to the carpet, and a haze of cigarette smoke hanging in the air.

There was a Rolling Stones concert on television and "Brown

Sugar" was cranked up so high, we had to shout just to hear one another. Emily, Anna, and I were sitting on the floor, our prom dresses bunched up in our laps, playing quarters with Eric Slater, Ben Stewart, Alex Korbington, and Chris Gaynard. Even though they'd been mean to me in the past, I still sort of had a crush on both Ben and Alex, but I knew it was all a lost cause. They were seniors now and they were the two cutest boys in our school. When I looked at Chris sitting next to them, I thought he was kinda cute, but in a different way from the other two. I thought that since I'd never get a guy like Ben or Alex, maybe he could be an okay boyfriend. He'd at least be someone to sit with at football games and he'd give me someone to talk about with my girlfriends. I must have been looking at him while I was thinking all this, because Chris was watching me watching him. Someone said something at that moment and Chris started to laugh. All I could see then were his teeth. I had to turn away.

For about the hundredth time that night, I caught myself thinking about my father and rehearsing what I might say to him the next day. Sometimes it came out as an apology, other times it turned into a screaming match. Each time inside my head, it played out a little differently. I didn't know how I was going to deal with him.

In the middle of "Let's Spend the Night Together," Eric Slater left to make a beer run, and while he was gone, Chris started talking to Emily. I don't know why, but it bothered me. They were sitting on the bed, kind of close together, I thought. They started laughing over something, so I asked Emily what time her curfew was. Chris answered for her, going, "She doesn't have an ob-ass curfew tonight." Emily giggled and he smiled, leaning back against the headboard. So I guessed that meant that Chris liked Emily now and that he and I weren't on a date after all. Then we heard Kara making rumbling and gurgling noises in the bathroom and Emily got up to go hold her hair back over the john.

That left me standing there, looking at Chris, who pointed to the bathroom and said, "That sounds totally ob in there."

I nodded, rolled my eyes, trying to giggle the way Emily had done for him.

He asked if I wanted to go outside and smoke a joint. I wrapped my arms in front of me, hugging my ribs. I wouldn't have known what to do outside alone with him. I was too afraid of that, so I shook my head all shylike and looked away at the clock on the TV console. It was one-thirty and I was already in trouble. I did have a curfew and I had already missed it. I knew my father was a light sleeper, and now this on top of the whole sweater thing made me just want to go home and get it over with. In the middle of "Get Off of My Cloud," I told Chris I had to go.

We didn't say anything on the drive back. Not a word. He couldn't get a decent radio station in, so we drove on, listening to a mixture of Peter Frampton and static playing "Baby I Love Your Way."

When we pulled up to the drive, the porch lights were on, casting a mellow glow over the lawn and trees.

"Well, thanks," I said.

"Yeah. Thanks."

"See you in class on Monday."

"Yeah. See ya," he said, and I noticed then that he was looking at my mouth. And I knew he was going to do it. He was going to kiss me. I braced myself for his beard. His teeth. I was thinking it was going to be awful, but then his lips were touching mine and they were as soft as his beard against my cheeks. It was a nice slow kiss. It surprised me.

When he was done kissing me, he leaned back on his side and said, "Yeah, so this was cool."

I was looking at him, at his mouth, wanting him to kiss me again, but he just said, "Well, see ya Monday."

"Yeah." I reached for the door and climbed out of the car. "See ya!"

Chris smiled and showed me all his bad teeth.

As soon as I opened the front door, I saw my father standing in the hallway in his bathrobe, the terry-cloth belt all twisted around his hips. The sweater was draped over the banister on the stairs, hanging there like a discarded rag doll.

"I never did thank you for the sweater, Dad," I said, surprised that after all my rehearsing, this was what I'd ended up saying.

"Is it really that ugly?" he asked, reaching over for one of the sleeves.

"It's really bad, Dad. It's awful."

My father cracked a smile. "Well, your mother and sister happen to agree with you." My father laughed and put his arm around me as my spaghetti strap slid off my shoulder. "Did you have a good time at least?" he asked as we walked side by side up the stairs.

"It was okay."

"Just okay?"

I nodded.

"Sweet pea, your next prom will be better." He kissed me on the cheek and said, "You really do look pretty tonight."

He clicked off the hall light, and I stood still for a moment, watching the streetlight outside the front hall window. I still wasn't sure if I'd been on a date or not that night. But I never did go out with Chris Gaynard again, so after about a week, I decided that it wasn't.

the guinea pig

By the time I was a senior in high school, I figured this was it. Other than my special makeup, there was nothing more I could do for my eye. Mostly, I tried not to think about it. I got up every day, applied my makeup, and sprayed my hair straight down over half of my face. I went to school, went to the Ballroom. I came home, took off my makeup, crawled into bed, and got up the next day and did it all over again. Life wasn't so bad. I wasn't miserable. But I wasn't happy, either. I was resigned.

But then my father found the doctors at the Cleveland Clinic. This time there was an entire team of specialists: two ophthalmologists and three dermatologists, all wanting to experiment on me. These doctors had been waiting for a case like mine. They wasted no time conducting the preliminary tests and ordering a CAT scan.

One week later, my parents and I were sitting in an examination room with the head doctor, Dr. Preston. My father took the lead, giving the doctor the rundown on my medical history. My mother sat next to him with her purse in her lap, her pipe sticking out the side pocket, watching us like a periscope. I was in a high-back chair and Dr. Preston was seated on a stool less than two feet away from me.

"Well now," he said, leaning forward, "let's see what we have here." When he went to push my hair back away from my face, it wouldn't move. It was solid as a wall, shellacked in place with too many coats of Aqua Net.

I bit the inside of my lip so hard, I tasted the salt of my own blood.

Dr. Preston made a face, cleared his throat. "Ah, maybe you can ah . . ." He tried to indicate something with his hands. "Can you just hold this out of the—yeah—way."

I reached up and lifted my hair like it was hinged to the top of my head. Dr. Preston kept going on about the ecchymosis due to the blood vessels beneath my skin and about my eyelid displaying significant ptosis. "Because the hemangioma has involuted . . . A lot of residual fibrofatty tissue along the eyelid . . . There's the pronounced ptosis itself . . . A six-by-eight-millimeter mass . . ."

It sounded even worse than I'd expected. I couldn't listen anymore until he got to the part about treatment.

"What we're recommending is to treat the vascular abnormality aggressively using what's called an argon laser. This is a new procedure that penetrates the skin with a laser beam. We would use it in order to coagulate the blood vessels along her upper eyelid and below, and wherever else she has discoloration. Of course, it's an experimental approach and there is a risk of scarring, but I'd say Nina is an excellent candidate for this procedure. We feel certain we can improve her appearance dramatically."

I unhinged my flap of hair and glanced at my parents and then down at my lap. These doctors promised so much, and I was afraid to get my hopes up. To me, lasers were something out of *The Twilight Zone*—science fiction, outer space. I'd taken the experimental route before with the injections, and while they had helped some, they didn't get the job done. I was older now. I'd earned the right to be skeptical.

My parents debated the laser's merits after we'd left the clinic. In the car, my mother and father smoked on their pipes, weighing the options. My mother kept saying she wished we knew someone who had been through the procedure before. "At least with the injections," she said in between puffs, "we had Bobbie Novak. She told us what to expect."

My father countered this, saying, "Sandra, you're acting like they haven't used the laser before. They've used it plenty. Believe me. What they're saying is, they've never used it before on someone like her."

Someone like her? Her was *me* and this was all too familiar. *Her* at four years old, riding in the backseat with my head covered in gauze, listening to my parents discussing why my operation hadn't been successful. *Her,* at ten, at eleven, twelve, and then thirteen, riding in the backseat with my eye swelling up, coming home from the airport, listening to my mother telling my father everything Dr. Waxler had said about that month's injection. And now it was *Her* again, at seventeen, riding in the backseat, listening to my parents discussing the laser like I wasn't even there.

Finally I had to ask the thing that concerned me most. "Do you think the laser could make it look worse?"

"Trust me, Nina. I've spent months researching these doctors. You're in good hands, toostie!"

"But Dr. Preston said there was a risk of scarring."

"There's a risk with everything you do. And remember, if we hadn't taken a few risks along the way, we wouldn't be where we're at today. Do you think I would let them do anything that would hurt you? Trust me on this one, sweetheart."

So we drove on and they talked some more. And I began to pry my mind open and let it consider the possibility. It had been years since I'd even thought anything could help. My father said to trust him, and bit by bit, I felt myself begin, once again, to fill with expectations.

The waiting room was crowded the day of my first treatment. There weren't three seats together, so my father sat by himself, over by the coffee machine. I was next to my mother, filling out release forms. I had a clipboard that was thick with forms, carbon copies in triplicate. The doctors wanted permission to videotape my procedures—fourteen in all, to be spread out over a two-year period. They wanted to be able to study my case later on.

I heard my father talking. "Did you know," he said to the woman next to him, pointing to a hospital brochure, "the Cleveland Clinic was founded way back in 1921? Isn't that something? Interesting, huh?"

I started back-kicking the legs of my chair. Why couldn't he keep to himself, just once?

The woman next to my father set her magazine in her lap and smiled back at him.

"Almost three thousand beds in this place!" My father pinged the pamphlet with the back of his hand. "Overhead's gotta kill 'em . . ."

I looked at my mother again. She watched my father as she twisted the ends of her hair about her finger, humming a Tchaikovsky piece.

When the nurse called my name, all three of us stood up, but she told my parents to stay out in the waiting room. I guess the doctors figured I was old enough to go it alone. But I wanted my parents with me. I may have been seventeen, but I was the kind of seventeen whose mother still came into fitting rooms with me when we shopped for clothes. Whenever I was on the phone, giving someone directions to our house, I'd end up handing the receiver to my father so that he could guide them the rest of the way. I was seventeen, but a young seventeen.

"We'd kinda like to be with her," my father said, walking toward the nurse.

But she told him I'd be just fine. "We'll take very good care of her," she said. "Really, it's better this way."

I felt the nurse's hand on my shoulder and I looked back at my parents, still thinking maybe they'd come with.

My father winked, said he had a good feeling about this. "Ain't nothing to worry about, sweet pea."

My mother smiled, too. "We'll be right here—soon as it's over. Go on, Neen," she said. "It's okay."

I followed the nurse down a long hallway and into a room in the very back. Dr. Preston and his team of doctors were all waiting for me in surgical scrubs, standing around an octopus of machinery. Dr. Preston was going through my chart and hadn't so much as looked at me.

A nurse in the back corner was adjusting the legs of the tripod for the video camera while a second nurse was taking the before pictures, close-ups, with a 35-mm camera. I hated cameras. My eye never photographed right. It looked even worse in pictures than it usually did. The nurse was coming at me with her lens and there was no place to hide. I knew the only way I could get through this was to pretend I was a fashion model on a photo shoot and that this was all very glamorous. "Head up," the nurse was saying to me now. "Look straight ahead, right here, right at my finger." The sound of the film advancing inside the camera made me hold my breath, waiting for the next shot.

After the pictures, Dr. Preston came over to me. "We're ready to get started."

I nodded. My mouth went dry.

Another nurse sat me in a chair, like the kind they have in a dentist's office, and while someone from behind collected my hair, tucking it into a cotton cap, Dr. Preston and the others talked about my eye. They had the results of my CAT scan up on the light board and they seemed unanimously surprised that the hemangioma hadn't affected my vision.

Then another doctor explained the argon laser to me step by step. And even though I'd heard this all before, that first day in Dr. Preston's office, I still didn't know what to expect.

But then it started happening. They put a plastic device, like a disk, in my eye to protect it from the rays. It felt like a thick contact lens, only bigger, harder to blink around. Before they bandaged my good eye, I saw all of them, even the one operating the video camera, putting on dark green goggles.

They said it wouldn't hurt, and it didn't. The argon laser felt hot, but not like it was burning. There was a clicking on/off sound all around me and I sensed the laser's rays even through the disk and my bandaged eye. I could feel where they moved it, covering a tiny section of the skin where the blood vessels were raised.

"How's the response?" I heard someone asking. That's when I remembered that I was their guinea pig. They didn't know what they were doing. I was their experiment. They didn't even know what to expect. I had no idea what I'd look like when they were done. What if this laser didn't work? What if it made me look even worse? I could end up with burn scars on top of everything else! My heart was beating faster and it took everything out of me not to flinch, not to scream. I was about to give in to my panic when suddenly the doctors were finished.

The plastic disk was removed and the bandages came off. They told me I did great. They were pleased with themselves, saying that the next time they'd do a larger area, that I had responded just as they'd hoped.

They handed me a mirror so I could see. My eye was red and a little puffier than usual, but you could tell where they'd treated the blood vessels. They said I wouldn't see the full effects of the laser for at least a month or so.

They propped my chair upright and one of the nurses took

more close-ups, the after pictures. I stared head-on, my breath rushing in and out with each slice of the shutter.

Dr. Preston was standing in front of me, talking about the possibility of my needing one surgery—after I'd finished with the majority of the laser treatments—where they'd raise my eyelid. "Just like a window shade," he said.

Would I be normal? I asked.

"It's going to take time," he said, jotting notes down in my file. "And we may be looking at that one surgery, like we said, but our goal is to get this as perfect as we possibly can . . ."

As perfect as we possibly can! No one had ever given me this much hope before. For the first time, normal was within reach. I almost started to cry right there in the examination room.

Dr. Preston glanced up from my file and looked at me. "And ah, next time, go easy on the hair spray, please."

❋

After I got home that day from the Cleveland Clinic, all I could think about was that now I had a chance to be made perfect. When all the laser treatments were done, I would look normal and everything would change. Everything! I wouldn't need to wear special makeup, wouldn't need to spray my hair over half my face. I told myself I wouldn't feel shy around boys anymore. Even the cute boys would like me because I'd have two normal eyes. A new world would start to open up for me. It was exciting, and yet at the same time, it felt strange to think of myself without my eye.

There was so much I'd been avoiding just because of my eye—my ultimate excuse. It got me out of gym class and going off the high dive. Too afraid of striking out, I told the coaches I couldn't risk being hit with the ball. I could pull a headache at any time and no one ever doubted it. When I was younger and my mother wasn't paying attention to me, I would tell her I needed a tea bag. When I was older and too afraid to ride the Blue Streak roller coaster at Cedar Point, I told my friends my eye couldn't handle the pressure. My eye rescued me every time. No one ever challenged my pain. My pain—my source of all unhappiness. The reason nothing in my life was right. If they took that away, I'd be put to the test. I might have to come to terms with the fact that it wasn't all about my eye. Maybe it was about me.

And then what about my father? My eye was the whole basis of my relationship with him. Growing up, he had cared more about my eye than he'd ever cared about my grades or school projects. He'd never once asked to read my poems or short stories. None of that interested him. I knew that the fastest way to get his attention was to complain about my eye, to pout about it. That brought him to me with all his anger and with all his impatience, but still, it brought him to me. Without my eye, how could I connect with him? Without my eye, what would we have in common? Part of me was afraid that if my eye went away, I would lose all that I had with my father.

the one left behind

Before we knew it, we were on the brink of adulthood. We had donned our caps and gowns, flipped our tassels to the left, and sang our alma mater for the last time. We were high school graduates about to face the world, and this was the last summer of our childhood.

It was early in the season, just after Memorial Day, and the McFaddens' pool, where we'd started to hang out the past year or so, wasn't ready yet. So, on the day after graduation, we decided to move our party from Patty's to the Akron Swim & Tennis Club. All they had out there was a big pool, a snack bar, and half a dozen tennis courts. Everyone we knew were members there because it wasn't as expensive as the big country clubs in town.

I was lying on the grass reading *One Hundred Years of Solitude* while the others were in the deep end. It was my first full day in the sun and I wanted to get a good start on my tan. I reached into my beach bag, looking for my suntan oil. It was buried in the bottom along with a deck of playing cards and my goggles.

Because of my laser treatments, I was back to wearing protective goggles in the water, though I couldn't bring myself to put them on. I didn't care what Dr. Preston said. I would rather not have gone in the pool at all than be seen in those frogman goggles. Besides, even though my special makeup was waterproof, I worried that the goggles might smudge it. And if I did go in the water, then I'd have to worry about my hair. I knew I'd never be able to get a comb through it after it got wet, because of all the hair spray. So instead of swimming, I decided to sit out like the girls did when they had their periods.

When the giant Coca-Cola clock hit three, the lifeguards rose from their stands, brought their whistles to their lips, and set off a shrill of chirps that ran the length of the pool. Kids protested, giving it one last splash before heading to the sides. This was the first summer my friends and I were old enough to stay in the water during break time.

Funny how we were the oldest kids at the pool now and yet, in less than three months, everyone was expected to scatter off to college. And then we would be the youngest, starting all over again from the bottom. The idea of leaving home was something I couldn't imagine. I still didn't know where I was going. I couldn't decide between Ohio University and Ohio State. I'd been accepted at both schools but couldn't bring myself to think about it.

Instead, I was clinging to my past, remembering all the summers I'd spent at this pool when we were little. In those days, when the lifeguards blew the break whistle, I'd head for the ledge of the pool with my goggles practically suction-cupped to my face. I'd run to my mother, who always sat beneath a big umbrella table, playing cards with the other mothers. I'd wait in line behind Lissy and Mitch, dripping and shivering while my mother pulled out beach towels and dipped into her change purse for coins so we could buy a Popsicle or cotton candy.

And then, one by one, we grew up, old enough to sit with our friends along a strip of grass by the fence, separate from my mother. We'd leave her at the sign-in gate, pretending she wasn't there until it was time to go home.

The first year I sat on the grass with my friends, we were twelve and the boys had spent most of that summer trying to yank off Patty's bathing suit top. That was the same summer that this one boy, already in college, would swim around us girls, trying to fit between our legs, trying to feel us up. He even did that to me! And like the others, I made a big fuss, calling him names, kicking water in his face, half-trying to squirm away. At night, we'd be down in the Ballroom, calling him a dork, saying how we wished he'd leave us alone. But when I'd get to the pool the next day, I'd look to see if he was there. This went on all summer, and none of us, not a single one, ever got out of the pool or complained to a lifeguard. I made it so he'd catch me, and when he'd try to swim through my legs, I prayed he'd go slowly so I could feel his skin against my thighs, feel the flutter of his kicks rush up inside me.

Knowing this was the last summer with all the gang, I grew nostalgic over the strangest things. Everything we did had the weight of finality to it. I knew the night we toilet-papered Eric Slater's house that it would be the last time I'd sneak across the Fairlawn Country Club golf course with the others, a flashlight in one hand and a roll of Charmin stolen from the linen closet in the other. There'd be no more water-balloon fights in the school parking lot, no more midnight bong-a-thon sessions in the Ballroom. And what was there left to do with Bev's Bust that we hadn't already done? Ever since they handed me my diploma, the countdown had begun. It was time to start growing up.

❁

In July of that year, I told my father I didn't want to go to college. All he could say was, "Why? Why! You don't have to do everything your brother does!" He let the tears stream down his cheeks. "What have I worked for? Tell me? Would you please?"

I couldn't say. All I knew was that I wasn't ready to leave home.

That whole notion—that I wasn't ready—had been growing solid and sharp within me all summer long. The only time I'd ever tasted college life was when Lissy was away at Ohio University. I had traveled down to see her at school for Little Siblings Weekend in a chartered bus full of other kids about my age.

That was the first trip I'd ever made anywhere by myself. I remember I was thirteen at the time and all I had to do was hug my mother and father good-bye in the parking lot, walk twenty feet to board the bus, and then wait to be delivered to my sister, who'd be standing at the other end, downstate in Athens. But still, I worried about being on a bus all that time, not knowing anyone.

But it turned out not to be so bad. There was a group of older boys sitting one row behind me in the very back and they passed their joint my way. I guess they thought I was cool, like them. Maybe it was because I was wearing a jean jacket and had a copy of *The Exorcist* in my lap. I took a hit and handed the joint back to a boy with hair in his eyes.

The next day, when Lissy and I were uptown on our way to see a movie, I passed that boy on the sidewalk. He saw me and just said a quick "Hey." That was all there was to it, but Lissy teased me for half a block.

"Woop-de-doo! Look at you, Nina!"

I could tell she was surprised, maybe even a little impressed that her baby sister knew a boy like that. I felt like a college kid then, and that was the fun part of being away.

But then there was the dorm—cold steel bunks, broken linoleum tiles, two of everything: desks, chairs, wastebaskets. I didn't want to carry my toothbrush and shampoo in a bucket, not ever. I didn't want to share a bathroom at the end of the hall with all those girls. They showered in front of one another, and even though the stalls had shower curtains, they were so flimsy that you could still see everything. And I remember I saw one of the girls taking a bar of soap and washing herself right down there, right between her legs. She got me thinking about soap in a whole new way. Growing up, if I had known everyone in my family was putting the soap in places like that, I would have demanded my own bar. Honestly, I didn't even know girls were supposed to wash down there. So I'd learned something, and maybe that was what it was all about. Maybe you needed college to learn what you couldn't figure out back home.

Still, I didn't want to go. Not until it was too late to change my mind. Not until we were counting the days until Anna—the first to go—was leaving for Tulane. Only then did I begin to understand that I was the one being left behind. Patty and Kara were heading for the University of Cincinnati and Emily was going to Miami, to one of those fashion colleges advertised in the back of magazines.

I'd lied to them all, saying I had to stay in town because of my eye. Even though my father said I could fly home for my laser treatments, I told them that Dr. Preston had to monitor me closely. No one questioned it. In fact, I started to believe the lie myself. I believed it so completely, I felt sorry for myself, because now it seemed that I couldn't go away to college like the others.

I think my father started to believe it, too. Or maybe he just wanted to. After a while he had stopped giving me grief about how I was ruining my future, how I was going to wait tables and bag groceries at the Acme the rest of my life, how I'd never find myself a nice young man. That part did get to me, but then I figured I'd probably never meet anyone anyway, so what difference would it make.

My father had stopped all that kind of talk. Deep down, I think, he was glad that I wasn't leaving home. He may have gotten Lissy back after college, but Mitch had slipped away from him for good. I knew that if I went to away to school, he'd be afraid that I'd stay away forever.

But I wasn't ready to leave home yet. Maybe in a year, maybe two. But just then, I couldn't imagine being out there on my own.

☼

By the time the leaves began to fall, I had developed a crush on Timothy McFadden. Suddenly he'd gone from just being Patty's little brother to being the one boy I would have done anything to please.

It was circumstance that brought us together. Timothy and I were feeling abandoned now that my friends and all the Mad Marauders had gone off to college. Even though Timothy was pretty much a loner and had never drawn a crowd of his own to the Ballroom, he was used to the chaos that centered around his house. Now the Ballroom was dark night after night. Timothy was bored, and so was I.

Neither one of us could bear the sudden quiet at his house, so we knocked around the mall together, or hung out in bookstores—Timothy would go to the art section, and I would lose myself in the fiction aisles. He always carried his drawing pad and I always had my journal with me. Sometimes we'd go to Sand Run Park, sit on the grass beneath a tree. While he sketched, I'd write and then we'd show each other what we'd done.

Though I'd known him since we were little kids, I'd never realized how funny Timothy was. I'd always thought of Keith as the clever McFadden brother, but really it was Timothy who had the sharpest wit. Just as his pen could capture someone's caricature on paper, his tongue could always nail a comic truth. He'd effortlessly rattle off sarcastic comments, making me laugh so hard, I'd have to beg him to stop so I could catch my breath.

And then one day, during a lull, after he had me laughing, it happened. We kissed. Afterward, we looked at each other and cracked up all over again, as if we couldn't believe what we'd just done. But it was nice, so we kissed again. And this time, once we started, we couldn't stop.

After that, we kissed a lot—in his bedroom, in my bedroom, in his backyard, underwater in the swimming pool, at the Summit Mall, on the hill at Blossom Music Center—anywhere and everywhere. Sometimes we touched each other, but mostly we were kissers.

I thought Timothy was beautiful. There was something about a guy with long hair, a slender, tapered nose, and soft eyes that always got to me. Ben Stewart was like that. So was Alex Korbington. And so was Timothy. The older he got, the more he looked like Gorgeous Greg. There was no question that Timothy was prettier than I was. And if someone as pretty as Timothy was willing to kiss me, I figured maybe that meant I wasn't as hideous as I feared. And if other people saw that he liked me, then maybe they'd start to think of me differently, too.

Timothy may have been pretty, but he had his struggles. Why he wasn't happier, being funny as he was, always surprised me. He was a senior in high school then, and having a hard time of it. It had gotten around town that he was seeing a psychiatrist. We never talked about it, but I suspected he'd been in therapy ever since his father died. Timothy never did spring back from that like the others had. There was something different about him, different from the rest of the McFadden boys and different from any other boy I'd ever known.

He'd never had a girlfriend before and I'd never had a real boyfriend. We were both still virgins and thought that meant there was something wrong with us. We thought having sex would transform us into what and who we thought we were supposed to be.

So I got a diaphragm. Timothy went with me to Planned Parenthood, and afterward we sat across from each other on his twin bed trying to figure out exactly what we should do with it. No one was home at his house, not like that would have stopped anyone from messing around there. But since the coast was clear, we knew we could have done it right then and there if we wanted to.

But we were both stalling. Even though we were clowning around like usual, I was embarrassed, especially when Timothy picked up the plastic container and gave the diaphragm a shake, as if checking to make sure it was still in there. The diaphragm was new and mysterious to him, to both of us really. And if they hadn't shown me how to use it at Planned Parenthood, I would never have guessed what it was for.

The case reminded me of the container that Lissy used to store her retainer in, and when I told him that, Timothy opened it up, took it out. For a moment I thought this was it—we were going to have sex. But then he squished the rimmed cup between his fingers, holding it up to his mouth like a hand puppet, and started doing a Groucho Marx imitation, going, "So a funny thing happened to me on the way to Planned Parenthood . . ."

I giggled with relief, and I was still laughing when Timothy placed the diaphragm on top of his head like a yarmulke, and adopted a Jewish accent, going, "Oy vey! Vaz da matter, younglady? You couldn't find a nice Jewish boy to screw around vith?" He even cracked himself up with that one. We were still laughing when he put the diaphragm back in its case and set it on his nightstand. I kissed him then and that started us kissing for the rest of the afternoon.

So nothing happened that day, or the next day, either. I was starting to get impatient, but there was no one else I could lose my virginity to. And besides, I couldn't have sex with anyone else because I had to keep the diaphragm at Timothy's, stashed in the bottom drawer of his desk, under his drawing pads and charcoal pencils. My mother cleaned too thoroughly. She would have found it, told my father, and then, I figured, he'd disown me.

He had once threatened to disown Lissy if she ever had sex

and wound up pregnant. I remember sitting at the top of the stairs, scrunching the carpet between my toes, eavesdropping while he lectured her about being promiscuous. He said if she ever slept with a man before she was married, he'd take one look at her and he'd know it.

He never seemed to scare Lissy with this, but he terrified me. That little lecture of his stayed with me for years, lodged in my gut.

One time, when I was nine years old, I imagined I was pregnant. My mother and I were standing in the frozen-food section at the Sparkle Market when I blurted this out. And what I can't believe is that my mother didn't laugh at me. She just squatted down in front of the frozen waffles, took both my hands in hers, and asked me why I thought I was pregnant. I think it had to do with a combination of that speech my father had given Lissy and my having pulled down my pants for a nickel in front of Tommy Bryant—a neighbor boy who carried matchbox cars in one of his mother's old purses. Standing there in the grocery store, I could feel life moving within me. I swore my stomach was bloating up and I was scared. I didn't want to be disowned. And amazingly enough, all it took to cure me and make my stomach go back down were the softly spoken words of my mother, who told me she was certain, "absolutely positive," I wasn't pregnant.

And so now I had a diaphragm. I was prepared, so I knew I wouldn't get pregnant. But still, I was sure my father would have disowned me if he knew I was having sex, or even wanted to.

For weeks the diaphragm sat untouched, resting in its case, waiting, like me, for Timothy. He said he wasn't sure he still wanted to do it, and I asked if it was because of my eye.

He looked at me, puzzled, slightly annoyed. "Nina, not everything is about your eye, okay!" He shook his head. "I don't even notice your eye anymore. The only person your eye bothers is you."

I wanted to believe him, but if it wasn't about my eye, I couldn't imagine what the holdup was. We had birth control. We had his whole house to ourselves while Bev was working, so why weren't we just doing it already? I felt too stupid and desperate to bring it up to him again.

And then, just when I thought I was destined to die a virgin, Timothy was finally ready to have sex with me. My parents were on their way to New York to help Mitch get out of a bad lease and into an apartment that wasn't roach-infested. Right after my parents left town, Timothy came to my house with the diaphragm and the tube of jelly stuffed inside his coat pocket. He must have been nervous, because he was humorless that day.

"So . . ." he asked without really having to ask, holding the case out to me.

So this was it. Finally . . .

I took the diaphragm from him. Ever since I'd been old enough to think about sex, I'd thought about this very moment. Only in my mind, it was nighttime . . . and I was in a fancy hotel room . . . and there were candles . . . and I was in a satin negligee and the man was in a silk smoking jacket . . . and there was champagne and soft music . . .

"Well," Timothy said, surveying the family room, "where should we go? Do you want to do it upstairs or down here?" He had no expression on his face. His blond hair had fallen forward, the ends brushing against the side of his face.

My mouth went dry. I started climbing the stairs. He was close behind me. Why wasn't he saying anything? Why wasn't I? My heart was going like I'd just run a hundred-yard dash.

I left Timothy in my bedroom while I took the diaphragm into the bathroom and did what I had to do. When I came out, I saw that he had moved all my stuffed animals to the spare bed. He was sitting cross-legged on the bedspread in nothing but his Jockey shorts. I'd seen his bare chest before—that was nothing new. But I'd never seen his thing before. We'd never really done anything below the waist except for maybe a few times over our clothes when we'd gotten really carried away.

I don't remember taking off my clothes in front of him. I just remember being under the covers with my bra and underwear still on. My clock radio was on and WMMS was doing a tribute to Queen. Freddie Mercury was singing "We Are the Champions." Timothy was lying on top of me. He had beautiful skin, smooth and warm. It felt nice, and just having our bodies touching like that would have been enough for me. I almost didn't need to go any further. But we did go further. We had to for both our sakes.

We started kissing a little and then stopped and looked at each other, amazed at what we were about to do. We kissed some more. And then I saw his thing. Queen had progressed onto "Crazy Little Thing Called Love."

So this was it. It was really happening. I was going to emerge from this as someone new, changed and transformed. All he had to do was put his penis inside me and, like magic, by the time he took it out, all my awkwardness would be gone. I felt him starting to do it then, and I let out a gasp.

"Should I stop?" he asked.

I closed my eyes and shook my head.

"But if it hurts, Neen—"

"Keep going." I needed him to keep going. I needed to be transported.

He put his thing even deeper inside me, and then he started pulling it out and then pushing it back in. His back was damp with sweat. I kept my eyes closed. We didn't say anything the whole time.

When it was over, Queen was singing "Another One Bites the Dust." I kept expecting Timothy to crack a joke about the irony of that, but he didn't. He just got out of bed like there was someplace he had to be. He stepped into his jeans and hoisted them up on his narrow hips, keeping his back turned toward me.

I looked around my room, at the books on my nightstand, the spare bed peppered with stuffed animals, the ruffled curtains drawn shut. Everything was exactly the same. I was exactly the same. I didn't feel transported. I felt stupid and sore.

As soon as he left, I don't know why, but I started to cry.

Timothy and I didn't do it again for three weeks. Not that I didn't try, surprising myself at times when I got so bold that I'd stand before him, unbuttoning my blouse or else reaching for his belt buckle. It wasn't even the sex that I was after. I just needed to know that I was wanted, and that he wasn't rejecting me because of my eye.

And then one day, when I least expected it, Timothy decided he wanted to do it again. We had his house to ourselves. We were upstairs, sitting on his bed with the movie section of the newspaper spread out before us. When we couldn't agree on what to see, he got up, went to his bottom desk drawer, and handed me the diaphragm. I didn't say anything. I just took it from him and went into the bathroom, trying to hurry in case he changed his mind.

⁂

WANTED: TOPLESS SECRETARY

Wants *top* pay and won't settle for *less* . . .

This was the ad my father ran in the *Akron Beacon Journal*. He thought it was great. "Is that not clever, huh? Huh!"

When no one responded to his ad, he asked if I'd fill in, answer the phones, that sort of thing. And that's how I started working for QBC. Lissy had tried working for him one summer. At lunchtime on her first day, my father handed her a twenty-dollar bill and told her not to come back. I guess I showed more promise.

At first I handled the phones and then I gradually started making sales calls with my father. He put me on straight commission, and after three months I was $375 in debt to him, but still I kept going back for more. I think he was hoping I'd be miserable enough to quit and go to college after all.

And I was unhappy with the job, but still I felt I owed my father this much. It hadn't worked with Lissy or Mitch, so I figured I would be the one to take over his business. It would be my way of giving something back to him—making it up to him because I'd messed up his most important music gig the day I was born. If it hadn't been for me, he would have been able to pursue his music career. Never mind that he had a family to support, I was convinced that if my father hadn't had me, he could have become a famous clarinetist, instead of having to sell carpet. I felt that the least I could do now was give him someone to leave his business to.

With all my heart I wanted to do good for my father, make him proud, but I wasn't a salesman. And when my debt reached five hundred dollars, my father fired me. It wasn't like I'd done anything wrong. I just couldn't make a sale, and the twenty yards I sold to my grandmother for her basement didn't count.

Besides, since it hadn't worked out with me, my father said he was thinking of selling QBC. I'd heard him say that hundreds of times before. It seemed he was always talking to an interested party. But as much as he said he wanted out, there was something inside him that couldn't let go. QBC was the one thing that had never failed him; it was one more place outside his home where people lit up to please him.

He'd started QBC from scratch. All these years he'd nurtured it, supported it with his life, and watched it grow and flourish. To him, QBC was like another child. He'd never be able to give it up.

the gals are back in town

It was just my father and me making the turkey run that year. I was nineteen, almost twenty. Mitch didn't come home for the holiday. He was still in New York, too broke for bus fare and too proud to ask my father for any more money. He was working at a printing shop in Chelsea, making minimum wage.

My father was upset that Mitch wouldn't be home for Thanksgiving, but he was certain that someday Mitch would return to Akron for good. I think my father wanted to believe Mitch would come back and take over QBC, but I knew that would never happen, not in a million years. Mitch may have been miserable in New York, but he was gone. He'd gotten away from Akron and from my father and was forever urging me to do the same.

"Family comes first," my father was saying while he backed out the drive. "Nothing could be more important than family." Then he started futzing with the radio dials.

We had been driving for a while and my father was still going on about Mitch. "Big-city boy forgets where he comes from. . . . Got no real job—he's making *bubkas.* Nothing! See what happens without a proper education, young lady? Huh? Huh!"

I looked out the window and sighed, stuffing my fingers in between the seat cushions. My father never had a so-called proper education. The scenery whipped past us. Everything looked rural now, long fields now dead for the winter, parked tractors waiting for someone to come ride them back to the barns.

"And I'm telling you, it's time you had some sort of direction for yourself. You're not a kid anymore."

"I have a direction." That fall I had enrolled in Akron University and was working part-time, selling shoes at Hoffman Brothers at the Summit Mall.

Even though I'd started college a year after all my friends had, school was going well for me. I liked my literature courses and my freshman composition class. My professor said I showed talent and he encouraged me to do something with my writing. When I told my father that, he said writing was a nice hobby but that I could never make a living at it.

As for my job at Hoffman Brothers, it was okay, easy enough. The hardest part was waiting on people I knew. People who had either stayed in Akron like me or else younger kids, like Anna's little sister, who still had a year to go before they'd graduate and leave town.

One day Greg and Matthew McFadden came in looking for tennis shoes. We stood at the register talking while I rang them up. Greg was still gorgeous as ever. He'd been living in Atlanta for the past year, painting houses with a college friend, and had just moved back to town to help his mother run the family wall-covering stores. Matthew was living in Arizona now, teaching phys ed and coaching high school basketball. He was back for just the weekend, for some big game, along with a bunch of guys from the old gang. They were having a party Saturday night and

Greg invited me. There was a time when I would have killed for Gorgeous Greg to invite me to a party, but I knew I wouldn't go to this one, even as I asked what time it started. I wasn't any good at parties. Boys would come up to me and say things like "Smile, it's not that bad." I'd want to slug them.

So I didn't have a great job or a great social life. I guess I didn't have much to call my own. I wondered if maybe my father was right about not having any direction. I daydreamed about being a writer someday, but I really didn't know what would become of me. All I knew was that I didn't want to be glued to my father forever, only I didn't know how to get myself unstuck. But even more than my father's hold on me, I was just beginning to see that everything I wanted for myself would take longer than I expected and would be harder than I thought it ought to be. Because of this I could see myself doing nothing remarkable with my life. God, how I didn't want to be mediocre. What kind of life was that? I would have rather been a complete failure than turn out ordinary. I was afraid I'd grow old in one place, stuck in Akron all my life.

For the first time, I understood why my mother and I never left that one block of State Street on our trips to Chicago. Like her, I lacked the spirit of adventure. I feared too much. And because of this, I knew I had already missed a lot in life. I wondered how much more I would let pass me by.

My father turned onto the long gravel stretch that led to Willie's Turkey Farm. Willie had passed away the year before, and now his widow, Mildred, ran the place with the help of her two sons. She came out of the slaughterhouse and met us in the driveway, pulling off her bloodstained gloves by the fingers, tucking them beneath her arm. I got the feeling she'd been watching for us, like maybe we were her only customers.

The youngest son, Willie junior, helped his mother load the birds into the trunk of the car. My father tried helping, but

Mildred wouldn't let him. Besides, that year it was only four turkeys, five counting ours.

Business was slow and once again my father talked about selling QBC. He wanted out of the carpet business. He'd had enough of the rat race. He'd worked hard enough, saved wisely, and was living off his investments. He was in a position to pack it all in, so why not? Why not just do it once and for all?

I knew this was just talk. And I knew that next year at this time, we'd be back here, my father and I, loading up the trunk with turkeys, even if we had only two or three to deliver. As we drove off, I turned back around and watched the old woman and her son climb the steps of the slaughterhouse.

Suddenly my life didn't seem so bad anymore.

❋

It was the Wednesday night before Thanksgiving. I was sitting around the McFaddens' kitchen table with the girls, drinking screwdrivers, eating Cheetos. I'd seen Patty and Emily whenever they came home, but this was the first time the five of us—Patty, Kara, Emily, Anna, and I—had all been back together at the same time since they'd left for college. None of us even thought about going downstairs to the Ballroom. It didn't hold the same appeal. We were older now and the party had moved upstairs.

Emily talked about how difficult fashion school was. Kara and Patty kept making inside jokes about their sorority, while Anna bragged about all the liquor she drank during Mardi Gras. It was only her sophomore year at Tulane and already she had acquired a slight southern accent.

Patty gave her glass a spin between her palms. I could tell she was getting drunk. Overall, she seemed happy and she had dropped about thirty pounds. I noticed the food scale with the Weight Watchers logo across the front on the counter. She'd brought that and a bunch of premeasured food with her from Cincinnati. Two or three times, she said she shouldn't be drinking. It wasn't on her diet.

"Oh God!" Kara suddenly got all excited about something and tucked a wisp of hair behind her ear. "Did you guys hear about Joyce Tauben?" Kara made a face as she took her finger and sliced it across her neck.

We all knew. It had happened about three months before. She'd hung herself in her parents' storage shed.

"You know, that girl tried to kiss me in the third grade!" Kara was pounding on the table, laughing too hard, her shoulders shaking even after she'd put her head down.

I watched her for a moment and decided that if I'd met Kara that night for the first time, I wouldn't have liked her. She lifted her beautiful face, all blotchy red from laughter. "Isn't that disgusting! Do you believe she did that!" She was staring right at me now, like maybe she knew something.

I got up, pretending to look out the window, watching Kara's reflection in the glass. What did she know? Was she trying for a confession? I was still ashamed of that first kiss I'd shared with Joyce Tauben in my parents' bedroom, even after all these years.

"Tell the truth," Anna said, changing subjects as she reached for Kara's arm, "did you really give Keith your first blow job?"

"*No way!*" Emily giggled as her fingers probed Patty's pack of Salems for a cigarette. "He was always so cute!"

"I'll tell you guys about Keith," Kara said, going to the refrigerator for more orange juice, "if Anna tells us everything that went on with her and Gorgeous Greg!"

"You guys, you know I really don't want to hear about you getting all hot and bothered over my brothers! It's gross. Give me a break. . . ." Patty shook her head and stared into her glass.

The girls didn't let up. "I'll tell you about me and Greg," Anna said, "if Nina tells us about Timothy!"

I shot Patty a look as I slipped back into my chair. She knew about Timothy and me. Even though Timothy said I shouldn't tell her, I confessed one night, called Patty at her dorm and told her everything. I mean *everything*! All she said before she hung up was, "Don't come crying to me after he dumps you."

"Timothy? You were with Timothy!" Kara's eyes went wide while she shook the carton of juice, holding the spout closed. "Little Timothy McFadden!"

In spite of Patty, I couldn't help smiling. Just having them know I'd been with someone as cute as Timothy made me feel like one of them. The details didn't matter; just the fact that it had happened was the important thing.

They didn't need to know that Timothy had told me we were better off being just friends and that he'd realized he didn't feel "that" way about me. And they didn't need to know that a month after that, I discovered why. One day, a couple of photos fell out of his sketchbook, and before he could pick them up, I saw two pictures lying faceup on the floor. One showed Timothy sitting on the lap of a handsome boy with a cleft chin, and the other photo showed the two of them kissing. It was shocking—not because Timothy was kissing another guy, but because he seemed so happy. You could see it right there on his face in the photos; all his sadness was gone.

"No way, Nina! You were with Timothy?" Kara was stirring her drink with her finger, looking at me the whole time. "When did this happen?"

"Wait a minute, wait a minute." Emily stood up, cigarette in one hand, lit match in the other. "Patty, am I the only one here who hasn't slept with one of your brothers?"

"Wait, wait, wait!" Kara suddenly stood up, too, and raised her glass. "Wait a second, everyone! This calls for a toast. I propose a toast!" Kara raised her glass an inch or so higher. "To the McFadden brothers!"

"TO THE MCFADDEN BROTHERS!"

As we touched glasses, I saw a change come over Patty's face.

She looked bored. I think she was glad then that high school was over, along with the days of everyone making themselves right at home in the middle of her family. I couldn't say for sure, but it seemed like she'd outgrown these girls who were still expecting her to provide them with her brothers, their friends, and, always, the next party.

We finished off our drinks just as Greg stumbled in. I could tell he'd been drinking, smoking some, too. His hair was long; his eyes were just slits. More than any of the other brothers, this one looked like Timothy. I still thought about Timothy all the time, but I knew we'd never be together again. We never even talked about the photos; we didn't need to. It was over for us in a lot of ways before it ever began.

"Well, well, well," Greg said, twisting out of his coat, "the gals are back in town!" He lifted the empty vodka bottle off the table and whistled. "Yup, the gals are back in town."

❋

The next day I woke up late to the garlicky smell of my father's turkey cooking. I heard the vacuum kick on then and Pumpkin started barking. In her younger days, she'd bark like mad the whole time, the hair on her back standing up, all teeth showing. The vacuum and the ironing board did it to her every time—that and dogs twice her size in her yard. Now I guess she was tired, too old for this. Four or five sharp yelps and she'd had enough, made her point.

I could picture my mother downstairs, cleaning like crazy, lining up all her Pyrex dishes, each with a strip of paper inside: sweet potatoes, three-bean casserole, dressing, cranberry sauce. The pantry was full of croutons and canned yams, bags of miniature marshmallows. Throughout the house I'd found grocery lists my mother had made and then misplaced. With Lissy's future in-laws coming, Thanksgiving had become a big production.

Even though Neil was a nice Jewish boy, and soon to be a Jewish doctor no less, my father still didn't think he was good enough for Lissy.

I remember the first time my father met Neil. It was a Sunday afternoon. Mitch was home for the weekend and Lissy had dropped by for a visit and to introduce everyone to her new boyfriend.

They'd walked into the family room while we were sorting through my father's pocket change. After years of letting it accumulate in a huge ceramic pot, he had decided he wanted it all counted and rolled.

My mother and I were assigned to the pennies, and at first my father had wanted us to divide them, separating out all the wheatbacks. "But they're worth two cents apiece!" my father had said after my mother had protested. "Two cents, Sandra!"

"Tough, Artie!"

My grandmother and Mitch were seated at the card table. She'd already built a nice shiny fence with her stacks of quarters. Mitch was working on the nickels. "I bet you've got a thousand dollars here," Mitch had said, sealing up a roll.

"More like two," my father had said.

"No way." Mitch had shook his head. "One grand—maybe."

"Is that a fact, huh? How much would you like to bet?"

"I don't want to bet."

"That's 'cause you know I'm right, huh? Huh!"

"You know," Neil had suggested, "they have automatic counters at the bank that do all this for you."

"Yeah, and they take a cut of the action, too," my father had said.

"But it's only something like two percent."

That had amused me. Back then, Neil had no idea who he was dealing with.

I heard Pumpkin barking again. I looked at the clock on my nightstand and decided it was time to get up. As I padded toward the bathroom, I saw my father standing in the hallway, half-dressed in a pair of beige slacks, holding two plaid shirts by their hangers.

"Does this go with this?" He twirled one of the shirts. "Or this one?"

"Either, Dad."

"Really?" He looked them both up and down. "They both go?" He seemed amazed he'd gotten it right.

"How come you're getting so dressed up?"

"This is so dressed up?" He pretended he didn't know what I was talking about. Thanksgivings past, my father slopped around in his weekend jeans and the college sweatshirts we kids had gotten him. He wouldn't say it, but I knew my father was dressing for Lissy's future in-laws.

Dr. Ulder, or Teddy, as they called him, was a surgeon with two sons following in his footsteps. My father didn't wear a suit and tie to work and he didn't have a professional degree. He was a reluctant carpet salesman, a frustrated musician, who had probably made more money than all the Ulders combined, but still.

"Which one would look better?" My father pushed the shirts toward me.

"The lighter one." I yanked on its sleeve and he pursed his lips, still contemplating. He seemed sad and lonely to me and I felt a tremendous ache for him. I couldn't take it. So I brushed past him on my way to the bathroom, leaving him standing all by himself in the hallway, holding the two shirts. I got about four feet from him before I stopped and turned back.

"Hey, Dad?"

"Hmmmm?" He was still deciding between shirts.

"Turkey smells great."

"She does, doesn't she, eh? Big-Joe-Daddy-O wouldn't have it any other way!" He smiled, like I'd just told him he'd won a million-dollar bet.

God, how he made my heart break! I couldn't look at him just then and went into the bathroom.

Later that afternoon, Neil showed up, along with two cars filled with the rest of his family. Neil looked like his father. They were both tall, had receding hairlines, and thick eyebrows that seemed to punctuate everything they said, like accent marks. His brother, Stewart, was shorter and quiet. The sister, Marla, had two small children who were running around, exploring.

My father asked Teddy Ulder if he could interest him in a little "libation." Around the Ulders, my father liked to use big words. Teddy Ulder was a boozer and my father had purposely stocked the liquor cabinet for him.

After fixing drinks for Teddy and the rest of the Ulders, my father poured himself a glass of whiskey. You could see my father wince each time he swallowed. He didn't normally drink, and the few times he did, he hadn't done it very well, usually ending up on the bathroom floor, moaning to my mother to bring him some Alka-Seltzer.

There was lots of wedding talk that day. My mother, Hilda Ulder, and Marla were discussing how nice they thought a spring wedding would be, and how they all preferred Rabbi Block over Rabbi Weissenstein. Marla broke away from the adult conversation when she noticed her two kids about to play catch with one of my mother's clowns. "Put that down this instant!"

My father was on his second drink, telling Teddy Ulder that he wanted Lissy and Neil to move into the basement. "Let 'em save some money. At least while Neil's still in med school." My father was trying to sound reasonable, but I knew he just wanted to keep an eye on the two of them. After they'd gotten engaged, my father had mentioned this to Neil, who just said, "Thanks but no thanks. We're going to need our own place." I remember Lissy had stood off to the side, pigeon-toed, twisting a piece of hair that had fallen from her ponytail. I think she was as amazed as I'd been that Neil had completely disregarded my father's wishes.

Teddy agreed with his son. Even if he had to help them out with the rent, he thought they deserved to have their own apartment. "My God, Artie," Teddy said, taking a long sip, "they're gonna be newlyweds. They'll need some privacy if I'm ever gonna get a grandson!"

"For chrissakes, Teddy, where's the goddamn fire? They're just a couple of kids themselves. They've got plenty of time."

"You know," Teddy said, "sooner or later, you're gonna have to let her go."

"Like hell I do!" My father drained his glass and went back to the bar to fix himself another drink.

One of the Ulders' grandchildren started banging on the piano. The little girl was so tiny, she could barely reach the keys. Marla grabbed the little girl's fingers, squeezing them in both her hands. "I'm afraid we aren't very musically inclined," she said, laughing.

"Ah," my father said, "you should hear this one play." He put his arm around my mother, who backed away, turning her face in toward his collar. "No, seriously, go on, Sandra, show 'em what you can do, huh! Huh?"

"Artie . . ."

"One song. Just one song. She's terrific."

"They don't want to hear it, Artie." My mother took his glass away from him, pointed to the buffet, and suggested he fix himself something to eat.

"Oh c'mon," Teddy said, "let's hear it."

"See, Sandra?" My father was smiling.

"Artie, please—" My mother shook her head.

"She's got perfect pitch—"

"Oh, I do not have perfect—"

"Tell you what, Sandra," my father said, jockeying for position, "you play something—anything you want—and I'll accompany you."

My mother must have recognized that tone in my father's

voice. He was one notch away from creating a scene, and that was usually the point where she'd give in.

"Okay, all right! Okay! One song, Artie, and then that's it."

Teddy Ulder got the rest of them applauding at this.

I caught the look Neil was giving Lissy. Not a good look. The eyebrows said it all.

"Love and Marriage" was the song my parents chose, and at least they played well together. They were not without talent. It was the same way when they danced at weddings and bar mitzvah parties. My parents were the couple in the middle, jitterbugging while everyone else looked on, clapping, admiring. When they were on like that, they dazzled.

My father gave the number a big finish, and if he'd stopped then, the whole thing could have passed for something sweet, touching, possibly impressive. But after "Love and Marriage," he wanted to do just one more song—and then, after that, he didn't need my mother anymore. She excused herself, then went into the kitchen to take a long-distance phone call from Mitch. My father just went on playing alone.

In the middle of "The Impossible Dream," Teddy Ulder inched over to the window and pulled back the drapes to see if it was still snowing. Stewart was drumming his fingers on his knee. Marla had one kid fast asleep on her lap and her hand on back of the other one's collar, holding him in place, going, "Shsssh, shsssh!" How could my father not see that people had had enough, that they were just being polite?

Hilda Ulder whispered, asking Lissy if she remembered where she'd put her purse, and Lissy went to find it. Neil followed her and I overheard him out in the hallway, going, "Just tell him it's getting late. The roads are getting bad."

"You don't understand," Lissy said. "I can't just say that to him."

"Melissa, he's a grown man. He can take it."

I gave Neil a cold look when he came back into the living

room and I clapped longer than anyone after my father finished "The Girl from Ipanema."

My mother got off the phone just as he was about to perform the song he wanted to play at the wedding. She burst into the room, as if she hadn't heard my father playing all the while.

"Artie," she said, "Mitch is on the phone. Don't you want to say hello?"

"Oh, go on, Art," Teddy Ulder said. "You take the call."

"I really think you should talk to him," my mother said. *"Now!"*

My father rested his clarinet against the back of a chair and followed my mother into the kitchen. Not a minute later, we heard him hollering. "HE'S NOT EVEN ON THE GOD-DAMN PHONE! Sandra, you said he was on the— Don't tell me to keep my voice down! What? You think I've had too much to drink? You think I'm boring everyone, is that it, huh? Huh!"

Only whispers came back from my mother and every face went tight around the room. It was a moment I would have taken back if I could have, plucked it clean from the universe and filled that gap of time with something pale and inconspicuous. If I could have, that's what I would have done.

"Well," my father said, when he and my mother came back in, "it appears that I owe every one of you an apology." He reached for his clarinet and began taking it apart. "I guess I just got a little carried away . . . Maybe I had one too many tonight. So I'm very, very sorry, and believe me, you're all free to go . . ."

"Oh no. Really, Artie," Hilda Ulder said, "we were enjoying it. But you two must be exhausted. We should really let you get your house back in order."

"After all," Teddy said, "it's getting late, and with the weather and all . . ."

But then it was Neil who stood up and said, "Would you do us one favor before we go? Would you play the song you want to play at our wedding?"

"Ah, no, no." My father waved him off. "Don't patronize me, Neil."

"He's not patronizing you, Dad." Lissy was on her feet then, too.

"Listen, gang, it's late. You're all tired."

"Please?" Neil said. "It'd mean a lot to us. Really it would."

"Nah." My father shook his head. "The weather's getting bad. Besides, I haven't played that in years."

"Please?" Neil wasn't giving up. He could be as relentless as my father. "You know me," Neil said, "you know how I am. I'd be the first to tell you if I really didn't want to hear it."

"This happens to be true!" My father pulled a laugh from the room and smiled in spite of himself.

"Go on, Artie," my mother said, smiling now, nodding. She could get sucked in just as easily as the rest of us.

"Well, all right, then, just this one. For my future son-in-law—but only because you insisted." My father began to play "Unforgettable," and it sounded so sweet and touching that it erased all the tension from just moments before.

I don't know, maybe it was contagious. But whatever it was that made us feel the need to please my father, keep him forever at the center of our lives and of our minds—whatever that was—I could see then that Neil had caught it, too. For the first time, it seemed he really could be a member of our family.

I suppose Lissy put it best the time she said, "If Dad went into therapy, we'd all get better." I was just beginning to see that in a way, we all were afflicted. We were all too affected by him. And this obsession we had with my father was already deep inside us. There was no getting beyond it. No matter where any of us went, how far away we got, it followed us. Mitch had proven that.

In a way, my father had spoiled us. Calm, nice, and simple would never cut it for us. Instead, I supposed we kids would spend the rest of our lives searching for someone of our own who could make us just as crazy, just as proud, and make us feel just as alive.

enough is enough

On my eleventh laser treatment, Dr. Preston introduced the CO_2 laser. It felt just the same as the argon laser, but they thought it could get those parts the argon had missed. Whereas the argon laser treated the blood vessels under the skin, the CO_2 laser treated the surface of the skin to smooth it out. It may have been a new laser, but there was nothing new about all this business for me.

When we got home that day, I locked myself in the bathroom and stared at my eye in a magnifying glass suction-cupped to the mirror. I analyzed the bubbled-up skin where my eyelashes started. Magnified like that, it looked spongy and there was a raw pink color from the laser. I leaned in closer and pulled the skin down on the lower lid to see inside. The scar tissue that once bloodied the white of my eye now looked like a sheet of dirty plastic. I let go of my eye and looked at it all swollen and irritated.

To me, the lasers were just making my eye look different, not better. The treatments had gradually faded the deep reds and purples to pinks and violets and then to nothing. The skin was all flesh color now, normal-looking, and I was happy about that part. But the lid and my brow were stubborn. Half the time, even after the swelling went down, I couldn't see the progress. The shape of my eye would be slightly different from the way it was before, a hint rounder along the outer corner, maybe a tiny bit flatter across the top. Then it seemed that the next treatment would reverse everything to the way it was the time before.

❋

One month later I was back in Cleveland for another treatment. This time my father came with us. That was because there were complications, decisions needing to be made. Dr. Preston and his team of experts couldn't get the eye quite right. From what I could see—and no one knew my eye's imperfections better than me—the only remaining traces of my hemangioma were a dime-sized bump above my eyebrow and a slightly drooping lid, which these doctors found unacceptable.

My team of doctors was going for a medical milestone. They were all about the before-and-after photos. They wanted to publish cutting-edge papers announcing new treatments in hemangiomas. They were looking to conduct seminars at major universities. They were consumed with seeing their accomplishments written up in medical journals. They were stuck in that place I'd once stood, where everything hinged on perfection. I'd been driven by heartache and vanity; they were driven by ego.

The one surgery Dr. Preston had spoken of early on hadn't done the job, and now he wanted to schedule more operations. "We're only talking one, maybe two more surgeries. All outpatient." Dr. Preston said this like I'd won a prize or something.

My father was sitting forward in his seat, not wanting to miss anything. My mother held her pocketbook in her lap, her sunglasses still in her hand. I was antsy, bobbing my leg up and down. I couldn't even think about surgery, outpatient or not.

"So what are the next steps?" My father was still sitting there, moving things forward, just as he'd always done.

"Well, first things first, we need to remove the excess scar tissue," said Dr. Preston. "Very simple procedure—minimal recovery time. Swelling should be down in five to ten days. Of course, the bruising could last longer . . ."

"That's nothing for you, Nina," my father said, giving me a wink. "This one here's a real trooper. You should see what she's been through." My father was smiling at me.

I was exhausted just thinking about all I'd been through. I closed my eyes for what felt like a long time, and when I opened them, I turned to Dr. Preston and then to my father. "I don't know if I'm ready for this," I said.

My father's eyes went wide. "What do you mean, 'ready for this'? We've come this far, haven't we? This is nothing compared to what we've been through."

What we've been through? "All I'm saying is, I'm not sure I'm ready for this. I just don't want to decide something like this right now."

My father waited until after we'd left the Cleveland Clinic before he said something. "Would you mind telling me why in the hell you don't want to go through with this surgery?"

"I didn't say I didn't want to go through with it. I just don't want a bunch of doctors who know nothing about me, who don't care at all about me as a person, telling me what to do."

"What, my opinion doesn't matter anymore?"

"But Dad, what about *my* opinion? It's my eye. Shouldn't my opinion be the one that really matters?" In the history of my eye, this was the first time that I was going to be the one making the decisions.

"I just don't know what there is to think about. They're saying they can do more to help you and you're not letting them.

Do you think I would steer you wrong? It's taken us years to get to this stage. Why in the hell would you want to stop now? Why would you not want to go ahead with the surgery?"

"Because, Dad, I'm just not sure I need it."

After I said that, my father lowered his face to his hands and rubbed his eyes, and when he raised his head back up, he was almost smiling. It was as if he'd been waiting years and years to hear me say that.

It had taken me all this time to come to this point, but I wasn't a child anymore. I was smart enough by then to realize that another tuck on the inner corner of my eye wasn't the answer. Neither was raising my lid another fraction of a millimeter. There wasn't another procedure that could make everything all better.

How often had I heard people say my eye didn't matter? "You look fine the way you are." "If you didn't point it out, I never would have noticed it." "You can't even tell which one's the bad eye anymore." What would it take for me to trust what other people said? And what difference did that make anyway? What more was I looking for?

Who said perfection was a prerequisite for love? I remembered seeing a man with boils all over his face, walking down the street, holding hands with a woman who looked perfectly normal. I saw a woman in a wheelchair at the Summit Mall being pushed by a man so handsome, I could still picture his face. I read an article once about two people with Down's syndrome who had found each other and fallen in love. Even when Patty was at her heaviest, before she'd lost all her weight, she had found boyfriends and even love.

When I was eleven or maybe twelve, we were at a cousin's wedding and one of the bridesmaids had a drooping eyelid. She was a pretty girl, even with her eye, and all the groomsmen kept asking her to dance. My mother pointed to her on the dance floor and whispered in my ear, "Now see, she doesn't let her eye hold her back at all."

I was starting to realize that people were far more forgiving of one another than I'd ever given them credit for. More forgiving than I had been of myself. I had cheated myself out of so much, and all because of an imperfection that had now been shrunk down to something the size of a dime. I could live with that amount of imperfection. If this was the end of the road, I could accept where I was at. I could handle knowing that my eye might never be perfect, that I might always have a knot above my brow, that I might always have a drooping lid, and that someone, somewhere, might come up to me and ask, "What happened to your eye?" And if that happened, if all that was true, would that be so horrible?

I didn't know all the answers, but I knew my problems were within me, lodged in a place where no doctors could reach, no experimental lasers could touch. My father had paid to fix me on the outside, but now the rest was up to me. The time had come to look in the mirror and be okay with what I saw. I didn't need another operation. I was done. Enough was enough. Dr. Preston would have to find another guinea pig.

☼

The day before Lissy's wedding, I threw out all my special makeup. As I was getting dressed for the rehearsal dinner, I pitched each jar and every tube into the wastebasket—the corrective base and tint, the compacts of pressed powder, the shaker of loose sealing powder, the jar of remover, the spatula that blended it all together, the worn-out wands of mascara. I got rid of it all, and my Aqua Net, too, and it tore at my heart to do so.

For months now I hadn't really needed it. I'd stopped hiding my eye behind my hair and now I could use regular makeup, the kind everyone else used. I had one of those beige concealer sticks and I could make my bad eye look normal with just ordinary pencils and shadows. Now I could create the same illusion from the tube of mascara picked off a display tree at Woolworth.

I had bought all new shiny compacts and beautiful tapered bottles. They were lined up on the counter, proud and waiting for me. I uncapped the sleek jar of liquid foundation. It even smelled pretty and felt light as raindrops on my fingertips. I applied it to my face in long, careful strokes. It looked good, it looked natural. It felt better, too.

I was doing okay and I might have been fine if only I hadn't glanced into the wastebasket. But that's when it got to me. There was all my special makeup, lying in the trash, abandoned like a favorite toy I'd outgrown.

I don't know why, but I started to tear up. I suppose I was still attached to that special makeup. Even though I had hated needing to wear it, resented the time it took every morning to put it on and every evening to take it off, it had become a part of me. It had served me well and now I didn't need it anymore. It was time to go it alone, naked.

I heard my mother calling up to me from the foot of the stairs. "C'mon, Nina. Everybody's waiting. We should have been at the temple fifteen minutes ago. Nina? C'mon. We're all waiting on you!"

I took one last look at myself and turned off the light. It was time to start down a different path, one that would lead me away from the mirror and into the real world. And if I couldn't be happy now, I knew I'd have no one to blame but myself.

cover me

Finally I met someone. And he was for real this time. Not a fantasy, not a crush, not a mirage that vanished when you got too close. His name was Michael Dempsey and he had curly brown hair and sleepy green eyes hidden behind a pair of wire-rimmed glasses. He was the only guy I knew who actually looked better with his glasses on. He used to take them off and either toss them on a table or stuff them in his pocket whenever we were kissing so they wouldn't get in the way. Another thing about Michael was he had the best Adam's apple I'd ever seen. I loved the way it jutted out, rising up and down when he swallowed.

Michael was in his last year at Akron U and I was a junior. I remembered seeing him one day at the student union. He was wearing a flannel shirt and Levi's. I liked the way he walked, the way he carried himself. About a week later, I saw him again. We were both waiting in line outside of the bursar's office and he just started talking to me. He wasn't the cutest boy on campus, but he grew into that for me. Before the semester was over, there wasn't anybody who looked better.

At first I was worried about his name. I'd had bad luck with Michaels, Mikes, Mikeys. It seemed like all my life a Michael or one of its derivatives had broken my heart. There'd been the Mike who barked at me when I wore tea bags over my eye, then Mike Farling, who ruined my life that day he sang that Beatles song to me. And there had been other bad Mikes and Michaels, too. It was just a bad name for me. I thought it was jinxed.

"You're crazy," he said when I confessed this. We were sitting on a bench outside the library, killing time before my next class. "So you think this isn't gonna work out with us because of my name?" He squinted as he lit his Marlboro. "Here's a thought," he said on the exhale, "don't call me Michael. Call me Henry. How's that?" He took another drag off his cigarette and smiled.

I reached over for one of his curls and stretched it out straight, till it touched his shoulder. "You don't look like a Henry." I sized him up, grinning. "Ralph," I said with a nod. "You look more like a Ralph."

And that's just the way it was with us. It was easy and I didn't have to try to get him to like me, or even love me. I didn't have to do a thing. He just turned up in my life one day, a happy surprise, like a lucky penny waiting for you to pick it up and change your fortune.

It wasn't until Michael that I realized how much attention I required from a mate to be happy, to feel calm, to feel reassured. He was perfect for me in that respect. He was the giver and I the taker. When I met him, I was empty to my core. You could have dropped a pebble down my throat and heard it hit bottom.

I think the greatest thing Michael did for me was listen. I needed listening to. Maybe if I'd had boyfriends all along, I wouldn't have had so much to say. But here I'd gone and stored it all up for him. I was a talker. That was my thing. And Michael heard everything, remembering every detail, remembering things I'd forgotten I'd even told him.

"How'd you know that? Who told you that?" I asked one night when we were sitting at the bar at the Ground Round, shelling peanuts and drinking beer. He had just recounted the tale of my first Spin the Bottle game in Patty McFadden's basement.

"You told me that." He cracked a peanut shell between his fingers.

"I did? When?"

"Uh, on our first date. We were sitting right over there." He pointed across the way to a table in the back. There was another couple seated there now, but just a few months before, it had been the two of us.

"Oh my God." I buried my head in my arms, hiding. "I told you that on our first date?"

He smiled, dropped a peanut in his mouth, and tossed the shell onto the floor.

So yeah, I talked a lot. About everything. Nothing was off-limits. I told him what the balance was on one of my father's financial statements that I'd seen on his desk, told him when I had cramps, told him one time that my underwear was riding up on me.

"You know, Nina," he'd tease, "you need to open up a little bit. You're too private."

I know I entertained him, but I was beginning to realize that in some ways I was just like my father. I needed so much attention. Everything had to be about me. At times I worried that I was too much for Michael. Like my father, I was a demanding person, difficult to love. I wondered what I was giving back to him. I couldn't understand what he was getting from me in return.

When asked, he took off his glasses and gave me a wide-eyed look. "Are you kidding me? I'm crazy about you."

Michael never had a problem with my eye. He accepted it, because he had accepted me first. Michael said he never noticed it until the night I pointed it out to him. We were in his Mustang at a drive-in restaurant, waiting for the carhop to bring out our food. "C'mon, seriously?" I laughed. I was skeptical. "You never noticed that my one eye is different from the other one?"

He looked at me and brushed the hair away from my face. "I think your eyes are beautiful. I like 'em both."

"You're serious?"

"I'm serious."

So I told him the whole saga. Michael heard about the name-calling, the medical treatments, the special makeup. He heard it all. And when I was through, I ran my finger along the lid, pointing out where it drooped. Then I reached across the gearshift for his hand and ran his fingertips across the knot on my brow. "See?"

"Does it hurt?"

"Nah." I shook my head. It used to be whenever someone asked about my eye, I'd tell them I had a tumor, or else I'd say I was going blind. Sometimes I'd even say I was dying. Michael had a look of concern on his face, and if ever I was going for sympathy from him, this would have been my chance. But pity no longer felt good to me. It was no longer a substitute for love. So I just smiled and said, "I can't believe you never noticed my eye before."

"I can't believe you went through all that." His fingertips left my brow and traced down along my cheek. And then he did it. He leaned in closer, pulled me toward him, and kissed what I once thought was my most imperfect, unforgivable, unlovable part. He kissed my eye and then he kissed my mouth, soft, sweet, tender. It wasn't our first kiss, but it was the one that meant the most.

The first time I slept with Michael, I found out that whatever I'd been doing before with Timothy was not this—not even close. With Timothy, I'd just laid there while he did whatever it was that he was supposed to do. I didn't know anything different.

But the first time with Michael, I was scared all over again, because I cared for him and wanted it to be good. And I didn't know what I was doing. Michael was on top of me and he just kept saying, "Relax, just relax." And then he kissed me and reached back for my legs, coaxing me to wrap them about his hips. And that made a difference. I couldn't believe that up until that time, I didn't even know what a girl was supposed to do with her legs.

And it was okay to show him if I liked something. He seemed to take credit for whatever I was feeling. He'd breathe heavily into my neck, going, "Oh yeah" whenever he'd see me losing myself in it all. And when we were finished, I'd want him to stay inside me, not move. I felt so full with him there like that. So complete. I feared that when he pulled out, he'd take part of me with him.

If I could have, I would have made love with him all the time. But it was hard finding places to go. He still lived at home, and so did I. So sometimes we made love in his car, sometimes in the park, sometimes at his house when his parents were both at work. Those were the times we could linger over it all. I'd rest my head on his chest, listen to his heart thumping, and say a quick prayer: *God, don't let this end.* There was always the fear that he might take his love back and shower it someplace else. Someplace more deserving. After all, his name was Michael and I'd come to expect disappointments. But for now, he was mine and I would have done anything to keep him with me. I was just so grateful to be loved.

❋

It was inevitable. Sooner or later, I was going to have to take Michael home to meet my parents. I thought a Sunday brunch would be the safest, better than a long, drawn-out dinner or family get-together. I was nervous but, at the same time, also excited. Part of me wanted to show Michael off to my father and part of me wanted to show my father off to Michael. I wanted my father to do something just outrageous enough so I could say to Michael, "See? And you thought I was exaggerating!"

That's what I was thinking when we arrived, and my father didn't disappoint me. He had gotten up early that morning and gone to Lou & Hy's Delicatessen to buy smoked fish and bagels. The first thing he said after we'd all sat down was, "Do you know they wanted twelve dollars a pound for that lox? Twelve dollars!"

"Wow!" My mother was sharing her sympathies when the buzzer went off, trilling from the kitchen. She popped up and dashed off to rescue her cake from the oven.

I glanced around the table and saw that my mother had kept the chipped plate for herself. Other than that, it didn't look like anything out of the ordinary had gone into making this brunch special, like they normally would for company. No flowers, no fancy serving platters. I wasn't sure if I was relieved about this or disappointed. There was a Tupperware bowl of ice, a couple bottles of Pepsi, and a cruddy-looking bottle opener on the table. The orange juice was parked to the side, still in its carton. I contemplated the lox, orange like sherbet. It was fanned out on a plate with rings of onions skirting it.

My father stabbed a few slices with his fork and passed the rest to Michael, going, "Now don't be shy, Michael. At prices like these, I'll be damned if I'm throwing any of this out."

I took a deep breath. Already he was starting with the money. The room began to take on the smell of cocoa from my mother's Texas sheet cake. It was the one dessert she always made, because it was easy—everything in one bowl.

"Ah." My father lifted the platter of smoked fish and did a quarter turn toward Michael. "When was the last time you had a good chub, huh?"

I could tell by the look on Michael's face that he'd never seen a piece of smoked fish with its head and tail still attached. The skin looked like golden crinkled-up foil and the eyes were murky, clouded over. It looked like something you were supposed to mount on the wall, not eat.

I was practically raised on smoked fish. Every Sunday for as long as I could remember, my father had gone to the deli and brought home chubs and bagels for brunch. When we were little, my father used to fix our plates for us. He'd unfold the fish from the oily skin and then with his fingers he would work his way through the meat of it, feeling for any tiny bones, discarding them on the side of his plate. Once satisfied that he'd gotten them all, he would hand us a pile of flaky, worked-over smoked fish. And we'd eat it. It wasn't until we were much older that we realized just how unappetizing this was.

To be polite, Michael took the runt, the smallest of the chubs. He scooted it to the outer lip of his plate to make room for a bagel. My mother was still moving about in the kitchen, icing her sheet cake and scooping out the creamed herring she'd forgotten to serve. I thought about asking if she needed help, but I was afraid to leave Michael alone with my father.

"So, young man, Nina here tells me you're graduating this year." My father reached for a bagel and tore it in two. He never sliced them in half the way you were supposed to.

"Yeah. Finally." Michael smiled, polite, innocuous, not one rough edge to get caught on, and yet my father found something.

" 'Finally'?" My father's eyebrows hiked up as he swiped the cream cheese, smearing it onto his bagel. "Christ, how long have you been in college?"

"No . . ." Michael half-shook his head. He hadn't meant it literally. "No, I mean . . . that's not what I meant . . ."

"Oh, well," my father said, wiping his hands on his napkin and setting his elbows on the table, "what exactly did you mean?"

"I just meant, you know, finally. Like finally—I'm finally ready to be out of school. Be out in the world. I'm all set to be on my own. Finally."

"Oh." My father nodded and took a bite off his bagel. With his mouth full, he added, "So you have a decent job lined up, then! Nina, you didn't tell me that."

I set my fork down. No one was better at not getting it when he didn't want to. My father could get stuck on a word and not let it go, like it was coated in glue. Michael shook his head again and stared at the chub on his plate.

My mother came back in with the herring and sat down. "So what did I miss?"

My father pointed to Michael with his broken bagel. "He has a job already lined up after graduation. Isn't that great!"

Michael set his fork down and straightened his glasses. I glared at my father, but he wouldn't look at me. Why was he being so difficult? And why didn't my mother pick up on this? She knew him. She knew the way he could get.

But all she did was smile and make things worse, going, "Oh, isn't that nice, Michael. What kind of job? Doing what?"

I felt the heat rising off Michael's face when he shook his curls, explaining, "I—I don't have a job yet. I mean, I'll get one. I just don't have one yet . . ."

"Oh." My father let his face sag like he'd just been told the market had crashed. "But you said you were ready to get out in the world. Be on your own. Finally. I thought that's what you said?"

I couldn't stand it. My father was wearing him down. And as the day progressed, it got worse and he got worse.

After brunch, my father challenged Michael to a game of pool. My father hadn't held a cue stick in years and suddenly we were all down in the basement and my father was clearing boxes and stacks of old magazines off the top of the pool table. It was cold and drafty down there, like a warehouse filled with everything we didn't use anymore—the roll-away bed, old file cabinets, a piece of broken furniture that my mother thought she'd have repaired someday. I felt exposed, like we were showing Michael our ugly, unkempt side.

As my father brushed down the felt top, he said, "What do you say we make this a little interesting, eh? Huh? Let's make a little wager."

"A bet?" Michael pushed up the sleeves on his flannel shirt and looked at the cue sticks leaning against one another in the stand.

"Sure!" My father smiled as he screwed his cue stick together—the fancy one that came in two parts and had mother-of-pearl diamond shapes running up the side. "Five bucks. Small stuff."

Michael selected his weapon, shrugged, and nodded. "Okay, I'm in."

"I knew you were a gamblin' man. I knew he was." My father winked at me, like we were in this together. Only I didn't want in. "Nina, who you gonna bet on? Huh? Which man's gonna win?"

My jaw was set tight. I couldn't answer. I wasn't going to choose between my father and my boyfriend.

"Tell you what, Michael, I'll rack 'em up and you break 'em." My father was leaning over the table, rearranging the balls inside the wooden rack—solid, stripe, solid, stripe.

Michael barely nudged the triangle of balls on the break but managed to scratch the cue ball. My father took over after that and started running the table. It sounded like heels on marble floors each time he took a shot. And then he launched into a speech about when he'd first met my mother. "Do you know I could not touch her until after we were married?"

"Oh Artie." My mother closed her eyes, shook her head.

Four ball in the corner pocket. Done. "And believe me," my father laughed, leaning over the table, taking aim, his one leg stretched out behind him. "I'd been around the block a few times." Twelve ball in the side pocket. "There were the girls you had your fun with and then there were the girls you married."

Michael put down his cue stick and looked at the floor. His Adam's apple inched up, then fell.

My father was going for the eight ball now. "Michael, man to man, I think you know what I'm talking about, huh?" My father took his shot: eight ball, clean in the corner pocket.

As soon as Michael left, my father started with his lecture about not buying a cow when the milk was for free, or something like that. He had me cornered in the kitchen, where I was helping my mother clean up. I was scraping fish bones into the garbage, chewing on the inside of my cheek. I couldn't look at him, I was so mad.

My father pressed on after hushing my mother. "Now you listen to me, young lady. That boy is out to use you."

"Dad"—I held up a dirty plate and fork—"he's *not* using me. He's *nice* to me."

"Yeah, because he wants in your pants, that's why!"

"Oh Artie." My mother was shaking her head, squeezing out a sponge under the faucet.

"You saw him, Sandra. You saw the way he looked at her."

My mother didn't have a response. She was scrubbing the Formica countertop with a vengeance, putting all her weight into it.

"You're nothing but his conquest," my father was saying to me now. "Once he gets what he wants from you, that'll be the end of it. That much I guarantee you . . ."

I went to the table and carried the platter of lox back into the kitchen. A dull ache was settling into my gut. What if he was right about Michael? My father could be so damn persuasive at times. Even though, according to my father, I'd already given Michael what he was after—I'd already slept with him, many times—and he hadn't dumped me, my father was still able to make me doubt Michael's love for me. It was my father's voice, his posture, the intense look in his eyes. Why couldn't he just let me be happy for once?

"I know what I'm talking about, Nina. You watch your step with that boy," he said.

My father walked out of the kitchen and I took the leftover slices of his twelve-dollar-a-pound lox and shoved them down the garbage disposal.

no looking back

Michael's parents were a lot more modern than my father. They didn't mind their son having a girlfriend. They had even invited me to go to Niagara Falls with their entire family. I was over eighteen. I guess I really didn't need permission, but I couldn't see taking a trip like that without my father's blessings. I tried to soft sell it through my mother, but she wasn't going to touch this one. When I asked, all she said was, "You'll have to take that one up with your father."

So I mentioned the trip to my father one night. He wasn't feeling well. He'd come down with the flu that afternoon and was sitting on the couch in his bathrobe, his body hunched over a huge bowl of boiling water, a towel tented over his head, trying to sweat it out. A TV tray was stationed to his right, holding aspirin, Vicks VapoRub, cough syrup, and the *Wall Street Journal*.

"But it's just two nights, Dad!" I said, sitting next to him on the edge of the couch.

"Wrong!" My father sat up, letting a cloud of steam escape,

the bath towel draped about his shoulders like a boxer's. My father's face was red and I wasn't sure if that was from the steam or me.

"But Dad—"

"Nina, you're not going away with him. End of discussion." He paused, trying to clear his throat, which turned into a strained cough. You could tell his chest was too tight to really give it up. He was getting redder in the face. It wasn't the steam. It was definitely me. My father sat back, patted his face dry, and reached for the jar of Vicks.

"But Dad, it's not like we're going alone. His parents are going to be there."

"Yeah, and where are you gonna sleep, Nina? Huh?"

I didn't know. I hadn't asked about that. I thought about telling my father that I was sharing a room with Michael's sister. But she was married, so that didn't make any sense. I thought about saying I was staying on a different floor, or at a different hotel. It was already getting too complicated.

"Uh-huh! That's what I thought . . ." My father was uncapping the jar of Vicks. He stuck two fingers inside, pulled out a glob, and swallowed it. He swallowed a gigantic glob of Vicks VapoRub!

I gulped, almost gagged. "Dad, you're not supposed to eat that stuff."

My father spread his hand across his chest and made another failed attempt to cough. "Trust me. I've been doing this since before you were born."

"Maybe that's why you can't breathe now." I was looking at the jar, right where it said *Do not ingest.*

"It's the only thing that'll loosen this crap up."

I was worried about my father eating Vicks, but he was way more concerned about my wanting to go away with Michael.

"Listen, Nina, you're not going away with this kid." My father reached for his towel again, getting ready to go back under.

"Not now. Not ever!" And then he disappeared beneath his hooded towel. Case closed.

Two weeks after the trip that I didn't take with Michael and his family, the two of us cut classes one afternoon and went to my house. It was rare that I had the house to myself, and I knew my mother had a luncheon at the Akron Jewish Center that day and my father was down at the store.

We raced up the stairs and into my room laughing, acting silly, speaking in ridiculous French accents. "Oooh la la!" I said, taking off his glasses and pulling his belt clean through the loops with a crisp snap. He unclasped my bra and swung it over his head like a lasso before flinging it somewhere over his shoulder. We were half kissing, half laughing as we stumbled onto the bed.

Pumpkin was whimpering, up on her hind legs wanting to leap up there with us. Everything slipped away and fell to the background, like the rest of our clothes that had fallen to the floor. I could get so lost in time when were together like that—the kissing, the touching, the legs and arms all entwined, Michael's curls brushing against my naval and thighs. Nothing else existed outside of this moment with him. Nothing else mattered because I had Michael. I had Michael and Michael had me.

I was kissing Michael with my taste still on his lips when I heard someone at the front door. We both froze, staring at each other. I brought both hands to my mouth as soon as I heard my father talking to the dog, going, "How's my Punky, huh? Huh!" I could hear the spare change jangling inside his front pocket, picturing him standing in the foyer, patting his leg, summoning her to his side.

My heart went still. Two in the afternoon? What was my father doing home? Michael and I were scrambling to get our clothes on, but it was no use. He was buckling his belt and I was pulling my sweater over my head when my father rounded the corner and appeared in the doorway.

. . .

Before Michael even got out of my bedroom, my father had grabbed his eyeglasses off my nightstand. "You're forgetting something." He chucked them at Michael and gave him a shove out of my room. Michael didn't even look back at me. He just fled down the stairs. He didn't even look back.

Part of me wanted to run after Michael, but I knew I couldn't. I didn't dare. My father had his eyes locked on me in such a way that my feet couldn't move. I braced myself for the outburst that I was sure would erupt at any moment. I was ready for that. I had it coming. More than a minute had passed since Michael had left and so far my father hadn't said a word. Not one word. He just stood there in the doorway looking at me.

I figured he was waiting for me to say something first, so I came out with "I'm sorry."

My father didn't respond. His expression didn't even change. He was set like a stone.

I tried again, thinking maybe he hadn't heard. "Dad, I said I was sorry. Okay?"

He sighed. That was it.

"Oh c'mon, Dad." I threw my head back and closed my eyes. "Jesus, say something, would you? Please!"

His eyes shifted and I followed the direction of his gaze. He was staring at my bed now, the perfect crime scene. All the evidence was in plain view, right down to the darkened wet mark on my sheets, which were crumpled in shame. My bra was resting on top of the blanket like a cherry on a sundae. Everything was so still and quiet, I could hear my father's wristwatch ticking, every second lingering, my agony playing out in slow motion.

"You might want to think about changing your sheets," he said. "I don't think your mother should have to do that." My father turned to the door and, with his back to me, he said, "I can't think of a time when you've ever disappointed me more." After that he walked out of my room.

I was standing there, stunned, listening to the steps creaking as he made his way downstairs, followed by the sound of his footsteps on the tiled floor below me. That was it? No screaming? No lecturing? This was too economical for my father and yet he had managed to slap me down just the same. What was I supposed to do now? How was I supposed to make this one better between my father and me? And what about Michael?

I snatched my bra off my bed and stuffed it inside my drawer. I started to strip the bed, but I couldn't get the top sheet untangled from the blanket and I didn't have it in me to wrestle them apart. That broke me and I buried my face in a handful of sheets and collapsed onto the bed. I wasn't even thinking about my father at that point. All I could think about was Michael. What if my father had driven him away for good? I was starting to panic, terrified that he would end things with me. I couldn't bear the thought of losing Michael. I had to go find him and talk to him. I had to explain my father to him. I had to make sure we were still okay.

I got off the bed and flew down the stairs. My father was sitting in his chair, leaning over an ashtray, packing his pipe. My purse was lying on the chair opposite him, right where I'd chucked it when Michael and I had first raced into the house earlier that day. I had to go see Michael, so I stormed into the room, grabbed my purse, and slung it over my shoulder.

"And where the hell do you think you're going, young lady?" My father's voice was low and penetrating.

I looked at him. I didn't have to say a word. He knew exactly where I was headed.

"Don't you dare go after that boy," he growled at me. "And I don't ever want to see him in this house again. Is that clear?"

"Oh that's just great. That'll just solve everything, won't it?" In an instant I felt my insides fisting up, ready to take him on once and for all. "What are you going to do next, Dad? Put a chastity belt on me? My God, this is the first time in my whole miserable, lousy life that I've ever been happy. Don't you get that? Do you have any idea what it's been like for me? You don't have a clue, do you! All my life I've felt like such an ugly, disgusting freak around guys. You don't know what they used to say to me—the things they used to do to me. I was nothing but a big joke, Dad. They called me names. I never thought anyone would ever want me—ever!"

My father started to say something, but I plowed over his words.

"You don't get it! I'm lucky that a guy like Michael wants me at all. And for all I know, you've ruined it for me. He might not ever want to see me again now because of you! Because of what you did!"

"Because of what *I* did?" My father's voice was full strength. He had his Zippo positioned over his pipe, the flame being sucked down into the bowl with each puff.

"You practically threw him out of my room!"

"Let me tell you something," my father said, his pipe gripped between his teeth. "That son of a bitch is lucky he was able to walk out of here today."

"That's it! I'm leaving!"

"Don't you dare walk—" But before he could finish his thought, my father a launched into a violent coughing jag. Deep, dry coughs rumbled from inside him, making his eyes water and his face and neck flush red. He looked panicked as he dropped his pipe into the ashtray and leaned forward in his chair. It sounded like he couldn't breathe. I thought he was choking.

"Oh my God!" I threw my purse onto the chair and headed for the kitchen to get him a glass of water.

He was still coughing when I came back. I held the glass out to him, but he wouldn't take it. Instead, he coughed some more and held up his hand, indicating he was okay. He kept coughing until he was able to settle back in his chair. And in between his wheezing, he managed to say, "Don't you dare leave this house!"

My eyes were burning into his as I slammed the glass of water on the coffee table and grabbed my purse. My father and I were glowering at each other, neither one of us blinking. This was the showdown.

I was the one who looked away, and as I reached for the car keys hanging on the rack, I heard my father say, "Not with my car you don't!"

"Fine. Then I'll walk." I threw the keys on the table and they skidded off and landed on the floor. I glared at him, unmoved. And then I saw what I'd been waiting for, what I'd been expecting all along: tears welling up in my father's eyes.

"Nina," he said, "don't you know that I only want what's best for you? This kid isn't right for you."

I had broken him. He thought I was leaving him for Michael. But I wasn't. I would be back in an hour, maybe two. I just had to make sure that Michael wasn't mad and that we were still together. More than my father's forgiveness, what I needed just then was to be with Michael. I was already reaching for the door.

"My God, Nina, he's the first boyfriend you've ever had. There'll be others. I promise you there will be—"

"I'm leaving," I said, pausing just long enough to glance back at him.

My father looked at me and I could tell he was lost and frightened. We both knew that something between us had shifted, once and forever. His daughter, his little girl, who had always obeyed him, never once defied him, who had lived her life only to please him, was pulling away and there was nothing that could bring me back. There was nothing he could have done that would have made me run to his side and sob along with him, apologizing and telling him what he wanted to hear. For the first time in our lives, we both knew he couldn't get to me. I was like that place in the center of your back that you couldn't reach to scratch. At last, I had found a way to get back at him for the past twenty years.

I just walked out the door. I never even looked back.

heaven has a trapdoor

My father went to the doctor. He just didn't feel right. He'd never fully recovered from the flu he'd had six weeks before. It seemed he was exhausted all the time. My mother thought he was depressed and I thought that was because of me, because of our fight. This was the fight that my father was pretending hadn't happened, even though it was still going on quietly, playing out inside my head.

The doctor conducted a routine physical and ordered a chest X ray to determine what was causing the coughing and wheezing. The tests showed nothing conclusive. Perhaps the fatigue was due to stress, he said, and it was possible that my father was experiencing a mild case of depression. Nothing to be concerned about. There was, however, something the doctor wanted to keep an eye on. The chest X ray showed a shadow, a spot on one lung. Just a speck. In a month they'd see him again, see if anything had changed.

We went about our family business. My mother played piano. Lissy dropped by for dinner whenever Neil was working late. Mitch called every few days defending his decision to live in New York, and I continued to hold a grudge.

Lissy and Mitch had already gone through their angry stages with my father. Now it was my turn. I was waging a one-sided cold war between the two of us. Ever since our fight, I hadn't spoken to my father unless I absolutely had to. I'd sit opposite him at the table, not making eye contact. I'd pass him in the hallway on my way to school, muttering a " 'lo" after he'd said good morning. "How was class?" he'd ask. "Fine." Did I want to go to the store with him? "No." I was punishing him, only I don't think he noticed. Actually, I know he didn't.

My father had selective amnesia. I was sure he had forgotten what went down that day and that I had walked out on him. He'd forgotten it all. And for all his conversation starters that he used like kindling, he never once mentioned Michael. He never asked where I was going or who I was going with. He didn't even know that Michael had moved into his own apartment and that those nights when I was supposed to be staying with Lissy, I was really with him. My father and I were hardly speaking as it was, and Michael was at the top of the list of things we weren't talking about.

A month passed by almost unnoticed, like a stretch of highway outside your car window. While we weren't paying attention, the spot—that "nothing to worry about" speck—on my father's lung was growing, and four weeks of indifference and speculation had turned to urgency. They were operating on him the following morning.

I still didn't get it because when my mother called from the hospital, she said it was just going to be exploratory surgery. That didn't sound so bad, and my mother seemed calm enough over the phone. She was on her way home and would explain everything when she saw me. When I offered to contact Mitch in New York, she said she'd just hung up with him.

"Oh . . ." I'd been doodling in my notebook. I stopped and set the pen down. "What about Lissy?"

"She and Neil were here with me all day. I tried to find you, Nina. I kept calling the house . . . I even called school to see if one of your professors could track you down. I tried, Nina, but everything was just happening so fast."

"Oh . . ." She couldn't find me all day because I'd been at Michael's.

After I hung up with my mother, I stared at the phone, debating whether or not to call my father. I was certain Mitch had already phoned in. And Lissy had been with him all day, so she'd done her bit, too. Proving ourselves to my father was something we'd done all our lives, each of us in our own way. Over and over again. Birthday and Father's Day cards were always covered front to back, pledging our love and devotion, praising his wisdom, his guidance. I never would have dreamed of signing a card to him with a simple "Love, Nina." That would have been an insult.

I cradled my head. It was throbbing. I didn't feel like talking to my father. I was still angry with him, and just because he was in the hospital, I wasn't going to forgive and forget everything. I thought about tearing up the scrap of paper where I'd scribbled down his hospital number. I acted like I wasn't going to call, even though I knew I would. I knew myself too well. Even after I'd walked away from the phone and poured myself a glass of water, I knew I was stalling, putting off the inevitable. I went back into the family room, broke down, and dialed.

My father answered the phone, sounding perfectly himself. He could have been upstairs on the extension, or at the store—anywhere really.

"We got nothing to worry about, sweet pea. Everything's gonna be just fine, Neen."

My eyes instantly began to tear up. I thought he was talking about the two of us. I thought he meant that in spite of our fight, we were going to be fine.

"They say there's a good chance it could be nothing. So don't you worry, tootsie . . ."

I went cold. I realized he wasn't even thinking about the two of us. I dried my eyes on the back of my sleeve. Honestly, I wasn't all that worried about him. According to my mother, they just wanted to rule things out. But I could never have let on that I thought this was just some routine procedure. He sounded fine and I found myself acting more concerned than I was because I knew that was what he'd want from me. Even flat on his back, that man had me falling back in line.

❋

The surgery took longer than expected. We were all gathered in the waiting room, sitting among old magazines strewn about, a vending machine spitting out weak coffee, and strangers trickling in and out until they got their news and left. I spent most of the afternoon sitting in the corner, reading *A Tree Grows in Brooklyn*. I was on page 31 when I sat down, and as the day wore on, the sunlight coming through the window moved its shadows across the page. By the time the surgeon came in to see us, I'd reached page 147 and the room had grown dim.

As the surgeon spoke, my mother leaned forward in her chair. Lissy was holding her one hand, Mitch had hold of the other. My grandmother had set her needlepoint aside. I went and sat on the arm of Mitch's chair, my leg swinging back and forth while I fiddled with the slats of the venetian blinds behind us.

The doctor began by explaining that they'd removed a small mass on his right lung. "Just a little over four centimeters . . . We're going to have to start him on radiation treatments right away."

I let go of the venetian blinds and sat up straight.

"But he's a lucky man," the doctor was saying. "If we'd waited any longer, with this form of cancer, we might be having a very different conversation right now."

After the surgeon left the room, my mother hugged us all and did something I'd rarely seen her do. She started to cry. My grandmother pressed her palms together and closed her eyes, going, "Thank God! Thank God . . ."

I watched all this, feeling removed from the rest of my family. I didn't share their sense of relief, because until this moment, I hadn't realized how serious this could have been. I never realized that what we were talking about was a malignancy, a cancer with all its tentacles. But the reality of it all clobbered me there in the waiting room and then again when I first entered my father's hospital room.

As soon as I saw him lying there, a dagger of guilt shot through my heart. I was hating myself then for the way I'd been treating him. Standing by his bedside, watching my father go in and out of sleep, still groggy from the anesthesia and pain medication, I replayed every mean, spiteful thing I'd said to him, every hug, every smile, every act of kindness that I'd denied him the past few months. He looked old and frail to me now, not at all like my father. The flowers on the windowsill, the Get Well Soon cards that had appeared out of nowhere, the balloons tied to the end of the bed—they all seemed so wrong, so out of place. What was my father doing lying there in a hospital bed in one of those awful gowns? It wasn't right.

Later on, when he woke up, I was still standing beside him, next to Mitch and Lissy. My mother was spooning gelatin and applesauce into his mouth, teasing him, going, "Open the hangar . . . Here comes the airplane."

"Uch . . ." My father made a face. "We need to work on your mother's aim, kids," he said, and I forced myself to smile for him as my mother dabbed the excess from his chin.

Visiting hours were almost over and my father was slowly coming back to himself and the grave looks on everyone's faces had begun to recede. We knew he was feeling better because he'd started giving his nurse a hard time, teasing that if she ever said "catheter" again, he'd leave a nice big surprise for her in his bedpan.

"Well," the nurse said, leaning over my father, rearranging his pillow, "just as soon as you start using that thing, we can send you home, Mr. Smarty Pants."

His nurse liked us and let us stick around for a while after visiting hours were over. We were all tired, worn-out from the day, and when it was finally time to go, my father seemed sad. He didn't want to be alone. I felt like a parent leaving my child at overnight camp for the first time. I stood in the doorway looking at him, and while the rest of my family made their way down the hall, I dashed back to my father's side, leaned over the railing of his bed, and told him I loved him.

"I know you do, sweet pea. I know you do."

❂

The next morning, I got up early and went to the hospital, arriving just after the doctors had completed their rounds. My father seemed relieved to see me. He looked terrible. His hair was a mess, he hadn't shaved in two days, and a subtle gray cast underscored the whiskers along his chin.

I pulled a chair up close to my father's bed and the two of us made small talk. He was saying how "goddamn noisy" it was in the hospital. "I don't know how they expect you to get any sleep around here, and as soon as you do fall asleep, they're waking you up, wanting to shove things in places where they don't belong. There's no such thing as dignity here, I'll tell you that much."

"What are you complaining about now?" his nurse asked, coming into his room with a cafeteria tray. "How do you put up with this man!" She winked at me as she rolled an L-shaped table over to his bed and set the tray down on it. The silverware and dishes looked fake, like they belonged in a dollhouse. "Now you be a good boy and eat all your breakfast, or I'll be back in here with an enema! You behave yourself now, you hear me?"

My father was laughing, being himself again for the moment, and then after his nurse left, he turned serious. "And what about you? Are you behaving yourself?"

"What do you mean, 'behaving' myself?" I lifted the dome off the plate of rubbery-looking eggs, glanced at my father, and covered them back up. "I always behave myself."

"You know what I mean. What about that boy?" he asked, scratching at his whiskers. "You still spending time with him?"

"So does this mean we're actually going to talk about Michael?"

"I was hoping sooner or later you'd say something."

I lifted the carton of orange juice off his tray and gave it a shake. "Listen, I know you don't approve of him. I know I should never have brought him back to the house. I know that. That was wrong and I'm sorry." I'd been trying to open the orange juice from the wrong side and was making a mess out of the spout. "I didn't do it to hurt you, Dad. And I'm not some little kid anymore. I know what I'm doing with Michael."

"And see, Nina, I don't think you do. That's what worries me."

"Why don't you let me worry about that." I set the orange juice down on the tray.

My father looked at the mangled carton and then back at me. "It's my job to worry about you. You're my daughter and I don't want to see you get hurt. Michael's not right for you. He's not good enough."

"Oh c'mon, Dad. No one's ever gonna be good enough for your daughters."

My father nodded. "I happen to think my girls are pretty special. You don't see it, but I'm telling you, you're a beautiful girl,

Nina. You've got so much going for you. You're bright and you're funny and you could have your pick. You don't have to settle for the first guy who comes along. And as your father, as someone who loves you more than anyone in this world, I'm telling you, Michael's not the one. He's not your crooked cover."

I ran my hands along the railing of his bed. The bars were cool and somehow calming. "But I want you to like him, Dad. Cuz I love him. I really do."

My father reached out his hand and touched my fingertips. "You know," he said, "I've been thinking a lot about something you said . . ."

I squeezed the railing and looked at him. I thought my father never heard a word I said.

"You told me something that day." We both knew what day he meant. "You said I didn't know what it was like for you. That I didn't have a clue what you'd been through. That I didn't know those boys teased you and called you names. That you were lucky that a guy like Michael wanted you at all."

I was stunned. He had been listening after all.

"You broke my heart that day, because I always knew how hard it was for you. I knew your eye was gonna be a toughie, kid. And why do you think I wouldn't let you use it as a crutch, huh? I couldn't sit back and let you feel sorry for yourself. If I did that, then I knew your eye would swallow you whole. You had to find a way to make your life bigger than your eye. So if I was hard on you, that's the reason.

"And the doctors and all—I didn't know if they could help you or not. But I did whatever I could so that someday, some young man would see you—my daughter—and not just your eye. Don't you see, I knew what you were going through. And when you grew up, I wanted you to have someone in your life who would make you feel the way this Michael makes you feel. I still want that for you. I just want that someone to be the right someone."

I couldn't find any words. I couldn't say anything. To have his sympathy now after wanting it for so long broke me down the middle. His pity stayed in the back of my throat; I couldn't swallow past it.

"You think I don't know my daughter? I know you, believe me. And I know I can't stop you from seeing this Michael. I know that, but just promise me you'll keep your eyes open. Watch yourself with him, Nina. Just promise me that. I don't want to see you get hurt."

I nodded as the tears ran down my face.

☼

Five days later, by the time my father came home from the hospital, my mother had gathered every ashtray in the house, washed them, and had put them away in the bottom drawer of the breakfront. Things were a little different around our house after my father's surgery. We all noticed the change in him. It seemed that the ordeal had mellowed him some. Situations that once would have launched a tirade now passed with a shrug or maybe a sarcastic remark. That was all he'd give you. What really surprised everyone, though, was his reaction the day Lissy came home and announced she was pregnant. For a man who had never been happy with her choice in a husband, my father couldn't have been more thrilled about the prospect of becoming a grandfather. When my sister told him, he cried, kissed her, and even hugged Neil.

After I told Michael about that, he telephoned my father and asked if he could stop by and see him. While Michael and my father sat in the family room talking, my mother and I stayed in the kitchen polishing the good silver, getting it ready for Thanksgiving, which was less than a week away. As I buffed a serving spoon with a rag that had once been my father's undershirt, we overheard Michael apologizing for that day in my bedroom. We also heard him telling my father how much he cared for me and that he would never hurt me. Not ever.

The next day my father said if I wanted to, I could invite Michael for Thanksgiving. "But he's not coming on the turkey run," he said. "That's just for you and me. Not him."

After that, I was more in love with Michael than ever. I started folding my life into his, smooth and easy. I kept a toothbrush at his place, and since I didn't like the shampoo he used, I had my own there now, sitting on the ledge inside the shower, next to my razor. A box of tampons was stashed beneath the sink. He took me to his parents' house for Christmas Eve and that year we spent New Year's Eve, my birthday, under a blanket on the floor of his living room. Sometimes on the weekends, we'd go for drives, admiring all the homes along Merriman Road, pointing to the Tudor mansion we said we'd own someday. We talked about having kids and getting a dog. We talked about the things we didn't like about our parents' marriages and what we would do differently.

Michael was my best friend. And I had allowed myself to fall in love with him. It was my bravest act of faith.

*

We survived the winter, and before we knew it, spring had arrived. Everything was in a state of promise. It was a Thursday night and Michael and I were meeting at the Ground Round. I had brought along some brochures about Italy. We wanted to go that August, only we hadn't told my father about it yet.

This was the first time I'd seen Michael all week. He'd been so busy lately, ever since he'd started his new job with the mortgage company. He wore a suit and tie every day now and had recently grown a mustache and goatee. He was thinking about getting contact lenses, but I was trying to talk him out of it.

He was waiting for me at a booth when I got there. I leaned

over to kiss his neck. "I've missed you," I said, sliding onto the bench opposite him. "Look what I got!" I fanned the travel brochures in front of him.

He didn't say anything. He just drummed his thumb against the tabletop. He wouldn't look at me.

"Michael?" I reached over for his hand. "What's the matter? What's wrong?"

He eased his hand out from under mine and shifted in his seat.

"Michael? What is it?"

Finally he looked up, pulled off his glasses, and set them on the table. His eyes were rimmed. "This is really hard . . ." His bottom lip was twitching. "I don't even know how to say this . . ."

I felt a burning in the pit of my stomach.

"Nina, I love you, I do. But . . ." He shook his head. "I can't do this anymore."

"What—what can't you do anymore?"

"You and me. It's just . . ." His voice trailed off.

"It's just what?"

"It's just not working, Neen. I'm not happy like this anymore . . ."

"Why? Why are you saying this?"

"I never meant to hurt you. And you know I'm always gonna have a special place in my heart for you . . ."

He was still talking, but I couldn't hear anymore. I didn't understand. We were happy. We were good together. We were going to have a future together. What about the house on Merriman Road, the kids we were going to have? I sat there, looking at the travel brochures growing cloudy through my tears. The waiter came over, looked at us, and then backed away without a word.

"Why are you doing this, Michael?"

At first he didn't want to say, but I pressed him. Finally, there it was. He'd met someone. The table, the glasses, everything whirled around me. I was knocked off kilter, dizzy from it all. She was older, by about seven years. She was recently divorced.

He had met her in a hardware store. He'd wanted to tell me sooner, but it just never seemed like the right time.

I don't even remember leaving the restaurant. I just remember standing in the parking lot and saying good-bye. That was where Michael gave me his last hug. And I wished he hadn't. Knowing it was the last time I'd feel his body pressed to mine, smell his neck, feel the tickle of his curls against my cheek broke open a fresh round of tears.

Before he walked away, he asked if I was going to be okay. Why do they do that? They don't really want to know the answer, do they? They don't really want to know what suffering they've just set in motion. Did Michael really want to know that the following morning my eyes would probably be swollen shut from crying all night? Did he want to know that I probably wouldn't be able to eat for the next five days? Did he want to know that I was the type of ex-girlfriend who would stake herself outside his apartment at night, hoping to get a glimpse of him and this new girl? Did he want to know that a week, a month, six months from now, I wouldn't remember what it felt like not to be in pain?

I got in the car, where I sat and sobbed so hard, I fogged up all the windows. I felt so foolish. How long had he been with this other woman? Had he been with me and then her and then back with me? How can one person be making plans for Italy while the other one is planning his escape? How could it be that one moment everything in my life was fine and now it was all destroyed? For a while, I had felt whole and happy, but now I could see that was all an illusion. None of that happiness ever belonged to me. It had all been borrowed, on loan from Michael. When I met him, I thought it meant that I'd overcome some huge hurdle in my life. I thought it meant that I had shed that lonely, miserable part of myself. But I hadn't. I'd just covered it up with Michael. Now he had taken all that was good away with him and I was left empty, hollow once again.

☼

When I got home that night, it was a quarter after eight and no one was there. It was so quiet when I opened the door, too quiet. Pumpkin barely stirred when she saw me. She just went back over by the door and lay there, like she was waiting for everyone else to come home. Then the phone started ringing, but I couldn't bring myself to answer it. Instead, I went into the den and slumped onto the couch, staring off into the room, thinking how the last time I'd sat here, I'd been happy. Now I was raw, and all of me was exposed without a single protective layer to cushion the pain. I didn't know what was upsetting me more—the thought of how much I was going to miss Michael or my fears of being alone and no one ever loving me again. Or was it just that he'd chosen someone else over me? They all hurt, and all in different ways.

The phone started ringing again and this time I answered it, thinking foolishly that it was Michael. He'd changed his mind. He'd made a mistake. He wanted me back.

But it wasn't Michael calling. It was Lissy.

"It's Dad," she said, crying into the phone. "He's back in the hospital—in intensive care. He couldn't breathe, Nina. Mom had to call for an ambulance. Mitch is on his way back to town. Just hurry up and get down here."

I don't remember the drive to the hospital. I don't remember turning on the ignition, or stopping for any red lights or making any turns. There were streetlights I'm sure, but I saw nothing but darkness. Everything went mechanical. I don't remember how or where I parked the car, and as I entered through the sliding glass doors I had a feeling that the next time I passed by this way, I would not be the same person.

My mother was in the waiting room, sitting next to Lissy.

"How is he?" I asked.

My mother shook her head. "The cancer's back."

A cold sweat came over me. We had so rarely ever mentioned cancer when we spoke about his illness. We'd talked about the surgery or his radiation treatments, but that was as far as we'd gone. Any mention of the cancer itself made it all too real. But now we were speaking of it because we had to. And all that we'd been too afraid to say before, now came rushing out. My mother and Lissy were talking about lymph nodes, stage IIIA, chemotherapy, more radiation.

While we were discussing all this, Mitch appeared in the doorway. My mother ran to him and I saw her legs buckle as soon as she knew he had hold of her. His garment bag was draped across the back of a chair, doubled over, already grieving.

They let us go back to see my father, two at a time. My mother and I went back first. Before we rounded the corner, she tried to warn me. "He doesn't look good, Neen," she said. But I wasn't prepared. I gasped when I saw him. He was hooked up to half a dozen tubes: one going through his nose, another down his throat. Monitors were beeping. Bags were dripping fluids into his veins. The skin on his arm was bruised and almost black from all the IVs.

My mother wiped a tear running down my cheek and asked if I was okay. I didn't know how to answer that. I knew I should have stayed there with her longer, but I couldn't breathe. I had to get away. So I wandered into the hallway, but there was no escape. Just more beds, filled with IVs and catheter bags, morphine drips, and other people's sufferings. Even at the nurses' station, there was no air to be had. It was all being sucked up by nebulizers, ventilators, and oxygen masks.

I went to find a pay phone. I had already dropped my dime through the slot before I remembered I couldn't call Michael anymore. He had removed himself from my life. And at a time when I needed him most, he was probably with his new girlfriend. I set the receiver back on the hook and saw where someone had stuck their gum inside the change return. I couldn't get my dime back, and this was more than I could bear. New tears were collecting along the rims of my eyes.

I headed back to the ICU. As I pushed the call button for the elevator, I told myself that if the car to my right came first, that meant my father would be okay. If the car to my left came, then that meant my father would die. Less than a minute later, the left elevator arrived.

☼

I stayed with my father in the ICU that night. I knew he hated to be alone. He was almost phobic about it, and I figured this would be the one thing I could do that would bring him comfort.

He slept for the first hour I was there. It hurt to see my father, of all people, so helpless and vulnerable. The things he couldn't control were the things that made him angry, and I could only imagine how frustrated and anguished he must have felt having tubes do his breathing, his eating, even a tube to do his pissing for him. How he must have hated being dependent on a morphine drip because the pain was too great.

This wasn't my father. It couldn't be. My father had raised us to believe he had God-like powers, that he was beyond the frailties that took down ordinary men. He'd given us a lifetime of stories that people outside our family found too outrageous to believe. Good or bad, he was the intensity in our lives. Without him, my family lost all its color. Without him, we would be as pale as the skin on his cheeks.

It was never dull being his child, that's for sure. We never knew what to expect from him. I remembered that one day, out of nowhere, he came home with a powerboat attached to a trailer, hitched to the rear bumper of his car. He named her *Miss Q.*, after Quality Brand Carpets. My father must have liked the idea of the boat better than the boat itself, because it made him nervous whenever he took us out on the water. Eight months after he'd bought it, *Miss Q.* sank in the harbor at Lake Erie during a bad storm. My father seemed relieved when he got the call. He never owned another boat.

I looked at my father lying motionless before me. There was something about him that went beyond special. And it wasn't just my family who felt that way. Even strangers were enamored of him. I was remembering then his story about the time he'd danced with Shirley MacLaine in a nightclub in New York. She was so tall that she'd had to take off her heels and had danced with him in her stocking feet. Afterward, she'd signed his shirt collar with her lipstick, saying he was "an original."

My father had charmed her. And, of course, me, too. One of my earliest memories of my father was when I was just five or six. He was getting ready to head to the driving range and I didn't want him to go. I clung to his leg, and with each step, my bottom was being dragged across the floor as he made his way to the door. I was sobbing, desperate for him not to leave me. I could feel that little girl's fear all over again. I wanted to cling to him now and beg him not to leave me. Not ever.

I realized then that there are moments when life seems to be happening to you. These are those moments that you later reflect on, wondering how you survived them. Getting the injections in my eye was like that. So were the laser treatments. It was even a little like that when I lost my virginity. These are moments that change and shape you, and they're so imposing that you can't stay present for them. So you slip away, someplace safe inside yourself, and wait for the storm to pass. So while I was there with my father, I was somewhere else, too.

There was an expression my grandfather used to use whenever things were going too good for anyone. He'd say, "Beware of all your good fortune, because heaven has a trapdoor that leads to hell." I'd never really understood what he meant until now. But I supposed something had to give. I wasn't one of those people meant to lead a charmed life. Everything for me had been going too well and for too long. Earlier that day, when Michael told me it was over, I'd thought that was hell. But that was nothing compared to this. Seeing my father in intensive care was way beyond hell.

My father had been right about Michael all along. How had he known this would happen? And how selfish was it of me to want to talk to my father about him right then? I needed to hear him tell me Michael wasn't right, that he wasn't the one. And what if we'd never get a chance to talk about it? What if I'd already had the last conversation I'd ever have with my father? What if that moment had already come and gone without my knowing it?

My God, could we be at the end so soon? I was just beginning to understand him and why he was such a difficult person at times, so needing of us and our attention. I was starting to understand how much it meant for him to have a family of his own. What it must have been like for him growing up without his mother or father. No wonder he couldn't stand to be alone. It must have terrified him. I understood that now, because I was afraid of being left alone in this world, too, without him.

And if this was it, if I had to lose him now, I knew what he'd want from me. He'd want me to pick up where he'd left off. If he couldn't be with me, I'd have no choice but to make my way using what I'd gotten from him. I knew that was what he would want, but it was too soon. I wasn't ready to let him go.

My head felt tight around my temples. It was throbbing. My whole face was wet with tears. There was no more room inside my chest for what I was feeling, and whatever this was, it didn't have a name. *Love* was too simple, too easy a word to carry this. There was no word for what I was feeling for my father at that moment. It was a tangle of thoughts and emotions, impossible to define.

My father's eyes began to flutter open. When he saw me, he tried to reach his hand out to me, but the IVs held him back.

I couldn't speak. I just leaned over the railing and grabbed his hand, afraid to squeeze too hard. The plastic bracelet around his wrist felt stiff to me and the name typed across the top seemed foreign: Arthur Goldman. Who was that? My father was Artie, Dad. He was never an Arthur.

My father closed his eyes and a tear leaked out.

I wanted him to say something, tell me something that would sustain me the rest of my life—something to live off of. But the only sounds I heard were the machines pumping, in, out, in, out. My father was lying before me. He had his oxygen, his morphine, and me—everything he needed to get him through the night.

moving on

The only thing harder than watching someone you love die is watching them struggle to survive. It took thirty rounds of radiation and six weeks of chemo. It took away all his hair and his dignity. It took having a nurse at home with him and too many emergency trips back to the hospital, each time the ambulance shaking our quiet neighborhood with its screaming sirens as it pulled into our drive. For months, I dreaded stepping outside to get the paper or the mail, having to confront neighbors who stopped to ask how he was doing.

It took over a year and took everything out of us and out of him. The progress was slow, but after fourteen months, the chest X ray and PET scan were clean. But the fear of the cancer's return hung over our family like a low-lying cloud. Even now, two years later, each time my father caught a cold, or even cleared his throat too loud, a tremor rippled through us.

I had mixed feelings about leaving him now, but I knew I had to move on. I was preparing to leave for graduate school—in

New York City, of all places. I'd been accepted in the MFA writing program at Columbia that fall. Initially, my father was against this, but after rounds of arguing and crying over it, I persuaded him to give me his blessing to go and make my way in New York.

My father was starting over again, too. He'd finally gotten out of the carpet business and was a consultant now—doing what exactly, I had no idea. But he had ended up selling QBC to Greg McFadden. Greg had been running his family's wall-covering business until they were bought out by an outfit based in St. Louis. Then, while my father was so sick, Greg had sort of handled things for him at QBC. Taking over my father's business seemed like a natural. So they had a deal as long as Greg promised to keep the QBC name.

It seemed everything about us was in flux, each of us looking forward, getting ready for what was next. Even my parents had decided to move. They didn't need such a big place just for themselves anymore, so they put a FOR SALE sign out front. They had scheduled a yard sale for the next weekend. My mother said this was our last chance to claim Barbies and catcher's mitts, old books and record albums. Everything else was either going to be pitched or sold. That brought Mitch and his girlfriend, Donna, back from New York.

My brother had been ready to surrender and leave the city when he met her, but Donna made New York tolerable for him. They'd been living together for six months in her studio apartment on the Upper West Side. She worked on Wall Street as an assistant to some big financial consultant. She had my brother wearing his hair shorter, pressing firm creases down the center of his jeans. He was talking about going into sales of some kind. He realized acting was getting him nowhere and that if he was going to stay in New York, he needed to start making money.

I wasn't sure about his girlfriend, but I was glad Mitch would be close by now that I was heading to New York, too. When I asked if he thought he'd marry Donna, Mitch arched an eyebrow and said, "She's a lot like Dad, you know."

With Mitch back home for the weekend, I woke to a house that was suddenly full once again, like when we were kids. Lissy had moved back into her old bedroom right before Jennifer was born. Eight months pregnant, and my sister had turned up in the middle of the night, announcing that she was leaving Neil. I wasn't surprised. From the start, they had argued, mostly about my father. Neil told Lissy that she had to choose: "Either you're my wife or his daughter!" Stupid ultimatum. Neil didn't stand a chance.

The night she left him, I listened to her bawling to my mother, going, "Nothing ever goes right for me! Never has and never will!"

Hearing her sob like that made me realize that even someone as beautiful as Lissy couldn't escape heartache.

I also realized that while I was about to break free from my father, he still held her in his grip. Even though she had found a new apartment, and even though she already had a new boyfriend, she was still staying with my parents, waiting until the last-possible moment before she had to move out. I didn't want to linger in Akron any longer than I needed to. I had things out there waiting for me. Even with all her blond hair and obvious beauty—for the first time in my life—I wouldn't have traded places with my sister.

Later that day, up in the attic, Lissy found the old projector with the reels of home movies we'd taken years ago, when we were little. Mitch set it up, projecting off a bare living room wall. We came across a reel taken the year we had auditioned for *The Phil Moran Show.* I remembered my grandmother standing there with the camera while we rehearsed. Lissy was waving, blowing kisses. Mitch was drumming away in the background, and then I got in on the act, fighting my way into each frame. And that's what amazed me, to see what a ham I'd been. I had put my face right up into the lens and smiled as big as I could. I moved like I didn't have a care in the world, even with my eye so bad. There was no fold back in those days and it looked like I had a lump growing out of my eyebrow. I'd forgotten how it used to look. Seeing it again made my throat go dry.

"Christ, have we come a long way, tootsie. How about that? Huh!" My father's hand sliced through the projector's beam, eclipsing my young face entirely. "You start to feel sorry for yourself, young lady, and you just remember where we started."

The next morning, we were in the basement, going through piles of junk, rediscovering hula hoops, boxes of my father's old 78's, my Easy-Bake oven. I came across my Etch-a-Sketch, and for a moment I considered keeping it and taking it with me to grad school. Mitch did the same thing with an old Batman T-shirt he'd worn when he was seven. Lissy was like that with a stuffed bear. We were having a hard time letting go. My father couldn't take it, either. He stayed upstairs and watched his granddaughter.

My mother was the one who'd cut all sentiment. With her silver hair pulled back in a rubber band, dressed in her weekend jeans and gym shoes, she was ready to pitch. The only things she set aside were my grandfather's violins. She wanted to keep one for herself and give the other one to my grandmother.

The garage was next. There was Pumpkin's leash hanging alongside the garden tools. I didn't know why we'd saved that, why we hadn't thrown it out along with her dish and all her toys when she died the winter before. In the corner, lying next to an old tire, were all my father's pipes, crammed into boxes, set aside to be sold. There was a label on top of each one: "Entire collection $50." They could have asked at least ten times that, but my parents wanted them out of the house, out of their lives. There was the old microwave oven, pushed back in the corner, next to Mitch's drum set.

While the others were still rummaging through things, I went back inside the house and upstairs to my room. I started sorting through my closet then, pulling out items one at a time. On the top shelf I found a big canister that I'd saved from grade school on. Inside it was filled with notes, intricately folded, tucked into perfect squares, my initials gracing the tops of each.

I spent a long time reading through that canister of notes. There were hundreds of them now flattened out in a pile on my bedroom floor. All of them filled with smiley faces, hearts, and one or all of the following statements: "So who should I like?" "Who do you like?" "I wish someone would like me."

The amazing thing was, I never remembered getting notes passed to me. I only remembered writing them to everyone else but never getting any in return. It seemed there was a gap between memory and reality, and that made me sad.

I had always thought of myself as the tagalong, the girl with the eye, the one the boys would never like. But the evidence was in front of me, sitting on my bedroom floor. In one note Patty wrote, "I think Ben Stewart likes you. He told Keith you're a riot!" And clearly, everybody had problems. In another note, Kara threw a fit just because "Alex wouldn't say hi to me in study hall today." Everybody got dumped. Half of Emily's notes were about Eric Slater wanting to break up with her. Anna's notes were filled with heartaches, too. Everybody cried. What made me think I was any different from the rest of them?

After reading through those notes, I realized that the childhood I thought I'd had was not the one I'd actually lived.

I guess even Michael was a part of being normal. God, it still hurt, even two years later. I wondered if he was still with that other woman. Every once in a while I'd be at the mall or the grocery and I'd get this feeling that I was going to run into the two of them. At least in New York, I'd never have to worry about that. New York would be all fresh—a new start—and I couldn't wait.

After I'd folded up my notes and sealed them back inside the canister, I went downstairs. Everyone else was taking a break, relaxing now in the family room. A Cleveland Browns game was on TV, but the sound was turned down to barely a hum. And there was my father—we called him "Poppy" now—with his granddaughter on his lap, a plastic juice bottle clutched between her hands. Everyone was quiet, heads turned toward my father, watching him. He was singing, serenading her and all of us: "Fly me to the moon/And let me play among the stars . . ."